DRAGON RESCUE

DON CALLANDER

D0191479

ACE BOOKS, NEW YORK

This book is an Ace original edition,
and has never been previously published.

DRAGON RESCUE

An Ace Book / published by arrangement with
the author

PRINTING HISTORY
Ace edition / October 1995

ISBN: 0-441-00263-3

ACE®
Ace Books are published by The Berkley Publishing Group,
200 Madison Avenue, New York, NY 10016.
ACE and the "A" design are trademarks
belonging to Charter Communications, Inc.

PRINTED IN THE UNITED STATES OF AMERICA

10 9 8 7 6 5 4 3 2 1

DON CALLANDER'S *DRAGON COMPANION* . . .
introduced readers to a unique world where dragons rule and mortal men are more than they ever dreamed they could be. Now, return to that world of unforgettable magic, menace, and mystery in . . .

DON CALLANDER'S *DRAGON RESCUE*

And Thrill to Don Callander's
Magical Mancer Novels:

The adventures begin when a young man answers a strange advertisement: APPRENTICE WANTED to learn the MYSTERIES and SECRETS of WIZARDRY in the Discipline of FIRE . . .

PYROMANCER
"THE SORCERER'S ANIMATED KITCHEN IS A DELIGHT, AS IS HIS BRASSY BRONZE OWL . . . THERE ARE NICE ORIGINAL TOUCHES HERE."   —Piers Anthony

Then the young Pyromancer meets his match—a beautiful and beguiling apprentice learning the Mysteries of WATER . . .

AQUAMANCER
"GOOD SENSE OF HUMOR!"   —Publishers Weekly

Finally, the Pyromancer and the Aquamancer try to free a tribe of men enslaved in stone by a treacherous Master of the EARTH . . .

GEOMANCER
THE MANCER NOVELS ARE "DELIGHTFUL . . . FUN TO READ!"   —South Florida SF Society

Ace Books by Don Callander

PYROMANCER
AQUAMANCER
GEOMANCER
DRAGON COMPANION
DRAGON RESCUE

While all my children, my grandchildren, and my step-children and step-grandchildren and even step-great-grand-children have been enthusiastic, interested, and encouraging spectators of my books, the one who has been at it longest and with the very least doubt that I would, in the end, get into print and sell is my oldest son, Miles Bruce Callander, of Falmouth, Virginia.

Bruce, I love you and your wonderful wife, Alane. As for my grandson, Andrew Morgan Callander, tell him the next book will be his when (and if) it's published.

Love you guys!

Don Callander
Longwood, Florida

What Happened Before . . .

IN *Dragon Companion*, Librarian Thomas Whitehead was suddenly transported to a strange land called Carolna. He was befriended by a fifty-foot, green-and-gold, fire-breathing gentle Dragon named Retruance Constable. Together they drove a force of Mercenary Knights from Overhall Castle, the Achievement of Lord Murdan, the Royal Historian.

Tom was hired as Murdan's personal Librarian and plunged into the struggle between mild-mannered King Eduard Trusslo of Carolna and his ambitious brother-in-law, Peter of Gantrell.

In flying succession Tom and his Dragon met a runaway Princess, helped her escape from Peter of Gantrell, and rescued Murdan's daughter and her three small children from Lord Peter's flunkies. Then Tom saved Retruance, with the assistance of Princess Manda and a woodsman named Clematis, when the Dragon was trapped inside a hollow mountain.

Murdan and Princess Manda, on their way to Royal Lexor, were captured by Lord Peter. Tom, in Lexor to protect Eduard's new wife, who was about to bear him an heir, hurried south to release them. Together the adventurers returned to court, assisted the King against the usurper's schemes, and drove Peter into exile.

Tom and Manda were married and planned to establish their own Achievement in Hidden Canyon and live happily ever after.

But now . . . the young couple receive news of an invasion by nomadic Northmen warriors—and the kidnapping by fiery Dragon of Manda's half brother, the baby Crown Prince Ednoll.

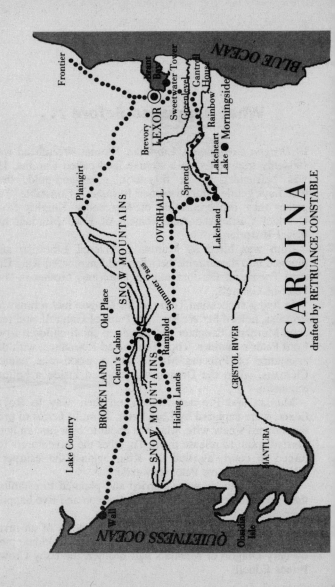

CAROLNA
drafted by RETRUANCE CONSTABLE

Knollwater
WATERFIELDS

GULF OF CAROLNA

Untracked Jungle

N

Map of Carolna

Scale — 1 inch = 50 miles

✵ 1 ✵
Librarian's Lot

RETRUANCE Constable was a masterpiece of awesome grace and terrible reptilian elegance.

His great, tapered black leathery wings stretched to their full eighty-foot span, trembling only a tiny bit at the trailing edges, curving upward at their far tips. Wicked emerald claws were held tucked close to his tummy and chest as he swung his spear-pointed tail as a rudder, guiding his course through the clouds.

He circled over the tropical shore flats and slowly soared over the deep velvet of jungle, his body lifted by the humid thermals from the blue Quietness Ocean a dozen miles to the west, then swept a thousand feet into the bright morning sky as the warm wind suddenly breasted the steep western slopes of the stark Isthmusi Mountains.

He was aware, as he turned south to glide silently along the rising slopes, of his brother Furbetrance Constable, thirty miles away to the north, sweeping an identical, ever-watchful circle over choked and teeming tropical forest.

The nearly impassable cypress jungles of the seacoast gradually thinned as they rose into the uplands. From the dark, oily green of the coastal wilderness the forest slowly turned to the lighter greens of tropical hardwoods: teak, ironwood, logwood, and mahogany.

The Dragons saw neither track nor trace of civilization below them, relying on Dragon instincts to sense what was hidden beneath the leafy canopy.

The topmost levels of the high forest were inhabited

by bands of shrilly calling monkeys, frightened by the swift-gliding shadows of the two huge Dragons overhead. The little brown-and-white simians hid under dense clumps of bromeliads and orchids, huddled together, whimpering in fear.

Nothing larger than the rare Great Condors of the Isthmusi uplands even approached the Dragons' size, wingspread, and slow, deliberate soaring. The monkeys feared the terrible beasts above sought prey—and hoped against hope that monkeys would not appeal to a Dragon's appetite.

IN the shadowy levels just below the tops of the tallest trees almost all movement and sound was stilled. Here lived, generation after generation, the Green Sloths, looking—and feeling, if the truth were to be told—very much a part of the foliage. Only once every hour or so a sloth would reach slowly out to pluck a ripe fruit from the underside of a leafy bough and slowly, slowly slide it into its mouth.

It chewed, ever so slowly, evenly, for a tremendously long time before it swallowed. Then it was completely at rest again, not even its tiny eyes moving.

Around the sloths darted clouds of brightly metallic ruby-headed hummingbirds, poking their long, curved beaks into this or that cluster of orange, red, or yellow vine flowers, sipping the heady nectar and scattering pollen in the soft wind when they darted on to the next flower.

The hummingbirds paid no heed to the sloths, nor did the slow animals pay attention to the brilliant, flashing hummers. Neither birds nor sloths paid any heed to the monkeys or the Dragons' fleeting shadows.

Below the flowered and fruited levels dropped long, straight brown or green tree trunks, a hundred feet or more down to the tops of younger growth struggling upward toward the sunlight. Too immature to bear flowers or fruit, they were ignored by the animals and birds in the higher tops.

The hundreds of feet of bare trunks seemed lifeless, yet they were vertical highways to a hundred billion tiny red ants flowing up and down from their nests below to the bromeliads above, which served them as water catchments.

The occasional young monkey, exploring the lower levels, might interrupt the ant's line of march but once— enough to teach even the dullest of the monkeys' children the folly of getting in the way of the red ant legions armed with their agonizing stings.

The sloths sometimes bestirred themselves to dine on ants. Their thick, interlocking fur and horny skins made a mere tickle of the ants' sting. Given the chance, most Green Sloths would have preferred a diet of ants, which could be scooped up like dark red honey from the trunks and limbs, but as a general rule the ants were safe. Ants moved too fast for the sleepy sloths.

Between a lower fringe of foliage and the dimly lit, spongy forest floor thrived 137 varieties of birds: basket weavers, bee eaters, insect- and honey-hunting darters and swallows, seed-cracking macaws, and raucous parrots.

Some foraged the upper levels for leavings, while others scoured the fern-covered forest-floor litter. These last were the only species who drank from the dozens of tiny rivulets that ran between the tree roots and trickled together to form shallow rills that flowed into the meandering rivers of the coastal plain and then into the western ocean.

Retruance was aware of the stir he caused among the little, fear-filled beasties of the rain-forest tops and regretted the terror his wide-winged form caused in their hearts. But it could not be avoided. With his brother Furbetrance, he was on a mission of filial duty. It required them to fly low and peer down through the several levels of the rain forest, ignoring the lesser life all about them, looking carefully for signs of a larger kind of beast.

They searched for Arbitrance Constable, their long-lost Dragon father.

ARBITRANCE Constable had been missing for over ten years, a short time as Dragons' lives go but long enough to cause worry to his family and friends.

At first they thought he might be indulging in the male Dragon's dual desires for wandering and treasure hunting, what Dragons rather euphemistically term "questing." But as the second decade began and Arbitrance's Companion, Royal Historian Murdan of Overhall, again and again called his mount to no avail, the Constables began to search for him.

It wasn't like Arbitrance to ignore his Companion's call.

When Murdan's tall castle had been captured by Mercenary Knights, they thought surely Arbitrance would return to assist the Historian. But he hadn't. Retruance, carrying his recently acquired Companion, Thomas Librarian, took his father's place and dropped in to drive the invading Knights from Overhall's walls, halls, and soaring towers.

When the adventure was over, the Historian's family safe and an ambitious royal uncle bested and driven into exile, still no word had been heard nor trace seen of the missing Arbitrance.

The search continued.

"We're off for Hidden Lake," Thomas Librarian of Overhall had said to Retruance some months before. "We need to take exact measurements for the new manor house and outbuildings, stables, and such. We want to start building next year . . . if that suits you."

Tom and his Princess, Alix Amanda Trusslo, had been married for two years. They'd been so very busy they'd just now found time to begin thinking about their own Achievement. It would be built beside a long, beautifully blue lake in a deep box canyon on the southern flanks of the western range of Snow Mountains, overlooking the empty desert known as Hiding Lands.

Furbetrance, Thomas, and Manda, as the Princess preferred to be called, had discovered the canyon and its lake while searching for Retruance when the latter was trapped in a cavern under one of the Snows' tallest peaks.

Right then and there, Tom and Manda fell in love with the secluded place. When Manda's father, King Eduard Ten, had offered Tom an Achievement of his own, the Librarian had immediately picked this Hidden Lake Canyon site.

The wedding had taken much time, but when it was accomplished, with all due pomp and ceremony, Tom had thrown himself into his work at Overhall's library, his first concern and duty. He and his new wife also spent a quarter of their time at the Alix Amanda Alone Palace in Lexor, the capital city, or at King Eduard's Sweetwater Tower overlooking Brant Bay.

The years-long task of setting the Historian's library in good order had settled at last into a routine that could be handled by Tom's handpicked assistants, and the couple finally could turn their thoughts to building a home of their own.

"What I'm saying," continued the Librarian to his Mount, "is that I know you're eager . . . anxious? . . . to resume your search for your father. Furbetrance, too, now that his kits are well grown. Why don't you do it?"

"I'd be very helpful at Hidden Lake, perhaps," said the Dragon reluctantly. "I've some of my grandfather's talent for designing castles."

Grandfather Altruance Constable had designed and built Murdan's Overhall Castle a generation earlier.

"Plenty of time to begin the designing," put in Manda, looking up from her needlepoint to smile at the great beast. "Tom says there's much to do, just to get the basic information, measurements and such."

Tom and Manda were sitting before Great Hall's number-two fireplace in Overhall Castle, for the late-summer evening had turned chilly. The Dragon actually was crouched outside in the main courtyard with just his huge head inside the Hall—there was little room for else, even in that huge room.

"We'll enjoy having some time to ourselves, I assure you," Manda went on. "Doing the measuring and the dreaming. We'll turn the really hard work over to you, dear Retruance."

"Well," said the Dragon, pleased by her compliment. "Furbetrance *was* asking me when would be a good time to start seeking Papa once again."

"Which direction will you take?" Tom asked, assuming it was all settled, then.

"South, into the Isthmusi Mountains and coastal jungles," replied Retruance. He'd obviously given it considerable thought. "We searched west and north and east last time."

"Besides," said Murdan, looking up from his reading in an easy chair on the other side of the fire, "I've given the Constables a message from an old merchant friend of mine who travels south each winter to gather spices and tropical wood. He's heard that a great Dragon has been seen there a number of times in the past few years. Terrified the poor natives! Primitives don't know Dragons as we civilized Elves do."

"We'll go to the Isthmusi, then," said Retruance, making a wry face at the Historian. He didn't consider most Elves all that civilized himself, present company excepted. "It's the best and the only lead we've had ever since Papa went lost."

The next day he carried the young Librarian and his Princess to Ramhold, Murdan's vast sheep station on the western short-grass plains.

Manda was no longer titled *Princess Royal* since the birth of her half brother Ednoll. He'd been given the honor of bearing the title of "royal." Ednoll would be

King of Carolna when he grew up, the only male heir to the throne of the Trusslos. Manda had gladly forsaken any claim she might have had to the Trusslo crown in favor of marrying Tom Librarian of Overhall and Iowa.

Wherever Iowa was.

They'd spent a few days visiting with Talber, the factor of Ramhold, an old and dear friend, before flying on to Hidden Lake Canyon.

They were greeted there by Julia, a rather conceited, imperious Jaguar who lived in the open pinewood glades around Hidden Lake. Julia was secretly pleased to have neighbors in that lonely spot, but hid it behind a veil of feline disdain.

"Just when it was getting quiet around here," Julia said to Retruance with a sniff. "Where can a lady get some peace and solitude?"

"I know a grand quiet place not too far off," said the Dragon, calmly. "Over that way . . ."

He gestured toward the towering Snow Mountains above the canyon head.

"Lake like a mirror. Plenty of fish, friendly as puppies and blind as bats. No one to disturb you, Mistress Julia."

Retruance had been trapped in that vast cavern once, suspended over a black pool within the mountain itself. He spoke from experience.

Julia recognized good-natured teasing when she heard it, and let the remark pass. Besides, she'd already explored deep under the mountains to satisfy her cat's curiosity. She really preferred sunlight and warm breezes, her school of golden fish in the beautiful tarn . . . and some decent neighbors to insult, at times.

RETRUANCE flew on to Mantura Bay at the mouth of the mighty Cristol River on Carolina's west coast. On a volcanic isle named Obsidia, in the great bay, he'd found his younger brother playing with his brood of Dragon kits—Dragon children are called *kits*—on a black sand beach of wave-polished glass pebbles.

They had been practicing fire jetting and smoke spouting.

"I keep telling you, Brazier," Furbetrance was saying to one of his children as Retruance landed. "You have to eat more anthracite and activated charcoal to get the best and hottest flames to jet."

"But, Papa!" protested the half-grown boy-dragon. "I just don't *like* the taste of that stuff. Foo!"

Furbetrance rolled his eyes at his big brother and coughed a gout of orange flame in parental dismay.

"Kits! Imagine! A young boy-dragon gushing *pink* fire! What will the other Dragons say?"

"Perhaps if you sauced the charcoal with a clove or two of garlic," suggested Retruance with all the wisdom of an unmarried uncle. "Or add a spoonful of red cayenne sauce. That usually helps the dry charcoal go down more easily."

"I'd like that!" young Brazier cried gleefully, and flew off to tell his sisters about Uncle Retruance's perfect understanding.

"I don't think I want to tell Hetabelle about your pepper-sauce theory," said Furbetrance when they were alone. "She's so concerned that they have the right diet for good teeth and strong claws."

"You should leave that sort of thing to your helpmate," advised Retruance. "There's important Dragon's work for us males to do. . . ."

"Work? A quest? A task? I yearn to get my teeth into a new adventure, I can tell you!"

"And a duty! No wife can deny her husband such a combination," Retruance assured his brother.

"Duty? *Ah*! You mean . . . looking for Papa! When do we leave?"

"Soon as you tell Hetabelle about it," his brother chuckled. "And only *you* can do that. I'll wait for you over on the mainland."

"Oh, no you won't!" cried Furbetrance, clutching his

brother's left wing firmly in an emerald foreclaw.
"You'll stand by me when I tell her I'm leaving . . . won't you? *Please!*"

As it turned out, Hetabelle was at once in favor of
sending her husband off again to pursue her long-
missing father-in-law.

"I need some time to myself, you see. Not that I don't
love you dearly, husband, and I've really appreciated
having you near the nest these past few years. I'd been
hoping to take the kits to visit my mother's aerie for
some time. Mama knows good Dragon manners and the
children need to get to know her better. But be careful,
beloved! And call me if I can help your search. Send
word if you are gone longer than you think you should."

Furbetrance sighed as he and Retruance launched
themselves from Obsidia Isle. "I'm relieved she took
it so well. And I'm pleased. But I'm also a bit . . .
well . . . *put out*. Do you know what I mean?"

"Thank your stars for unlooked-for blessings," his
big brother advised.

FIVE days later the two green-and-gold Dragons were
circling the upland rain forests at the feet of the sharp
mountain range that ran north to south through Isthmusi,
looking and feeling for signs of their missing parent.

✦ 2 ✦
Mountain Springe

RETRUANCE Constable rolled over on his back and waved a claw to attract his brother's attention. Furbetrance waved back and the two flew toward each other to consult.

"Shall we go on after dark?" asked the older brother. "We can't do as well by starlight. The moon's not up 'til after midnight, and it'll be a mere crescent."

"Hate to waste the time, but you're right," replied Furbetrance, doing slow wing-overs to maintain his altitude.

"I've a strong feeling that Papa passed this way, and not too long ago," added Retruance. "I've never had so strong a *sense* of him before."

"I trust your good senses, as always," Furbetrance said. "I feel it, also. Rather strained, I must say, but definitely Papa."

He pointed a wing eastward, where the heavily forested uplands swooped up to the range of rugged, bare peaks. These stood shoulder to shoulder, cut only by one immensely deep valley filled with an unnamed river.

"Somewhere up there, I should say." he said, turning away. "We can spend the night counting southern stars or catch a little sleep before the moon rises."

Without waiting for Retruance to reply, he shot on ahead, aiming for the riverine pass between the towering peaks. One of the wildest and noisiest rivers he'd ever seen flowed through the narrow water gap and down to the jungle, toward the distant Quietness Ocean.

Retruance lingered to test again the wisps of Dragon

scent in the humid air, and then followed several miles behind.

All the better, he said to himself. *Furby can make camp for us on some cool mountaintop.*

He was greatly impressed by these high mountains. They were surely the tallest peaks anywhere on the continent. Their feet were buried in the thick, tangled jungle, their lower slopes were densely clad with giant hardwoods. Higher up the cover changed to soaring pines, alternating with high, grassy alpine meadows. The bare upper third of their slopes rose steeply, almost straight up. Thick clouds washed over the peaks, frequently dumping sheets of rain to the accompaniment of lightning flashes and rolling thunder.

Hello! he thought. *There are people of some sort living on the middle mountainsides, I see.*

He was about to shout to Furbetrance, in case he'd missed the round, stone huts perched precariously just at the timberline, when he saw his brother dive toward them.

He's seen them, Retruance decided.

He began a more moderate descent, dropping as he did so through a heavy layer of wet, gray clouds that masked his view of the tiny native village and the other Dragon for several minutes.

Now where could he have got to? he wondered, not seeing the younger Dragon when he himself finally emerged from the mist.

He pivoted into a tight circle and dropped closer to the treetops, sensing something was wrong.

Unless he's gone through the pass to the other side. No, he was definitely headed for a landing when last I saw him!

Retruance wove back and forth on the strong updrafts, flying not far from the tiny village, ducking in and out of the lower clouds. A small crowd of people were clambering along a goat path above the village, going around the shoulder of the mountain that edged the water gap.

As he banked to follow them he heard their excited shouts.

"We've snared the child snatcher! Hooray! Hurry!"

Women's voices came, also, saying, "Now be careful, Lofters! Snagged he may be, but hot is his breath, recall!"

"Snagged!" cried Retruance. "For Pete's sake! They've got old Furbetrance fairly netted down there— like a plump pie pigeon!"

If it hadn't been so dangerous, the scene might have been comical, for poor Furbetrance had flown headlong and heedless into a net knotted of tough ropes stretched from side to side across the riverine pass. When he'd hit the strands, he'd flipped head over pointed tail several times, trapping himself in the ropes and binding his wings tight to his sides.

"He's lucky the net's holding him up," thought Retruance aloud, "or he'd have had a pretty bad fall into yonder river!"

HE landed, unnoticed in the excitement, on a narrow ledge several dozen feet above the dangling Dragon. He considered an immediate charge on the natives, flames spurting and fearsomely bellowing, but he hesitated. How to get Furbetrance down? The trappers must have some idea how to disentangle the Dragon . . . perhaps.

If I do it, I might drop him. Where he hangs it's much too narrow to get our wings spread!

He slid to a landing behind an outcrop of gray stone to watch the action. It occurred to him that these mountain men might possibly have some idea of Arbitrance's whereabouts. Otherwise, why would they have gone to the trouble to set up a Dragon-sized snare? It could only be a trap for a full-grown Dragon.

Scantily clad Lofters easily climbed the sheer walls of the gorge, uncoiling great loops of heavy rope as they went. In a surprisingly short time they moved into position above the writhing Dragon, and began to jockey their lines into place to support the Dragon's tremendous weight once the net was cut loose.

"Hi, Dragon!" a loud voice hailed. "If you stay still and hold your fire, we'll get you out of this fairly quickly. Agreed?"

Furbetrance, who'd been trying unsuccessfully to twist his head about to blast through the twisted netting, realized suddenly that, were he to do so, he would plunge into the raging river far below. Sensibly, he ceased his struggles and nodded agreement.

"I've little choice, I see," he said. "No flames and no biting, then."

The mountain men expertly lassoed the trapped Dragon's head and both wing tips in such a way that, when the net was suddenly cut loose from its moorings, the Dragon's heavy body merely swung with majestic slowness to the left and came to rest in a narrow green strip of alpine meadow halfway up the wall of the gorge.

The rest of the villagers quickly whipped their lines about the boles of several twisted but sturdy pines and snubbed them tight. Furbetrance remained firmly bound but at least he was no longer dangling upside down, in danger of falling into the chill torrent.

"May I ask, then," he said, putting the best face on his predicament, "what's next? Do you intend to make pot roast of me or perhaps Dragon stew? Or hold me for ransom? That's your best bet," he decided. "There must be a few Dragons and friends back home who'd part with some of their treasure to set me free. My good brother, for example . . ."

He broke off, remembering that Retruance had been only a few miles behind him when he'd flown into the net. He rolled his eyes about, trying to catch a glimpse of Retruance, but failed. His bindings wouldn't allow him to twist his head enough to look upward.

"Neither roast nor stew," said a figure behind a full-length hide shield perched on a rock lip not far from Furbetrance's nose. "And we have little use for your gold or jewels, living here as we do.''

"Why bother, then?'' asked Furbetrance.

His normal Dragon equanimity had returned after the first few chancy moments in the net. "What can I do for you?''

"Listen!'' called the man on the rock, laying aside the shield but keeping it close to hand.

He was a burly man of middle years, well muscled and deeply browned by the tropical sun. He was dressed in a scarlet-and-white striped, calf-length kilt, unlike the rest of his tribe—men, women, and children—who wore only short skirts about their hips and nothing much more.

Retruance, watching from above, noted the men carried long scabbard knives strapped to their bare thighs. Most also carried short, recurved mountain-sheep's-horn bows in one hand and long, cruelly barbed arrows in the other.

They hadn't notched their arrows to make ready to shoot, however. Although his brother's situation seemed perilous, Retruance knew a Dragon's tough scales and immense strength could withstand almost any such puny weapon. His brother could, fairly easily, tear the strands that held him to the pines, now that there was no further danger of falling in the river.

The tribal chief, if that's what he was, waved his arms and shouted at the younger Dragon, "Harken to me! We'll let you go on your way if you promise on a Dragon's most solemn word of honor never to bother us again.''

"How have I bothered you?'' wondered Furbetrance, sounding puzzled. "I've never passed this way before, I assure you!''

The native leader seemed surprised by this earnest remark and took a few moments to consult with the group of tribal elders who stood behind him.

"My sharp-eyed councillors,'' he said to Furbetrance at last, "point out to me that you are indeed slightly

smaller and more of a greenish cast than the terrible
Dragon who's been terrorizing us for the past several
years. It's possible you're right, Dragon! We intended
our springe for another Dragon altogether. If so, we are
prepared to release you with our sincere apologies.''

"Let's talk about this," suggested Furbetrance, completely calm by now. "It happens we've been looking
for just such a Dragon, my brother and I."

"Talk all you want," called the chief, "but you don't
go free until we have your sacred promise never to fly
around here again."

"Easily given, especially if you can tell us where this
other Dragon went," rumbled Retruance, moving out of
his hiding place.

The sudden sight of a second, even larger Dragon
caused a frightened stir among the mountain men. Most
of them moved hastily away from the meadow, hiding
among the straggly stand of dwarf pines below.

Retruance spread his wings to glide down into the
meadow. The villagers darted even farther back into the
covering pines to avoid being flattened by the descend-
ing beast.

"*Two* dratted Dragons!" shouted their chief, falling
back several paces himself. "Stand steady and ready,
men! No false moves, either of you! You might squash
us in a trice, but we can do some damage before you
kill us!"

"Now, now! Simmer down," snapped Retruance, a
bit impatiently. "We came in peace and we intend to
depart the same way, if you'll let us. And for what it's
worth—which is a great deal—you have two Dragons'
promises never to come your way again, if you don't
want us."

The chief thought this over, came to a decision, and
signaled to his rope handlers. With a few deft twists of
the binding ropes Furbetrance was free. The handlers
stepped back to coil their heavy lines.

Furbetrance crouched in the grass with a sigh and gestured to his brother to join him.

"Now, perhaps you'll agree we deserve some explanation of your unprovoked attack," Retruance began.

It was beginning to grow dark as the sun dipped below the edge of the distant ocean. The older Dragon gathered and arranged a pile of deadfall branches nearby, setting it afire for light and warmth with a burst of his breath.

"Come, let us warm ourselves and speak together as sensible people," he added when the Lofters still hesitated. "We'll keep our promise and promise not to harm you, also. We're merely searching for our long-lost father. We believe he flew this way."

"I am called Quillan," said the long-robed chief, drawing nearer. "I am headman of our village of Timberside."

Retruance gave the Lofters his name and Furbetrance's as well, and spoke briefly of their origins in Carolna.

"We've heard stories of Carolna," Quillan said with a nod. "Welcome! And accept our apologies for the netting."

"Tell us how it came to be here," replied Furbetrance politely, rubbing his massive shoulders where the rough cables had scraped his green scales rather badly. "Describe this other Dragon, please."

"We've seen entirely too much of him—at least, we believe he was a male," replied Quillan, taking a seat on a ledge where he was just below the Dragons' eye level.

"Just less than three summers back he came to our mountains and made a nest up there, on that highest peak overlooking the gorge. We thought nothing of it at first. We had no reason to fear Dragons. The few we've met were always quite polite and friendly enough."

"*This* Dragon was rather uppity, we thought," said a woman from the crowd. "My elder daughter sought to make a friend of him and he chased her away and warned us all never to bother him."

"That doesn't sound like Papa at all," protested Fur-betrance. "He's most fond of people and especially of children of all ages—as friends, I mean, not as dinners. Dragons are most particular about their meat."

"He stayed up there alone for a number of months," continued the woman. "Then, about two years ago, he upped and flew away . . ."

". . . and returned six moons later," continued Quillan to recapture the explanation. "And then he stole one of our babies!"

The villagers muttered and nodded shocked affirmation, attesting to the chief's accusation.

"You *saw* him do that?" cried Retruance, shocked to his very tail tip.

"Yes! Took a little girl right from her cot outside her parents' hut," Quillan insisted solemnly. "Carried her off for a full day and a night! We mourned her as dead. Sang the death wish for her spirit!"

"But the . . . the Dragon returned her?" Retruance asked, hardly able to speak clearly in his fear.

"The next day!" cried another woman. "She is my daughter, you see."

"Harmed?" inquired a very worried Furbetrance. "This is quite, quite serious!"

"Unharmed," admitted the chief. "The baby was but two years of age and seemed to take it all as a lark. There were certainly no signs of her being hurt."

"I just can't *imagine* . . . ," sputtered Retruance. "I can't imagine *any* Dragon doing such a thing, let alone our gentle papa—who has never harmed anyone, to my certain knowledge!"

"If it *was* Papa," put in Furbetrance.

"As big as your brother," Quillan described the kidnapper. "Much more gold on his topside, so he glittered magnificently in the sun! Red-and-purple underbelly, I remember. Grand black boot markings on his feet . . ."

"Certainly *sounds* like Papa," muttered Retruance to

his brother. "Did you notice if he wore . . . ah . . . any sort of jewelry?"

"Yes," said the first woman. "He wore a wide collar of flat gold links fastened rather tight about his neck. It had a raised rune or a letter of some sort dangling from it."

"Letter *M*, by any chance?" asked Returance weakly.

Such a collar had been a gift from Murdan the Historian. Arbitrance had worn it constantly.

"I couldn't say about that," said the woman, "being that I never learned any letters, Sir Dragon!"

Arbitrance had disappeared after keeping the baby girl for a day and a night.

"If it *was* Arbitrance," said his sons, still unwilling to believe the evidence.

But it certainly appeared it *was* their papa who had done such a strange and wicked deed.

"That's not all," Quillan added sadly. "After another half-year the Dragon, this same Dragon, gold collar and all, set up camp again on the top of the mountain."

"What did you do?" Retruance wanted to know.

"What could we do? Move away or try to drive him off—and he could easily beat us in a fight, what with those sharp claws and his fires and all."

"Understandable," agreed Retruance. "What happened next?"

"We were undecided—and greatly afeared. Then he came one night and stole a second child!"

"*Great heavens!*" cried Furbetrance with a blast of red fire. "There's something very, very wrong here."

"Wrong is right!" agreed Quillan emphatically.

His people nodded their heads and looked very serious.

"Who was it this time?" asked Retruance, almost afraid to ask.

"A boy of five or so," the chief of Timberside told them. "Young Diamont there, son of Diamont, it was.

Snatched him from his evening play and kept him for three whole days!''

''We were about to sing the death song for him, too,'' wailed a woman identified by the chief as the boy's mother, ''when Diamont wandered back into camp on the morning of the fourth day.''

She pushed forward a lad of six or seven, looking very frightened but determined to seem brave facing the two enormous Dragons.

''Diamont, my lad,'' said Furbetrance most gently. ''No need to fear old Furbetrance and Retruance! If that . . . *other* . . . Dragon harmed you or frightened you, it was because he was . . . sick, it may be, or somehow out of his head. I think he may have been enchanted.''

''Yes, sir,'' said Young Diamont.

''Did he—this other Dragon . . . his name is Arbitrance Constable, did you know? Did he hurt you?''

''N-n-n-no, sir,'' the boy admitted slowly. ''Carried me up high, is all.''

''What did he say to you, this Dragon?'' Retruance asked.

The lad shivered—more at the present circumstances than the memory of his captivity, Furbetrance thought.

He gently picked the lad up in his right foreclaw and set him beside his chief on the higher ledge. Quillan put an arm about the boy's shoulder and gave him a reassuring hug.

''Tell us—tell these great beasts, I mean—what they want to know and tell them truly, laddy. The . . . the *other* Dragon, the one who took you off? He was their father, you see, and they are terribly upset about it.''

''I see, yes, sir!'' said Young Diamont carefully. ''Great Dragons, I'll tell you whatever I can. But will you hurt him, then? Your father, I mean. For he wasn't bad to me at all and gave me good food to eat and played games with me, you see, sirs.''

''No, we won't harm him. He's our papa,'' Retruance reassured him softly, ''and neither a Dragon nor a young man like you, my boy, wants his very own papa ever harmed, does he?''

"No, sir,'' agreed Young Diamont.

"Well . . . if *your* papa were . . . *deranged* . . . or, more likely, enthralled by some magician or wizard,'' Retruance went on, "you'd want to find him and help him back to his senses, before . . .''

"I see,'' said the boy, and everyone in the village nodded and murmured in sympathetic agreement.

"What did you two talk about, though?'' asked Furbetrance. "You were together three days?''

"Two days and two nights and half a day,'' replied the lad concisely. "We played games—like 'eye spy,' you know? In his nest, that was.''

"I remember playing that with Papa when I was a kit,'' said Furbetrance, nodding solemnly. "Go on, Young Diamont, please.''

"Well . . . he said he would teach me to fly, he said, but I said I didn't have any wings, you see, sirs. So he didn't teach me to fly.''

He seemed genuinely disappointed at that.

"A natural thing for a Dragon father to say to a youngster, I guess,'' said Quillan. "We teach our young to hunt and fish and climb mountains. You Dragons teach your young ones to fly.''

"Precisely!'' agreed Furbetrance with another nod and a mournful sniff.

Young Diamont was warming to his subject now. After all, it had been a year or more since anyone had asked him about his strange adventure.

"He took me on his head and . . . and I held fast to some of his ears. And we flew through the air over the low jungles and down to the ocean shore!'' he said eagerly. "I'm the very first of my tribe ever to see the ocean's waves from up close! Nobody believes me, sirs! Tell them that some waves are higher than a grown-up man's head. Much higher!''

"It's quite true!'' said Retruance, nodding to Diamont's mother and father. "The lad didn't just make that up."

"We caught fish in our bare hands for a fry!" continued the lad. "The Dragon made a fire by blowing on a pile of dry sticks—like you just did! And we swam in a sandy-bottomed pool where the water was as clear and still as in Mama's cooking pot. There were colored fish all around us!"

"And he said to you?" his mother prompted.

"He asked me my name and I told him and he said I was a good boy and big and brave for my age," replied Young Diamont proudly. "And he carried me across the mountains to see the far water, the Gulf as he named it, and there was a terrible storm, but we flew high over it and came straight home. Then he said good-bye and set me down a short walk from our house and told me to go home."

"He told you not to tell anyone about your ... adventures?" Retruance asked.

"No sir, Dragon, sir! He was very nice to me. We picked melons from a wild melon patch and ate them for breakfast just before he set me to home again. I do hope no harm comes to him."

"One more thing," asked Furbetrance quietly. "What did he ask you to call him? Did he give you a name?"

The lad thought about this hard for a long moment, then shook his head.

"I called him 'sir' and later 'Dragon,' is all," he replied.

"Well!" sighed the older Dragon brother. "Well and well!"

"Twice more the same Dragon, this Arbitrance as you name him now, flew down and captured one and another of our babes. Once a lass of twelve who was picking berries beside the river," said Quillan. "He kept her for only an afternoon."

"Is the girl here? Could we speak to her?" asked Furbetrance.

"Well, ah, no," replied Quillan. "Her parents thought it best to take her off to stay with her cousins over near Brittlestone Quarry."

"The Dragon didn't harm her, did he?"

"No, not as far as we could tell from what she said, but . . ." Quillan shrugged. "The last time was just three months back and it was then we finally decided to weave and hang the net to catch him if we could and warn him to stay away from us . . . or kill him if we had to. Although nobody's been hurt, you can imagine how fearful we are of . . . what *might* happen."

"I wish I could tell you why Papa did what he did," said Retruance with a sigh, loosing a cloud of white steam, "but we just don't know! Can't even imagine! Who was the last to be snatched up, did you say?"

"A five-year-old lass," Quillan told them. "Same as with Diamont, but she was much more frightened. She'd heard us talking about the terrible Dragon and it put a fright into her, near as I can figure. She cried and carried on all the time and wouldn't play games with the terrible, ugly lizard . . . ah, your poor papa, that is . . . and he brought her home after less than a day. Her family took her and moved down the mountain to Fishkill Ponds, for good and ever. I can't say as I blame them much, either."

It was full dark and there was no moon yet, so the Dragons asked Quillan's permission to spend the night in this meadow, which he gave readily, and he even offered them what food the village could furnish.

"Thank you! We don't need it, however. You've helped more than we could expect under the circumstances," Retruance answered. "Good night, all! We'll be leaving with the rising of the moon."

"Er," hesitated Quillan. "Ah . . . about not ever coming back here? I don't think you need keep that part of your promise."

"When we find Papa . . . ," said Retruance. "Well, he may want to come back and apologize—and see his little friends again, you know.''

"Warn us in advance, is all I ask," said Quillan, smiling for the first time that evening. "He can come then."

"YOU know, then, which way to go?" Furbetrance asked when the villagers had left them alone in the mountainside meadow. The dry meadow grass rustled in a chill breeze dropping down from the peaks, and the stars were as clear as silver bells.

"Well, he isn't *north* of here, we know for sure, nor is he *west* of here. That leaves south or east. What's to the south, d'you know?"

The pair settled side by side in the soft, cool grass. Dragons seldom took more than a few hours sleep a night. For them, eating was always more important than sleeping.

"As I recall my geography, there's nothing much at all south of here," Retruance continued sleepily. "Hot, humid wilderness and lots of lions and snakes and such. Very few Dragons have ever gone there, I'd say."

His brother sighed.

"The continent between the two oceans narrows to a proper isthmus four hundred miles south of here, I've been told," Retruance went on. "At one point the two oceans are less than thirty miles apart. Mama told me that. She visited there once, a long time ago. What happens beyond that . . . who knows? Maybe someday I'll take time to explore and map it."

"But you think eastward has possibilities?"

"Greater possibilities and the chance that, if what Papa is doing is due to an enchantment, the magic comes from the east or north. East and north have always been the most magical directions, Murdan once told me."

But Furbetrance was asleep, snoring slightly and blowing slowly rising puffs of smoke with each exhalation.

•   •   •

"BAILIFF Kedry!" the magistrate of Lakehead called. "Come at once! I need you!"

The burly—some would say corpulent, others insisted on saying just plain fat—court official sighed, set down his jack of midmorning beer and crossed the square of the city at the head of the lake to where the magistrate was waiting on the top step of City Hall.

It was a pleasant early-fall morning, cool and breezy. Flocks of gray-and-white lake gulls circled and cried to each other over the docks, hoping that the overnight lake boats would soon empty their breakfast leavings into the harbor, providing a rich meal without demanding very much labor from them.

The housewives of Lakehead, in striped aprons and lacy mob caps, stood about in groups, waiting their turns at the city pump, at the far end of the square.

Townspeople and visiting sailors nodded respectfully to Kedry as he rumbled past them. Very few were quite sure they really *liked* the huffy, puffy bailiff of Lakehead. But fewer would have wanted his job.

As for Kedry himself, he rather enjoyed it. Except when duty interfered with his midmorning quaff from the tapped kegs of Head o' Lake Tavern.

"Sir!" he greeted the magistrate.

"Sorry to bother you at your ... morning meditations," Fellows said, grinning at his subordinate. "I've just had important word from Lord Granger of Morningside by post pigeon. Come inside. There's important work to do."

Kedry nodded, tugged his forelock respectfully, and followed the mayor into City Hall, down a wide corridor, up the stair, and into the mayor's room at the second-floor rear.

"Sit you down," Fellows directed his bailiff.

He himself dropped into his leather-upholstered, high-backed chair behind the large, shiny, smooth table and spread the message from their liege lord between them.

Kedry, having peeked to confirm the letter was just

what the mayor said it was, plopped his ample posterior onto a straight-backed chair and prepared to listen.

"Lord Granger tells us a large force of Northmen is advancing south from Frontier on Lexor!" Fellows began.

Kedry's face, usually set in an easy, happy-go-lucky grin, suddenly became white and grim.

"Lord High Chamberlain has issued a call to arms to all Achievements, large and small," the mayor continued, studying the message. "We must call muster at once, Bailiff!"

"No problem there, sir," said the court officer. "Will do so at once, Magistrate!"

"There's more! Morningside has already sent the call to Lord Granger's own holdings. He orders that we detail lake sailors to establish a patrol on the lake. There're reports of bands of roving invaders—believed to be Rellings from the Northland—appearing on the lake above Rainbow and headed this way!"

"No problem there, either, sir," Kedry said, after a moment's thought. "I'll put Captain Boscor Sack and his brother Trover in charge of that. They're both in port right now. Armed, would you suggest?"

"These Rellings aren't here on a fishing trip, Bailiff! If they come this way, they're to be stopped, killed if they fight, or captured and held until Lord Granger tells us what to do with them."

"Meanwhile, I'm to muster the militia?" Kedry asked, struggling to raise his bulk from the chair.

"In the square. At four o'clock this afternoon. Swear them in and give them until tomorrow at dawn to get their arms and baggage and to elect their petty officers."

He ran his eye over the paper in front of him, marking his place with a forefinger.

"I'm to lead them to Rainbow, then up to Lexor, Lord Granger orders, to meet the other militias and help the Royal Army defend the city and drive the Northmen back to their ice and snow. We're to meet Lord Granger there. You'll stay here to keep order in the town and county, of course.''

The bailiff tried very hard to look disappointed. In a way, he actually *was* . . . for a moment. On second thought, however, he nodded in satisfaction.

''Yes, Lord Magistrate!''

''Very good, Bailiff Kedry! Find the pigeon trainer and send him to me at once. I must send the message on to Ffallmar and to Lord Murdan at Overhall.''

Kedry bobbed quickly and left the mayor's office, frowning and muttering to himself, rehearsing in his mind everything that needed doing and saying—all at once.

Mayor Fellows raised his voice to bellow for his clerk.

''RELLINGS?'' Kedry said, pondering the question aloud.

He searched his memory for some idea of the enemy. Rellings? Snowfield tribes—that was it! They were, he'd heard, fierce fighters. Allies—or co-conspirators—of the exiled Peter of Gantrell. Men of the snowy wastes in the Northlands beyond the kingdom's frontiers to the north and east.

On the broad front porch of Lakehead City Hall he began to shout orders in all directions. There were always idle early tipplers at Head o' Lake's public bar and lazy malingerers sitting on wharf benches and iron bollards, whittling large pieces of wood down to small pieces and swapping tall lake tales in the morning sun.

''Find the pigeon seller!'' the bailiff called to a group of boys and girls on their way to school. ''Lord Mayor wants him at once!''

''But, Bailiff Kedry . . . ,'' one of the older lads objected.

''Now!'' Kedry barked. ''Someone tell the school-marm there'll be no classes today—nor until after the militia muster is completed and the men have marched tomorrow morning. Go!''

The children, surprised and not entirely displeased by

his orders, shot off in all directions, shouting the exciting news at the top of their shrill voices.

A war patrol on the lake began within hours.

Before the town merchants, farmers, the sail makers, rope walkers, and shipyard carpenters of Lakehead had gathered excitedly to muster in the town square, fully two dozen sturdy, swift lakecraft of all types and sizes had hoisted sail and headed for the horizon.

Inshore, their leader was Captain Boscor Sack, aboard his fast ketch-rigged sloop *Windsong*. Farther down the lake, smaller and faster boats such as *Felicity*, belonging to Boscor's brother Trover, caught the freshening westerly breeze and formed a forward picket line from north to south.

The lake at this time of year was filled with all manner of watercraft, hurrying east or beating to the west to complete one last voyage before the first winter storms could catch them too far from their home ports.

The Outer Fleet was busy inspecting each westbound ship and boat as it approached the fleet. Captain Trover was diplomatic.

"Advise you to go on to Lakehead at best speed," he yelled to a lake bargeman he knew quite well. "Better to be away from the fighting, unless you relish land warfare with them Rellings, Fross!"

"Thanks for the warning!" Captain Fross yelled back. "Dine with me at the Head o' Lake, tomorrow night, eh?"

"If I could, I would, with pleasure," Trover bellowed. "We're liable to be out here on the rough, cold water for some time yet!"

As they pulled away from the slow barge, Trover's nephew, Giffom, *Felicity*'s best lookout, called a new sighting.

"Small boat, dead ahead," he hailed from *Felicity*'s foremast head.

Trover strode to the bow's peak to catch a glimpse of the new sighting.

"How many men in her?" he shouted up to Giffom.

"None I can see, Uncle Captain!" the boy replied at once. "Seems to me she's adrift."

"Run her down just the same," the lake captain decided. "Bear a point to starboard, Henric!"

"Aye, aye, Captain!" responded the helmsman, expertly twirling the spokes of the wheel.

In eight minutes Trover was peering down into the small rowboat. From the looks of it, it was the kind the lake fishermen used to tend their nets—badly needing paint, clumsy, bluff of bow, and flat of keel. Trover spotted no oars in her, which was unusual to say the least.

In the bottom, curled like a sleeping baby or a sick old cat, lay a man dressed in wet gray-white furs.

"Ahoy!" shouted the captain, forming a megaphone with his hands. "We're taking you by the board, mister! Name of Magistrate Fellows and the good Lord of Morningside!"

The figure in the boat stirred, lifted his head, and groaned in pain.

"Get down there and see what's the matter," Trover ordered one of his hands. "Careful now!"

The young sailor dropped expertly into the fisherman's skiff, scarcely making it rock. The man in the bottom moaned loudly and tried to lift his head again.

"He's badly hurt!" the sailor yelled back after a quick examination. "Lots of blood all about! And no oars in the boat, Captain!"

"Hoist him aboard, then, but carefully, carefully," decided Trover.

Even from the foredeck he could see the bloodstained bilgewater around the man in the skiff.

A stretcher was quickly rigged from the main gaff and the wounded man in bloodied furs was hauled up, swung inboard to the main deck, and hustled below, where he was lifted carefully into one of the bunks.

"He's an awful hole in his belly," whispered Trover, almost to himself. "Lost a lot of blood, must be."

He did what he could to make the stranger comfortable in the bunk. The wounded man gasped for water and the ship's boy brought a mug and held it to his lips.

"Easy! You'll choke him if you give it to him too fast!" his captain snapped. "Cover him with plenty of warm blankets and stay by him. Tell me if he comes to and wants to talk."

"None of the lakeshore fishermen I ever met," said an older member of *Felicity*'s crew. "Strange cast to his features, too."

"I can see!" growled Trover, turning to return to deck. "Keep a close eye on him, boy! Yell if he comes to enough to talk."

On deck he hailed the nearest blockade ship.

"A Northlander, or I miss me guess! We'll take him back to Lakehead," he explained when she closed on the *Felicity*. "Keep an eye out for more stray boats, Fellish! I'll be back after dawn, I judge."

"Who is he?" Fellish wanted to know.

"Not sure. Looks like he might be one of them Rellings the bailiff spoke about!" replied Trover. "Wounded close to death!"

He turned his eyes inboard. "Hands to the sheets! Prepare to go about! Helmsman, port tack for Lakehead! Hop to it! He's in a bad way, or I'm no judge, whoever or whatever he might be, poor soul! May not live to see the bailiff's gaol!"

⋆ 3 ⋆
Call to Arms!

THE ten-day overland journey from Hidden Lake Canyon to Overhall was pleasant, especially in this early fall of the year when dry southerly winds alternated with sudden light showers and cool gusts off the distant Quietness.

At first Tom and Manda rode along the east-west range of the Snow Mountains, enjoying the spectacular scenery of snowcapped peaks on one hand and flat, featureless desert on the other. Riding at a relaxed pace by day and camping out at night were rather pleasant, a change from the hard work of beginning a house in the canyon.

When they had reached a point several days' ride to the east of Hidden Lake Canyon, the land began to roll gently and the yearly rainfall there was sufficient to encourage lush grasslands but very few trees. This was the western edge of Murdan's Ramhold, and his huge flocks of sheep grazed here in the winter and spring before summer dried the water holes and springs, and the rams and their ewes had to be herded up into the foothills to the north for yeaning, to spend the summer and early-fall days.

The grasslands were not quite as empty as they seemed. Every day or so the travelers came to upwelling springs, many of which had fostered the growth of prosperous ranches and even a few villages. This broad, fertile land was the bread basket of Carolna. Seemingly endless grasslands became seemingly endless fields of

wheat, oats, corn, and barley and pasturelands for horses
and fat cattle.

The Librarian's party overtook and passed long trains
of wagons being hauled by teams of stoic oxen, down
to the Cristol River, where the wheat and barley would
be ground at water-driven mills, bagged, and shipped by
flour barges east to Head of Navigation, a day or so
south of Overhall and west of Lakehead.

From there the cargoes were carried by ox train over
the shallow divide to Lakeheart Lake, and transhipped
another time into sturdy lake barges for the next leg—
to the more populous east. Much of the wealth of the
powerful Gantrell family had come from controlling this
trade and its traffic, Manda explained to Tom.

Like the loads of milled flour, Tom and Manda were
carried the middle third of their journey up the slow,
winding Cristol. The river barges, driven by the steady
autumnal westerlies, were quite comfortable and roomy.

Their fellow passengers were a varied lot; hardworking smallholders on their way to the eastern cities
with their wives, children, and servants to sell their
grain, buy seed, purchase new clothing and winter supplies, and see the sights; commercial travelers returning
east to restock their trade goods and report to their em-
ployers a successful summer; an occasional circuit court
justice and attendant cloud of lawyers and clerks excitedly looking forward to the Fall Sessions at Lexor.

If not the men, their wives immediately recognized
Princess Alix Amanda and made much of her presence.
Tom talked to their husbands about farming and building
houses in the west, while Manda was told how to raise
chickens, cows, and children so far from the amenities
of castles and cities.

Evenings were filled with music—many of the travelers brought fiddles and harps and flutes along for just
this time—and stories and news. The barge crews furnished plain but plentiful food and drink. In this way,

the long days of early fall aboard a river barge were pleasant and never lonesome.

AT the confluence of the Cristol and its largest tributary, Overhall Stream, Tom and Manda had their horses and sumpter mules unloaded from the livestock pens on the foredeck, saddled, and reloaded in a grove of ancient riverside willows, and rode up Overhall Vale to the Historian's tall castle, by far the most pleasant part of their long journey.

On every hand Overhall tenants and neighboring freehold farmers stopped their late-summertime work to come to the roadside to greet the Princess and her consort. The young couple was known everywhere, but nowhere more cordially greeted than here, near Murdan's home Achievement.

The countryfolk well remembered the capture of Overhall by the Mercenary Knights, the fight against Lord Peter of Gantrell, and the victorious return of their lord after Gantrell had at last been forced to flee into exile.

"We could swing around to Ffallmar Farm and spend a day or two with Rosemary and her family," suggested Manda.

She'd been the only woman in Hidden Lake Canyon all summer long—the rest being menservants, surveyors, and young second-sons who had been selected by Tom and Manda to work his new Achievement.

"I miss Mornie, too," she admitted wistfully. "I wonder how she fared in Broken Land this season!"

"You're travel weary as it is," protested her husband. "But if you really want to take the extra time . . ."

Tom was an indulgent husband. Fortunately, Manda was an independent woman who seldom took advantage of his good nature.

"No, no!" she said with a sudden brilliant smile, "I still am a city and castle girl, you know. I'll be happiest when we ride into Overhall's front gate once again. Besides, you must report to your employer. Murdan'll be impatient to hear how we've fared out in the wilderness.''

Tom urged his mare to a gallop, leaving the mules to follow at their own pace. Manda followed Tom. They rode swiftly along Overhall Stream until they started up the greensward hill leading up to the Overhall foregate.

Pulling his horse down to a walk again, Tom said, ''Well, in a few more summers and winters, we'll have a place as populous and pleasant as Overhall, all our own. Well, maybe not quite as populous.''

''I know that!'' his wife said with a laugh. ''I've absolutely no complaints, really! I've enjoyed our summer at Hidden Lake as much as any I can remember—and I'm ever so old, you know.''

They had been seen and recognized coming up the vale, and by the time they rode through the barbican gate, across Gugglerun Draw, and through the wide-open inner gate, a crowd had filled the outer bailey, shouting their welcome.

Murdan was in their midst, beaming broadly behind his full black beard. With him stood his daughter Rosemary and her three young children, waiting for them to dismount so they could engulf the arrivals with their love and joy.

''I *do* like homecomings!'' cried the Historian, stepping back so others could salute the Librarian and his beautiful Princess. ''We've laid on a real Overhall dinner party for tonight, after you've rested and washed up and gotten settled in.''

''I can start right now!'' exclaimed Manda, forgetting her travel weariness at once. ''Oh, Rosemary! I was just now saying how much I missed you. Next summer you really must bring the children to Hidden Lake for a long stay. It's well worth the journey!''

Rosemary's youngest, Eduard of Ffallmar, jumped up and down with excitement at the thought.

"Will I see rattlesnakes? Will I ride on a riverboat? Will I . . . ?"

"Eddie," cried one of his sisters in the matter-of-fact exasperation common to all older sisters, "you've seen mountains before! And the ocean, too. Remember when we were stolen away to Wall?"

"But that," said Eddie, just as a matter of fact, "was years and years ago. Now I can ride a horse as well as anyone."

Tom settled the matter for the moment by asking Eduard and his sisters to lead their sweaty horses up to the stables under Aftertower and make sure they were rubbed down, watered, and fed a heaping measure of oats with brown sugar in reward for being so good as to carry their riders a thousand miles with not a bit of trouble, not even a lost shoe.

"All goes well beside Hidden Lake, then?" asked Murdan of them both.

He led them into his Great Hall at the bottom of Middletower, where a light lunch—three tables filled with it—had been whipped up by Mistress Grumble, Murdan's capable housekeeper, on very short notice.

"We got all the lines and angles measured and staked out and the elevations figured," Tom told him eagerly. "Retruance can begin designing the house and the grounds, now that we have the proper figures. If all goes well, we should be able to start some construction with the new year."

"Do you still not intend to build curtain walls about your castle?" asked Graham, Murdan's Captain of the Overhall Guards.

The old soldier thought all great houses should have thick stone walls and tall watchtowers and deep moats, all the crenellated defensives of his beloved Overhall.

"No walls, except for flowers to climb upon!" said Tom positively. "What use? The only way for an enemy to reach us will be either up the canyon, where ten men could hold off an army of a thousand . . . or drop straight down almost a thousand feet from the rim. Manda thought of putting up towers, as towers are elegant, but Retruance and I talked her out of it.''

"Towers," admitted his Princess, "would look not just strange but downright silly in our canyon, I suppose. The tallest would reach no more than a third the way to the rim.''

"You're right, of course," admitted Graham, giving up.

He piled thinly sliced red roast beef slices on a slab of dark, seeded rye bread and slathered the whole with a generous dollop of hot brown mustard. "Still . . .''

"Have you heard anything from Retruance and Furbetrance?" Tom asked, turning to face the Historian. "They've been gone for almost four months now.''

"How well I know it!" sighed Murdan. "I'd never admit it to your good Dragon Mount, but I miss Retruance and his brother almost as much as I've missed their father. A Companion without a Dragon is only part a whole elf, as the saying goes.''

"Oh? I never heard that one," Manda said, laughing. She was doing her best to surround a steaming meat pasty filled with tomatoes, onions, and hot peppers.

"Ho? I can't imagine why not," said the Historian with an innocent smile. "I made it up myself, not long ago.''

"Say, thirty seconds ago?" Manda teased.

Murdan wrinkled his nose at the Princess but said to Tom, "No, no word as yet. Not that I expected any this soon. I did hear from Hetabelle, however. She said that the boys headed south into Isthmusi.''

"Well, they've tried every other direction," said Tom. "They'll have fine tales to tell when they do return.''

ONCE at Overhall it was easy to fall into the familiar routine of the Historian's castle. Tom spent his mornings supervising his own staff, gathered to arrange and care for Murdan's vast personal library, his official papers, and the seemingly endless and entirely muddled papers of the late architect-Dragon Altruance, the builder of Overhall Castle.

"There are some files missing, sir," said his chief assistant, a bright lad from Sprend, a village a half day's walk toward Ffallmar Farm and Lakehead. "They appear to deal with tunnels and passages that aren't there, whatever that means."

"Make a note to ask Retruance about them," answered the Librarian. "I've long suspected that good old Altruance built some secrets into these walls. His grandson may have some ideas where the notes got off to."

Manda, as a Princess and a member of the Royal Family of Carolna, mistress of a number of important and valuable properties, threw herself into their administrative details and related social matters. She was assisted by her own staff of butlers, majordomos, and factors, but mostly by a dour middle-aged woman named Mistress Plume.

"Have you ever heard any more from Plume?" Manda asked the woman.

"No, thank goodness!" the fugitive's wife said with some heat. "Nor do I ever wish to."

"I think you're right, I must admit," the Princess said with a sigh.

Mistress Plume's acid and arid little husband had proved a spy and a traitor within Overhall in the pay of Lord Peter of Gantrell, Manda's wicked and ambitious uncle. He'd disappeared into the far Northland of the Relling nomads, following Lord Peter into exile four years before.

Mistress Plume was neither glum nor acid, and Manda was very fond of her. The secretary now took a fat sheaf of papers and began to sort through them, telling Manda of their subjects as she riffled.

"You've been asked to sponsor the Fall Sessions Ball," she noted. "Did I tell you that?"

"No, but I knew Father was going to ask. When I was Princess Royal all I had to do was go to the ball. Now that I'm just an ordinary married Princess, I have to work at it."

But she loved such doings and came to her bed each night still elated and happy with her daily tasks.

MURDAN was already preparing to go to Fall Sessions, still two months off, and that called for a series of social events at Overhall as he gathered his delegates, wined and dined Small Achievement neighbors, and planned petitions and political strategems.

He had, at last, hired a new secretary of his own—a young, rather serious and scholarly young man named Flaretty—and spent long hours closeted with him in his Foretower office dictating letters and drawing up memoranda by the ream.

But in all this confusion of preparation there was time and opportunity to ride off to a shucking bee or a harvest fair at this or that nearby Achievement or tenant holding. The Lord of Overhall was expected to make an appearance at each gala affair marking the end of another good growing and harvesting season.

The three of them, accompanied by Flaretty, rode down to Ffallmar Farm to escort Murdan's daughter and her lively three children back to Ffallmar, Rosemary's farmer husband, a prosperous, honest and thoroughly delightful man.

As they neared the Ffallmar Farm gate, they were met by Ffallmar himself, bluff, ruddy, and solid, accompanied by three officers of the Royal Courier Service in their orange-and-brown uniforms and tall plumed hats.

It was said their uniforms had been designed by the King himself, in colors and plumes that made a Royal Courier easy to spot, even at a great distance.

"Hello and most welcome home!" shouted Ffallmar as they approached the gate. "Most welcome home, sweetest wife! Obedient and loving offspring!"

Rosemary leaned out of her saddle—she rode astride, not in the new-fashioned sidesaddle manner that ladies of fashion were recommending to accommodate the season's longer, tighter skirts—and gave her man a fierce hug and a long kiss, although they'd not been apart for more than a month.

"Manda, my beloved!" cried Ffallmar. "And good old Tom Librarian! So glad you're back from the far wilderness. Wonderful to see you, Murdan, my liege!"

"We've been eagerly looking forward to seeing you, your farm, and Rosemary's home-cooked meals," laughed Tom, shaking the farmer warmly by the hand.

Murdan and Ffallmar slapped shoulders, Manda gave the farmer a kiss and a hug, but they were distracted by the presence of the three Royal Couriers.

"We do have important words for you from Lexor," admitted their senior officer to Murdan as soon as the greeting had quieted down a mite. "It can wait a short while, Lord Historian, until you are dismounted. But not much longer. It *is* urgent!"

"Lead the way to the house, son-in-law," Murdan commanded Ffallmar.

There were farm lads and lasses lining the long, elm-shaded drive to greet them. A bouquet of huge chrysanthemums in brilliant reds and golds were presented to Manda—the traditional Ffallmar greeting to a visiting member of the Royal Family.

"We can't disappoint them," apologized Manda to Murdan. "Tom and I will look at the new piglets and the colts, as they've planned for us. You go ahead to the house and hear what news comes from Father."

Murdan nodded silently and gestured to the Courier officers and Ffallmar to follow him. They dismounted and climbed three stone steps onto the wide front veranda of the wide, rambling Ffallmar House, where they could talk in private comfort.

Manda and Tom went off, dragged almost bodily by Eddie and his sisters, Valerie and Molly, and followed

by the farm men and maidens, all dressed in their very
best for the occasion.

"Come see my new horse!" cried Eddie. "No, *not* a
pony! I love old Patch to death, but in a year, Papa says,
my feet'll be dragging in the farmyard dirt when I ride
her. So he gave me a real, full-sized horse. Her name is
Challenger."

Listening to the children's excited babble and truly
admiring the farm buildings, barns, stables, coops, sheds,
tall silos, deep cellars, and the broad fields all around,
the young couple spent a congenial two hours, hoping
and planning someday to do almost as well in Hidden
Lake Canyon.

They returned to the manor house at last, glowing with
pleasure, a bit dusty, with wisps of golden wheat straw
adhering here and there to their clothing, somewhat out of
breath and rather sweaty from all the running about.

The Royal Courier Service officers were more relaxed, having loosened their gold-frogged jackets and
put off their extra-tall plumed bonnets to take a glass of
cider, cool from Rosemary's icehouse.

Murdan looked distracted. As soon as it was polite to
do so, he drew Manda and Tom aside and showed them
the letter brought by the Couriers.

"It's from the Lord High Chamberlain," he said.
"It's worrisome—certainly quite serious."

"Tell us about it," said Manda. "To save us from
having to read old Walden's circumlocutions."

"It's actually pretty straightforward for Walden,"
said Murdan seriously. "I'd better read it aloud to you."

He rustled the parchment with its azure ribbon and
red-wax Royal Privy Seal. Walden had been left in
charge of the royal establishment in Lexor while the
King and his family chose to travel.

Murdan read aloud:

> *"Lord Murdan of Overhall, Royal Historian, post
> haste (by way of Royal Courier; for his hand only!)*

"My Lord:

"Two events of supreme concern have come to my attention this moment.

"First, the acting commander of the garrison at Frontier has sent urgent word to us that a large force of heavily armed Northmen, led by the notorious Grand Blizzardmaker of the Rellings, several days ago bypassed the post of the garrison at Frontier. His message was sent, he said, just before he was going to be surrounded and invested by vastly superior numbers. It is his understanding and judgment that the Rellings and their wild allies intend to war on Carolna immediately and are marching on Lexor with the purpose of taking and leveling the capital, looting the warehouses and great houses in order to finance a long and bloody war of conquest.

"We have no further word about this invasion at this point in time, but I am making all possible preparations to resist the Northern hordes when they reach the capital walls.

"I have sent what information I have toward Knollwater, where the King and his family are currently visiting, but I understand that heavy rains have made the roads impassable between here and there. The Couriers bearing this message are instructed to carry copies to the King by a roundabout route, as necessary.

"As more information becomes available, I will forward it to you and to the King at Knollwater. Word has already been sent to all Achievements ordering them to call their militia to arms in the King's name, and lead their soldiers toward Lexor at once.

"The second matter is less clear but even more frightening.

"The mayor and magistrate of Lakeheart, one

Fellows, last night forwarded to Lord Granger for presentation to the King a report made to him by his bailiff Kedry. Kedry says he on Monday last attended a Relling prisoner in his gaol who had been wounded and was expected to die.

"When asked to account for his wound, the Relling, who had been caught on Lakeheart Lake the day before, admitted that he first joined and later fled from a troop of Relling soldiers who were moving south to Waterfields with the intention of stealing and looting in the wake of a disturbance they expected to arise following a major uproar at Knollwater during the King's visit.

"With his last breath—no medical care was able to save him—the prisoner told Kedry that the 'uproar' the Relling band expected would be the kidnapping of the royal children! *He died before he could give more details.*

"I beg of you, Lord Historian, to come to the aid of Lexor as quickly as possible, *and also to do what you can to warn His Majesty of the threat to the infant Prince Royal and Princess!*

"Perhaps from your position you can advise the Couriers on the fastest path to Waterfields to reach Knollwater with the warning before it is too late!

"Awaiting further word on both matters, I remain your obedient and loyal—and very frightened—servant . . .

Walden of Sweetwater."

"The poor, poor little babes!" cried Manda, clutching Tom's hand. "We must do something, and at once!"

"Ffallmar!" shouted Murdan.

The farmer, who was talking to his guests, came running at once.

"Couriers! On your way at once! Ffallmar, how can

they most quickly reach Knollwater? I hear the rivers
are over their banks.''

"There's been an inordinate rainfall in the southeast,''
said the farmer. "But, Murdan, there're no direct roads
between here and Knollwater! There's no other option.
They will have to ride to the headwaters of the Cristol
and backtrack to Waterfields. It'll take them several
days!''

He sent a servant to his small library for a detailed
map of the area.

"What can *we* do?'' asked Manda, recovering her
composure quickly. She was, after all, a Princess.

"Recall Retruance,'' said Tom. "He can get here and
take us to Knollwater quicker than Couriers can ride
there.''

A Companion and his Mount shared a special rapport
that allowed them to sense when one was calling the
other, even at long distances. Tom had never tried it
from this far away—no telling how far south the Constable brothers had gone—but he was sure it would
work.

Murdan advised him to call at once and the Librarian
went off to a quiet corner of Ffallmar's orchard to do
so. Manda watched him go, a worried frown creasing
her usually sunny face.

"I'll go to Knollwater with Tom,'' she said. "My
place is with my father and stepmother. We may be able
to help prevent the kidnapping—if we are on time.''

"Yes, do that,'' agreed the Historian. "Ffallmar, issue
a call to arms! I intend to go to Lexor immediately myself. Gather our combined levies and follow me as fast
as you can march.''

Ffallmar called for his stable hands to saddle horses
and began assigning to each rider an Achievement and
a rallying point. Rosemary rushed inside to begin writing
the call to muster each would carry, so there would be
no doubt of their authority to call the United Small
Achievements to war.

Murdan stripped an ornate old ring of gold, set with a red stone, from his finger and handed it to Ffallmar.

"Use my signet as authority. My people know it—and you—and will follow at once!"

Before sunset the Royal Couriers had ridden southwest on fresh Ffallmar horses toward the watershed where Cristol River rose.

Ffallmar himself galloped off to Sprend, designated as the mustering place for all Overhall lands and farms, after hurriedly kissing his wife and children and pulling on his half-armor and buckling on his sword as he ran for his horse.

Tom and Manda did all they could to assist Murdan.

"By fastest horse to Lakehead," the Librarian advised the Historian, pointing to the map. "Mayor Fellows'll find you a sloop to carry you to Rainbow. From there, Granger Gantrell should be able to furnish you transport either by fast ship along the coast, or by horse across Overtide and through Greenlevel Forest."

"Raise my forester militia at Greenlevel Royal," Manda reminded him, handing him a note addressed to Strongoak, the Chief Forester of her Royal Forest. "They can reach Lexor faster than Ffallmar and his midland farmers."

"I'm off!" said the Historian grimly. "Good-bye, lad and lass, daughter! I don't know what I can do in Lexor, but I hope to be able to aid Walden in withstanding the attack on the capital. Leave military strategy to me and militia matters to Ffallmar, you two. Protect the King and Queen and the royal children—what you do there in Waterfields is at least as important to the Kingdom as fighting the Rellings in the field. Did you hear from your wandering Dragon, Tom?"

"He answered, but I don't know how long it'll take him," said Tom. "A Constable Dragon can be pretty fast when he must!"

"So can I," muttered Murdan. He slung his leg over his saddle, stuck his booted feet in the stirrups, and shot off down the farm lane, not looking back.

"Come inside and have some supper," urged Rosemary. "Try to get some sleep. No telling when Retruance will come dropping down out of the sky."

A moment before, if you'd asked him, Tom would have sworn he wasn't hungry, but the Historian's daughter's words made him realize how famished he really was.

He and Manda stood embracing each other for a moment of mutual comforting, then followed Rosemary into the warm and brightly lighted farmhouse.

"Oh, come *on*, Retruance!" Manda cried fiercely. "I wish I were a Companion myself!"

"Sooner than later," Tom promised, comforting her. "Come on, yourself! Let's prepare for what is coming by filling our stomachs and getting a bit of rest."

Manda nodded, in control of her emotions and her mind.

"If *we* can't do it, nobody can!" she said firmly.

EDDIE of Ffallmar yielded his father's place to Tom with only a little reluctance. With Ffallmar away, Eddie felt he was entitled to sit at the head of the table. Tom accepted the honor with grace and served bowls of steaming, savory chicken stew with dumplings and rich squares of golden cornbread. Eddie contented himself with passing the cornbread squares and making sure the milk pitcher was passed to his guests, his mother, and his sisters.

Everyone retired as soon as the supper dishes were cleared away. Tom, an old campaigner by now, fell at once into deep sleep but his wife lay awake at his side for a long time, thinking worriedly of her stepsiblings and of her father and his Queen.

At last, when the lights in the kitchen and pantry were blown out by the servant girls on their way to bed, she moved close to her husband's sleeping form and composed herself for sleep.

⁎ 4 ⁎
Knollwater Uproar

RETRUANCE and his brother sat on a sandy Gulf of Carolna beach, paddling their tails in the warm salt waves and wondering what to do next.

"Just peters out!" cried Furbetrance, irritably. "Do you think he went out to sea? There're a lot of islands out there. But Papa was ever a Mountain Dragon by choice, you know. Would he have hidden himself on an island somewhere?"

Retruance shook his head but didn't reply.

Furbetrance turned to demand an answer but recognized the faraway look in his brother's golden eyes.

"What! What is it?" he asked, anger and frustration forgotten.

"It's Tom. Calling me. I must fly to Ffallmar Farm at once!" said Retruance, rising and shaking the sand and saltwater from his tail. "I've got to go!"

"Of course you do!" agreed Furbetrance, also rising. "But what shall *I* do? Go along? Stay here?"

Retruance lifted his enormously powerful wings in preparation for a fast takeoff, but paused a moment to consider his answer.

"Try the nearer islands you see out there," he suggested. "See if the animals or the birds have seen anything of a wayward Dragon. I'll get word to you as soon as I find out what's going on . . . if I can. Good-bye, little brother! Tom wouldn't call if it weren't urgent, you know."

"I know," said the other, wistfully watching him soar

into the blue tropical sky. "I often wish *I* had a Companion myself."

He took off eastward, more gently and thoughtfully than Retruance had flown northward, mulling over in his mind the matter of a Companion.

Dragon Companions weren't all that common. Perhaps one in ten Dragons found such a close Companion in his lifetime. *When one comes along, you're supposed to know it at once, no matter who or what,* Furbetrance thought to himself. *That's the way it was with Murdan and Papa, I've heard them both say, and with Tom and Retruance, too.*

"I've always been very much drawn to Princess Manda myself," he said aloud as he flapped along low over the gulf waves. "Why have I never gotten up enough nerve to ask her? Because she's a Princess, I guess."

He slowly circled the first of a thousand small islands that dotted the vast Gulf of Carolna. Most were uninhabited except by birds and turtles and such. Or so he'd heard. Little was known of the gulf, actually. No Dragon he knew had ever lived or even visited there.

"Which is a good reason to look for Papa there, I suppose," Furbetrance said, sighing.

He lowered himself toward the closest white sand beach, fringed by graceful coconut palms. A great cloud of seabirds screamed into the air, startled to see the huge stranger arrive. They were cautious but not especially afraid.

TOM was awake when he heard his Dragon land in Ffallmar's farmyard. The rooster in the chicken run had just announced the rising of the sun and, looking up, had choked out a frightened *gurk!* when he saw the dark, reptilian form dropping down upon him.

He and his hens scattered, clucking and bawling in panic. Things that dropped from the sky meant only one thing to chickens: danger! Hawks! And hawks meant death and bloodshed and sudden bereavement.

"Oh, hush!" Retruance snorted after them. "Good morning, ma'am!"

This last was to a startled farm lass who'd just come to the hen coop to gather breakfast eggs for her mistress.

"Good morning, Sir Dragon," she said hurriedly, to cover her start. "Welcome to Ffallmar Farm! You are the Dragon Retruance Constable, I know."

"Right! Come for my Companion, Thomas of Overhall. Is he here still?"

"Here and ready for breakfast," Tom hailed from the bedroom window. "Be right down!"

He finished dressing hurriedly, not worrying about waking his wife. Manda could sleep through a riot usually, and the day before had been trying, at best.

She did murmur his name and turn toward him as he opened the bedroom door.

"Wha's?" she asked.

"Retruance is come. I'm going down to tell him the news. Getting up?"

"Of course!" said Manda, sliding out from under the comforter and shaking her thick blond tresses vigorously. "Be right along."

By the time she'd quickly bathed and dressed in a comfortable and serviceable traveling costume and come down the stairs to the breakfasting room off the big farm kitchen, Tom had already told Retruance the information the Lord High Chamberlain had sent the day before.

Retruance was shocked and more than a bit angry.

"Let's go at once!" he rumbled.

He was standing in the barnyard with his head at the open kitchen window. His voice shook the house and brought Rosemary running, followed by her children.

Eddie ran to give Retruance a hug—or as much a hug as a small boy could manage on the huge Dragon—and the girls piped their delighted greetings. Retruance was a great favorite with them all.

Rosemary leaned out the window, kissed Retruance

on the nose, and said, "Now, give them a minute to wake up and have a bite of food, Retruance! No one should go flying off into certain danger without some of my eggs and hickory-smoked ham and pecan pancakes inside."

"You sound just like your father," the Dragon said good-naturedly with a snort. "Oh, all right. I'll give them time to eat, at least. I'd welcome a bit myself, if you can manage it."

He allowed the nightdress-clad Ffallmar children to climb merrily over his head and shoulders and slide down his long, scaly tail while he ate a vast quantity of pancakes submerged in maple syrup and butter. Manda and Tom ate breakfast quickly, all the while discussing their route with the Dragon.

"How long to reach Knollwater?" asked Manda.

"Five hours or so from here, if we fly fast and high. I generally avoid flying low. It tends to frighten children and chickens, you see," answered Retruance with a chuckle. "Now, my good little barnstormers, your mother has your breakfast ready for you and Uncle Retruance has to rush off and save the kingdom once again, so slide into your places and say good-bye, for we are off!"

Tom helped his wife to her accustomed place on the Dragon's broad, smooth head between his foremost pair of ears and then climbed up next to her, saying his farewells to the Historian's daughter and her brood.

"I wish I could come along this time," called Eddie wistfully.

"But someone has to stay here and forward important messages and protect your mother and sisters," his mother told him. "Militiamen will be asking all sorts of questions, and someone must be here who knows the answers. I'll need all the help you can give me, Eduard."

The boy gracefully accepted the responsibility, even though it didn't involve flying off on a Dragon.

"I hope your father'll be all right, Rosemary," worried Manda. "He should be in the capital by Thursday night—if he travels fast."

"Father can take care of himself," insisted Rosemary of Ffallmar loyally. "And my husband will be back for a few hours, before the militia marches, I'm quite sure. Say good-bye to the Princess and Sir Tom, children, and get dressed to do your chores. Colts, calves, and chicks must be fed! Lessons start right on time, in an hour."

"Lessons! When the kingdom is in awful danger of invasion and the royal babies are threatened!" protested ten-year-old Molly.

But young Eddie clapped his hands sharply and said, "Daddy would want us to carry on here as usual, so he can go to war without worry."

"Yes, Eddie!" said both his sisters, amazingly obedient considering he was the youngest of the three.

They waved once more to Retruance and his riders and dutifully trooped off to make their beds and don their working-day clothes.

IN considerably less than the five hours he'd predicted, Retruance swooped down on a large and graceful, rambling old mansion flanked on all sides by wide verandas and surrounded by sweeping lawns and carefully tended flower gardens, set among a glistening network of canals and connected ponds.

This was Knollwater, the childhood home of Queen Beatrix of Carolna.

"Easy now!" cried Tom, leaning far forward over the Dragon's brow. "Look out! Soldiers seem to be expecting an air raid!"

Below them formed tense ranks of soldiers with raised pikes and shouts of defiance, grim officers with drawn swords, and archers with bows bent, as if they were expecting an order to shoot.

"Ho, whoa!" roared Retruance, sliding to a halt in the graveled courtyard. " 'Tis but me, Retruance Con-

stable, and the Princess Manda and the Librarian of
Overhall. Where're the King and the Queen! What's
happened?''

An officer looking greatly distressed rushed up to
them, waving his sword in salute and wiping tears from
his eyes.

''Thank goodness you've come, Dragon! Princess! Librarian! Port your arms, men! Stand at ease!''

Manda slid from the Dragon's lofty forehead, followed by her husband.

''What news, Colonel?'' she asked at once.

''The poor little babe's been stolen away! Snatched
during the early-morning hours, soon after breakfast. It's
just horrible, my Lady Princess! No one saw or heard
him come 'til it was too late! We could do nothing to
stop him!''

''Babe! *Which* child?'' demanded Manda, running full
tilt toward the main entrance to the mansion.

''Get yourself together, man!'' Retruance snapped
quite sharply to the shaking officer. ''Order your men to
put up their weapons before someone gets hurt!''

Tom followed Manda at a run.

They were met at the main door of Knollwater House
by King Eduard Ten himself, who through his bedroom
window had seen them arrive.

''He took little Ednoll!'' groaned the King, catching
his older daughter in his arms and holding her tight. ''A
Dragon came and stole my son! It was . . .''

''Arbitrance?'' asked Tom, who had discussed his
suspicions with Retruance as they flew.

''Was it *truly* Papa?'' wailed Retruance, aghast at
hearing the thought said aloud.

''I . . . I'm afraid it was!'' the King admitted with a
catch in his voice. ''Several people saw him who know
him well. As he departed . . .''

''But . . . *just* Ednoll, Father? What about Amelia? Is
she safe?''

''She's with her mother,'' Manda's father assured her,
relaxing his embrace enough to clasp Tom's hand and

put his hand on Retruance's forepaw. "Up in the master bedroom."

"I want to look about and ask these guards some questions," muttered Retruance quickly. "Go comfort the mother, Companion! I'll try to find out where Papa flew off to when he left here, and all else I can."

Tom nodded and followed the King of Carolna and the Princess up the sweep of stairs to the second floor. On either hand stood Knollwater and royal servants, many in tears and all with shocked, sad, or angry expressions. Their eyes fearfully followed the Dragon as Retruance turned to speak to the guard officer.

"The danger's over for the moment, I suspect. Fall your men out, Colonel! Tell me what you know to have happened."

Beatrix seemed calm but greeted her stepdaughter and son-in-law with an unaccustomed frown, pale countenance, and strained voice.

"It was Arbitrance, they say," she said to Tom as Manda embraced and kissed her and then took the little Princess Amelia on her lap to stroke her hair.

"I'm afraid 'tis so, ma'am," replied the Librarian. "All indications point to it, at any rate. As soon as Retruance gathers information from those who witnessed the terrible deed, he and I will set off in pursuit. If anyone can find Ednoll, it's Retruance."

"Retruance and you, Tom!" said Manda, turning to her stepmother. "Oh, if we had only come a few hours sooner."

"Nothing you can do about that, and you came as soon as you could, I'm certain," said Eduard Ten, seating himself wearily on the foot of the canopied bed and taking his four-year-old daughter on his own knee. "I'll go with you, Tom. My son . . ."

"No, and I'm sorry to say it to you, but there's more to this than just a wanton kidnapping," said Tom, shaking his head.

He told the royal couple of the invasion of the kingdom from the northeast and the expected attack on the capital.

"It can only be that wicked Peter Gantrell!" cried the Queen. "Who else would do such a terrible, terrible thing to a mere child, to us, and to Carolna?"

"We don't know that, my dear," said Eduard. "A King, I fear, has more than a single enemy."

"We'll certainly discover who's responsible," Tom assured them. "First, however, we must rescue little Ednoll and try to save Arbitrance. He's under some sort of a spell, we think. Everyone agrees that Retruance's papa is normally a most gentle beast. He's Murdan's Companion, too."

"I'd forgotten that," sighed Beatrix. "Does it make the matter better—or worse? Now, little Princess, 'tis time for your lunch and past the time, at that. Go find Mistress Nannah and see if she's set it in the arbor as we asked."

"But I wanted Ednoll to eat lunch with me," wailed the little girl, with tears in her huge blue eyes. "What *am* I to do?"

"Ask Nannah to invite your cousin Merry to lunch with you. You've wanted to show Merry your new dishes, have you not?"

"Well, all right," sighed the four-year-old Princess. "Will you come to see my new luncheon service, Manda? It has all kinds of birds painted on it, you know."

"For a little while, darling," her half sister agreed, taking her hand. "Let's go find Nannah, shall we?"

"We'll go see if Retruance has discovered anything we can use," the Librarian suggested to his distraught father-in-law. "Come with us, madam," he added to the Queen. "No need for you to sit alone and fret."

"I'll come and still fret," said the young mother with a slight smile. "I feel much better now you and Manda are here, my dearest Tom. You always have a way in such emergencies."

They descended the wide, winding stair to the central hall and went out into the hot, humid Waterfields sunshine of a formal garden.

Retruance was there, surrounded by a score of servants and soldiers, under a spreading oak festooned with gray-beard moss. At the approach of the King and Queen with Tom, the servants bowed quickly and scattered back to their duties. The soldiers braced to attention.

The Dragon turned solemnly to greet them.

"Oh, Retruance, my very special, dearest Dragon friend!" cried Beatrix, rushing to hug the beast. "Can you find my baby boy? I'm so very sorry it was your f-f-father! I never met him, but everyone who knows him says he must be enchanted by some powerful wizard to do such a terrible, t-t-t-terrible thing!"

"Dearest Queen, my lovely Beatrix," murmured Retruance soothingly, circling her waist with a gentle emerald claw. "Yes, I'm positive Papa is a victim of this as much as poor little Ednoll. Yes, we'll go at once to his rescue, Tom and I, you can be sure."

"Have you found out which way Arbitrance flew when he left?" Tom asked.

"Seen clearly by at least five guards and three household servants. He stooped like a hawk and took the child in his fore-talons just as the boy left the house to go riding this morning," the Dragon answered, sitting down in the shade of the old oak, the better to talk to the royal parents and his Companion. "Amelia had music lessons at that hour, so she was not present. That was less than five hours ago, I understand. The guard had just been changed."

"Yes, that's what they told me," agreed Eduard Ten.

"And he mounted up straight away and shot off to the west," continued Retruance. "That's about all anybody could tell me as sure and true. It certainly *was* Papa, however, from what they said. No doubt about that. He didn't breath fire nor roar. What he did, he did coldly, not in any sort of anger or heat!"

"I could send for several good wizards the Crown retains," Eduard told Tom. "They would be able to assist. But with the rivers up north running over their banks, it'll be days before they could arrive, I'm afraid."

"If it will make you and the Queen feel better, do so anyway! Mayor Fellows of Lakehead warns of a company of Relling soldiers marching this way, bent on pillage and creating confusion. A crowd of wizards could only help."

"I'll order my Guards Company to intercept those Rellings," the King assured him. "How many, do you know?"

"Not exactly—likely just a small handful. Probably acting for their own gain, I think. Retruance and I discussed it at length. They've stolen a boat or two on their own hook, we believe, acting on information about the kidnapping they somehow learned about as their forces approached Lexor."

"My soldiers will welcome action, and it'll be good for their morale, after what happened here this morning," Eduard thought out loud. "I'll set it in motion at once!"

"We'll not await the outcome, however," Tom decided. "Retruance and I are best suited to deal with this rogue Dragon, however enchanted."

"Magic has little effect on Tom," Retruance reminded the King and Queen. "He's Human. We'll go this very moment! No time must be lost, although I cannot imagine Papa harming the boy or anyone at all. Still . . ."

"What should *I* do?" asked the King and Queen together.

"We'll send word of anything we discover, and bring the child to you as soon as we rescue him," Tom answered. "Manda will escort you and the little Princess to Overhall."

"To Overhall?" asked the King.

"Lexor is about to be attacked by the Northerners,

Walden wrote,'' Tom reminded him. ''If it isn't *already* under siege or even captured. We can trust old Walden to make a stout defense, given the chance, with Murdan there soon to help him, but you and the Queen and the Princess will be safer in Overhall. And it'll be to his own castle that Murdan will return, if he can, once he's organized the defense of the capital.''

''Perhaps . . . well, yes, you're right,'' said Beatrix, sighing, and the King nodded.

They went off together to find Manda and Amelia in the sunny flower garden.

✦ 5 ✦
Dragon Chase

MANDA saw the wisdom of taking the Royal Family to Overhall at once, although she said she'd much rather fly with her husband and Retruance.

"I know the way," she told Eduard. "If we leave at once, we can ride through to Overhall in three days—or less, if the floodwaters have subsided. At any rate, a moving target—"

"Is harder to hit, yes," her father agreed with a firm nod. "We'll travel light and fast, then. I'll send my guards here to Lexor, after they've caught this marauding bunch of Rellings and clapped them under lock and key. I'll take only a half dozen, my best archers, with us. I'll go on to Lexor after. That's my place, I deem, with the army and levies."

IN little more than three hours after the Dragon's arrival at the Queen's parents' house, both parties were ready to depart.

Tom held his wife close for a long moment but said little. Manda was very good in emergencies. She had a more level head than even her father, the King, at times like this, and experience of dangerous adventures he had not. She was solid, smart, and unflappable.

"Go!" she said to Tom and Retruance. "We'll make haste to Overhall. Come to us there when you find the boy or send us news. We'll be anxious—very anxious!"

Tom bowed to the King and would have bowed to the Queen, except that Beatrix threw herself into the Librarian's arms for a farewell embrace.

"Are you going to find Edney?" lisped Amelia when he picked her up to give her a buss.

"I am that! You can depend on Retruance and me, little Princess," Tom promised, wishing he felt as confident as he had made himself sound.

FOREWARNED by the Librarian and his Dragon, the remaining royal escort and the local levies rowed off by canal boat to intercept the raiding party of Rellings. Before nightfall they discovered the ten men in furs, trying to ford a deep, dark channel, sweltering in the unaccustomed humid heat of the southern land.

"Surrender *at once!*" cried the Captain of Guards, waving his sword threateningly. "Move, and you die to a man! You are our prisoners—or you may choose to fight us or drown!"

"Mercy!" begged the renegade Rellings as one.

They'd come south on their own venture, they soon admitted, deserting the army of Rellings and allies well to the north of Lexor.

"We surrender! Take us away! This is a terrible, fearsome land!"

"I suppose it seems that way to men used to snow and ice nine months of a year," chortled a veteran Royal Guards sergeant. "Bind them tight and lead them back to Knollwater! There's a nice, dry barn there to keep them safe!"

"How can we trace him?" asked the Librarian, once they were aloft.

"How can I hear you call from half a world away?" retorted the Dragon. "I'm sure I don't know, but I seem to smell or feel or hear or taste or see my father somehow, Companion. We're as close to Papa as I've been in years, I know."

Tom fell into silence, letting the great scaled beast find their way over the endless-seeming land of thick-set woods, ponds, canals, and cattailed marshes to the north and west of Waterfields proper.

He tried to sense the strange Dragon He'd never met, also, straining his eyes and ears and even his sense of smell, but to no avail. The wetlands of Waterfields sent up a dank and musty odor that might have masked the presence of the rogue Dragon.

"Fortunately," said Retruance after an hour of silent flight, "the wind is still, so any trace of . . . of Arbitrance this morning is still in place."

"We'll have to depend on *your* senses, then," decided his Companion, settling back. "I detect nothing except the marshes and the slow-running streams. What lies ahead?"

"According to my geography of Carolna, we're heading out of Waterfields proper toward a vast area called Sinking Marsh. It's not really a swamp, you realize, but a very broad, flowing river, mostly very shallow and often choked with vegetation."

"A sort of Everglades, I suppose," Tom thought aloud. "And the waters come down originally from the Snow Mountains, then sink under the Hiding Lands desert, do you think? Yes, and emerge once again south of the Cristol. Interesting!"

If he heard the Librarian's musings, the Dragon didn't answer but flew swiftly on, making wide sweeps to left and right to focus on the faint trace of his poor papa.

THE royal party, riding fast as the King had decreed, passed the first night on the road just short of the farthest northern border of Waterfields as guests in a rickety old stone-and-timber keep long since near ruin. It was inhabited by a large family of cattle herders who had preempted the stone walls and replaced the ancient wooden roofs of the castle with woven reed thatching.

"Never met a King of any sort before," said Frost, the boisterous head of his clan. "I'm admitting to being flattered, even if ye're running away from yer enemies.

Discretion being the better part of . . . whatever the saying is, Sir King.''

"We'll pay you for our night and food," said Eduard, somewhat testily.

He was tired and sore and unaccustomed to such casual treatment, even if it was basically polite and even cordial.

"Nonsense!" cried Frost's enormously fat wife, whose name they were never told. "Anyone travels this way, we puts 'em up and thank 'em for the company!"

"I appreciate your hospitality so very greatly," sighed the Queen. "May we help you with supper? We've brought some foodstuffs that we would share with you."

"Now here's a *real* lady!" cried Master Frost with a pleased cackle.

He had seven sons, an unspecified number of daughters and daughters-in-law, and several other dependants whose relationship to them was obscure. Plus what seemed to be two dozen or so children of all ages running about, shouting excitedly.

Manda and her stepmother speculated between themselves but decided not to ask more deeply as to who, exactly, was who in this boisterous crowd. It didn't seem to matter to the Frost clansmen. A few awkward minutes after their arrival at Pinkleterry, as Frost called his old keep, daily life resumed its even if rather noisy way.

Several of the young menfolk quickly rounded up a half-grown beef and led it off outside the crumbling curtain walls. When the King's party next saw it, the beef had been skinned and was basting, turning slowly on a spit over a bed of glowing oak coals that lit up the outer bailey of the ruined old castle.

"Do you rest easy," Frost advised jovially. "Be a while yet afore the bobby-cue is burnt enough to chaw. Take yer ease away from the smoke, Majesties. Me 'n' the boys have herds to bed down and hogs to feed and the ladies, bless 'em, have cows to milk and baking to attend to, and such.''

He showed them to an open-air pavilion of beautifully cured and tanned leather hides stitched neatly together and supported by slender poles, not far upwind from the open fire pit. There were surprisingly comfortable old chairs and divans to sit upon, brought from the castle, Manda assumed.

One of the women brought the Queen a horn cup of fresh milk, still warm from the udder, for Princess Amelia. Beatrix had doubts about its cleanliness and contents, but the King nodded for her to give it to the tired child.

Amelia had no such qualms, and within ten minutes the little Princess was sound asleep on a soft, clean lambskin on the dirt floor beside her mother's chair.

"A King ought to travel thus to get to know his people," observed Eduard to Manda. "These are rough, bluff folk but honest and good-hearted and hospitable to strangers."

"I recommend you don't lay your wallet aside when you sleep, and keep your knife handy, too," advised his oldest child in a low whisper. "You must beware of surface appearances, Lord King."

"Princess Alix Amanda Trusslo!" cried the King, shocked.

"Well, that's my advice, free for the taking," retorted Manda with a fond chuckle. "Take it or leave it, Papa dear! Personally, I plan to keep my blade near to hand and sleep with an eye and both ears open."

As it happened, they were fed huge quantities of deliciously roasted beef, entertained with fireside tales of birthings and deaths in the back country, of ancient doings and yesterday's musings.

They all slept—with both eyes closed tight—in complete safety on the second level of the ancient keep, and woke at first light to a hot breakfast of coarse yet very tasty porridge with fresh cream and wild honey, and wild raspberries and cranberries with the dew still upon them.

They said many grateful thank-yous—it was all that

Frost and his wife would accept in payment—and cordial good-byes, then rode on, waving back at the sturdy herdsmen and their waving women and prancing progeny.

✦ 6 ✦
The Grand Blizzardmaker

THE bone-weary Historian shifted his aching bottom on the too-small saddle, borrowed along with the tough, lanky gelding from Lord Granger Gantrell's Morningside stable.

He wished he'd waited while young Granger had mustered his pikemen and archers. The road was cold, empty, and lonely.

He'd crossed the broad Samber by the ferry and ridden through the quiet, cathedral aisles of Greenlevel Forest. He'd stopped only to order Manda's Chief Forester, Strongoak, to issue the call to arms to his men in Manda's name—it was her forest and they were her retainers—before pushing on through a light snowfall in the late afternoon, refusing escort again as he had in Morningside.

The walls of Lexor were now a dark loom in the frost-gray late afternoon. No sound or light came from either the city or the villages and farms clustered about the capital's southwest gate.

The southwest high road that circled the capital walls was completely deserted, he thought. He'd just turned in toward the city gate when a dozen white-fur-clad men in steel-pot helmets leapt from a close-set stand of dark cedars, bearing him and the Morningside horse to the ground with a loud bump and startled double snort from the man and his poor mount.

"Hold up there, stranger!" snarled a guttural voice in his ear.

He felt a sharp prick near his Adam's apple and

caught the dull flash of cold steel.

"Hold on, here! Ye've found a home in our army, I'd say!"

"Rellings!" muttered Murdan in a hoarse gasp. "I'm not surprised."

"Softly, now," snapped his captor. "Truss the bloody rich man up!"

To a chorus of rough laughter, leather thongs were whipped about his wrists and elbows. His sword and dagger disappeared in a trice. His horse was set on its feet again and led away into the gloom.

"Rather eat walrus!" said someone leading the animal, laughing. "Still . . . beggars can't be too particular!"

Someone thrust a nasty-tasting gag into the Historian's open mouth before he could protest or even utter a curse. The Rellings jerked him rudely to his feet.

"Drag him to old GB now," ordered their leader.

Mutters answered him.

"None of your nasty fun and sassy games, says I! GB won't take it at all kindly if the prisoner can't be interro . . . interrog . . . ah, questioned. Hustle, you sons of eared seals! Get back here on the run! Others may be following this one."

Smelling of rank sweat and rancid fish oil from long days of marching and meals of salted fish, the soldiers hauled the Historian along the perimeter road at a fast clip, laughing when he stumbled, but waiting until he regained his footing on the slippery pavement before moving forward again.

Two hundred yards beyond the tightly barred and heavily fortified west gate, the band turned onto a path that followed the high wall around to the north. The going became more difficult; the snow here was deeper. Murdan had time and breath to glance about.

He glimpsed movements on the top of the city's outer wall and sensed the presence of Carolna soldiers up there, keeping careful watch. His captors moved carefully and silently, just out of range of longbow shot, obviously fearing a sortie in the dark from behind the silent walls.

The city had been warned of the invasion and had managed to slam shut its gates before the invaders could force an entry, that much was clear.

Lexor was under siege.

Two hundred or so paces farther along, as they slogged through the deep, soft snow, the guard sergeant halted his men with a growl and plowed forward to mutter a password to a snow-covered sentry. Beyond him, the Historian could just make out groups of heavily armed men in white fur huddling together for warmth about tiny campfires.

The soldiers and their prisoner left the road to enter an open field. A bit farther they climbed a low stone wall and crossed a narrow, wooden bridge over an ice-glazed moat, frozen black by the early cold. They passed through a double-towered gate guarded by a company of archers, their bows held at the ready.

"Brevory, by the gods' toes!" swore Murdan to himself.

He recognized the Achievement of the traitor Fredrick of Brevory, long since stripped of his property for kidnapping Murdan's daughter and grandchildren under the orders of Peter of Gantrell.

"Lively, now!" snapped the Relling sergeant, taking Murdan's arm as they came to rising steps. "GB'll be at supper. Speak up and speak truth, stranger. He'd as soon slice your gullet as toss you in a snowbank."

They marched into the dim entry hall of Brevory Castle's square keep, stamping caked snow from their boots and coughing at the smoke that filled the air from cook fires laid on the bare flags.

Here inside it was overly warm, Murdan thought, and he soon began to sweat profusely. His bound hands wouldn't allow him to loosen his coat buttons or remove his scarf.

"Be the culprit armed?" asked a heavily furred officer, returning the guard sergeant's salute negligently.

"We've not stripped him, but he seems unarmed, sir," replied the soldier. "We didn't want to take the time and keep old Coldness waiting. Such were our orders."

"Fools!" snarled the officer. "Incompetents! Nitwits! He could be an assassin or a magician! He may carry a short, sharp dagger in his boot, ready for all sorts of foul deeds! You should have searched him right down to the shivering buff! Do it at once!"

Cowed and sheepish, the Relling sergeant ordered two of his men to untie the prisoner and remove all his clothing. In a minute Murdan was standing, naked as a plucked turkey, in a widening puddle of ice-cold meltwater. He tried to look as though it were perfectly normal to stand thus.

"He's unarmed, Sergeant!" called one of the searchers.

"He's completely disarmed, sir!" reported the sergeant to the officer.

The be-furred Relling officer walked around Murdan three times, slowly, closely inspecting his naked body for hidden weapons. He kicked at Murdan's discarded clothing, dumping them also in the middle of the spreading puddle.

"Who are you?" he shouted suddenly, leaning into the Historian's face. Murdan jerked back in surprise. The officer smelled of fire, fish, and sour ale. "Here, you stupid walrus, remove that gag so he can answer!"

"Murdan of Overhall," replied Murdan as soon as he could speak.

He had, in the maneuvering to remove his clothing, managed to step out of the puddle onto a thick rug nearby.

"Some puffed-up, bottom-kissing, mid-country lordling, eh?'' sneered the officer.

''Well, I do have the title of Royal Historian,'' said his prisoner.

''*Historian!* What bloody sort of title is that, I ask you? What do you do? Sit in a leafy bower and scribble on scented parchment all day?''

''More or less, yes,'' answered Murdan mildly. ''Do you mind if I put my clothes back on now?''

''No questions, prisoner!'' shouted the other. ''Give him something to wear,'' he added to the sergeant. ''It's not seemly he should come before Grand Blizzardmaker naked as the day he was born!''

The soldiers gingerly plucked several sopping items from the puddle and handed them to the Historian, who nodded his thanks, wrung as much of the cold water from the clothing as he could, and began to redress.

From beyond a thick door at the other end of the entryway came a shout of loud laughter and louder clapping. The officer gestured for the sergeant to bring Murdan and stalked stiffly through the door into Brevory's Great Hall.

THE scene within was a riot of sounds and smells due to the heat of two vast hearths, one at either end. A hundred Relling warriors were seated at long tables, eating, drinking, and shouting in laughter. A gaudily clad jester was singing a song of some sort in a nasal, piping voice, accompanied by a badly played flute and a flat-toned drum. The aroma of steaming wet leather and fur was almost overpowering.

At the head table, dressed all in snow white fur, sat an enormously fat man with a sour red face, the color continuing up to the top of his bald head. His beady eyes were almost buried in fleshy cheeks and his ears were crumbled and chewed like those of a catch-as-catch-can wrestler.

''That's Grand Blizzardmaker,'' the officer muttered to Murdan. ''Answer his questions and be respectful, I advise you. He has a sudden and foul temper!''

"Agreed," replied Murdan.

For several minutes they stood watching and listening—Murdan, the sergeant, and the officer—near the door. Murdan strained to catch the words of the salacious ditty the jester was attempting to project over the noise, but to no avail.

Grand Blizzardmaker suddenly roared and the crowd fell silent. The jester sang on a moment or two, then let his song fade away, unfinished. The fat Northern War Leader waved him away and the jester and the two musicians fled from the hall by a rear door. Murdan thought they looked rather relieved to get away.

"What've you got there, Fraggle!" roared Blizzardmaker. "Bring it forward, sirrah!"

Murdan was pushed down the narrow serving aisle between the long tables. The audience of Northmen stared at him with curiosity and made uncomplimentary remarks about his state of undress. One or two threw bits of bone or fat at him, laughing uproariously when someone scored a hit.

The guards halted in front of the nomad War Chief and waited while Blizzardmaker studied Murdan and gulped a full goblet of Fredrick of Brevory's best fortified brandy.

"Now, sirrahs! Who is this?"

"Murdan of Overhall, he says he is, sire," answered Fraggle, bowing deeply.

"Royal Historian to His Majesty Eduard Ten, King of Carolna," added Murdan.

"Eduard? Ten? Oh, your lord and master, I presume," rumbled the obese War Chief thoughtfully. "Historian? What do you do?"

"He scribbles, sire," said Fraggle.

"Of course he does," GB jeered. "A lot of people in this kingdom do silly things like that. When I finish my—our—conquest, I intend to outlaw all writing and reading on pain of a long, slow, and painful death!"

He hitched himself forward in his chair and reached for another full goblet, knocking over two others in the process. Murdan couldn't decide if he was drunk—or just clumsy.

"Where is your Eduard Ten?" GB asked suddenly.

"Last I heard—" Murdan began.

" 'Last I heard, *sire*!' " growled Fraggle.

"Keep out of this, Fraggle!" cried the War Chief of the Rellings. "I can snarl for myself."

"Aye, War Leader!" said the officer humbly.

"Answer me! I am addressed as sire! Majesty! Lord High War Chief! And, and, and . . . stuff like that," sputtered GB at Murdan.

"The last I heard, *War Chief*," resumed Murdan evenly, "our King was visiting his Queen's ancestral home in the southeast."

He decided there was no profit in concealing it. This GB undoubtedly had other sources of information.

"At Knollwater, then," grunted GB, betraying that he did, indeed, have other sources. "What actions do you see him taking, when he hears his capital city has fallen?"

"Issue a call to arms. Raise an army from his loyal Achievements everywhere," said Murdan quickly. "Lead the Royal Army into battle against you."

"And where will they muster, this army?" asked GB slyly. "Tell me you that!"

Murdan thought rapidly.

"I can't say for sure, but probably at Peter Gantrell's Morningside, in Overtide. Or perhaps at my castle at Overhall."

"Morningside, I know of," said the fat Relling monarch. "Never heard of Overhall . . ."

He reached for a greasy slice of cold roast, slapped it on a piece of bread, and took a tremendous bite. It reminded Murdan of his missed meals all that long day.

"So, where is your Overhall?" Grand Blizzardmaker asked through the mouthful of beef.

"Five days' ride west of here," Murdan told him.

He was suddenly very hungry, even while watching the disgusting way the Relling chief gobbled his food and spilled his drink.

GB continued questioning him for several minutes more, consuming another open-faced sandwich, two more goblets of watered brandy, an apple, and three pieces of something that looked . . . and smelled . . . like fruit cake doused in rum.

He belched loudly, fell silent, and contemplated Murdan with hooded eyes—or maybe he was just sleepy. The room was hot and stuffy. Freddie of Brevory had obviously liked his brandy very powerful and very plentiful. The assembled Rellings and their allies were quiet, listening or dozing, heads on their arms.

Someone coughed loudly and GB popped his eyes full open, startled.

"Well, nothing to be learned further from this bumpkin." He belched again. "Toss him in the stockade or whatever they call 'em in these parts."

"Sire," said a courtier near the head of the head table, "there are no stockades or dungeons in this palace."

"No gaols? No lockups?" cried the War Chief in vast surprise.

"Just three short towers and a large wine cellar," the official told him apologetically.

"Well . . ." GB drew the word out. "Lock him in one of the towers, then."

"Hmmm," replied his informant. "The tower rooms are already filled with our—your—officers and their . . . er . . . lady friends."

"Damnation!" cursed the War Leader. "Hell's fire! What do I do with important prisoners, then, Fraggle?"

Fraggle said quickly, "Leave him to me, sire. I'll find a safe place to lock him up."

"Do it! Now I'll go to bed. Tomorrow we burst the flimsy walls of Lexor and slaughter the defenders in glorious, bloody battle. By tomorrow night I'll sleep in this

King Eduard's own soft bed, over there in his dainty
city. After that, it makes no difference what Eduard Ten
does or says.''

The crowd roared in rather sleepy approval and applauded as the enormously fat man struggled to his feet
and waddled off, accompanied by a number of courtiers
to keep him from stumbling over his own feet and plowing into the doorjamb as he staggered out.

No one laughed—at least not out loud.

THE crowd of officers heaved a collective sigh of relief,
or yawned, and began to filter from the hall, ignoring
Murdan, Fraggle, and the Relling sergeant.

''Where?'' asked the latter, remembering just in time
to add, ''Sir?''

''Oh, it doesn't matter,'' snarled the officer petulantly.
''I need a breath of cold, fresh air. Do with him what
seems proper and necessary, Sergeant Spring.''

He turned on his heel and stalked toward the door,
ignoring the Sergeant's parting salute.

''Well!'' snorted Sergeant Spring. ''I suppose I could
take you back to camp. But I'd rather find us a corner
near the fire here, where at least we'll be warm for the
rest of the night. I could tell the captain it was GB's
idea, couldn't I?''

''Precisely,'' agreed his prisoner, who had no desire
to march back to the southwest gate and sleep in the
deep, wet snow. ''Good thinking, Sergeant!''

The noncom sent a cowering Brevory servant to fetch
the rest of Murdan's clothing and helped the Historian
spread them to dry—along with some of his own—on
the warm hearthstones.

''You're not a bad sort, Sergeant Spring,'' com-
mended Murdan as they settled down before the glowing
coals. ''What do you think of such things as invasions
and usurpations?''

''Invasions I approve of,'' said Spring stoutly. ''What
soldiering is all about, says I. Usup . . . usurp . . . whatever

you said . . . taking over a proper King's throne? Well . . .
I can't see the use of it, sir. I really can't! 'Specially where
it's so hot here most of the year. Whew! I prefers colder
climes me-self.''

After a while Spring fell asleep, forgetting to bind the
Historian's arms again. Before he drifted off he asked,
sleepily, ''What *does* a Historian do?''

''Keeps track of mistakes, so they won't be repeated,'' explained Murdan.

''No use to us, then,'' yawned the soldier. ''Relling
never makes a mistake the *first* time.''

Murdan smiled to himself.

Spring began to snore softly; by then forty other men
and a few rumpled women enjoying the stuffy warmth
of Brevory Grand Hall were snoring, too. The combined
rumble was somehow soothing.

Murdan of Overhall fell asleep.

✦ 7 ✦
Prisoner of the Rellings

MURDAN awoke in the dimly lighted Great Hall of Brevory just after dawn, groaning as he stretched stiff muscles, cramped from a night on the cooling stones of the hearth. The Great Hall smelled foul and damp of sour wine, acrid wood smoke, stale sweat, and old urine.

The fire was nearly out and the stone hearth had turned icy cold. His clothes had dried nicely before the embers died, however, and he dressed quickly. He added a handful of split kindling to the low embers and, when they'd caught, put three half logs of pitchy pine on top of them. The morning chill became almost bearable.

Sergeant Spring rolled over on his back and squinted up at his prisoner. He had managed to wrap a hearth rug about himself for warmth.

"I intend to go find some breakfast," the Historian told him. "Coming?"

"No, no. Why leave such comfort for an unheated mess hall?" the other responded. "You can't get far. As soon as I show any sign of life, some stuffed-shirt officer'll pop up and order me back to my outfit. Let me enjoy this luxury for a short while yet."

"If you say so," Murdan agreed with a chuckle. "I'll bring you something, if I find any food left in the mess."

"Good man!" mumbled Spring, and before Murdan had turned his back he was fast asleep again.

The Royal Historian had visited Brevory Castle once or twice before and had a good idea where to look for breakfast. Down a wide corridor carpeted with sleeping soldiers he followed his nose, the smell of bacon and fresh-baked bread guiding him along.

In a side room he found a number of stout tables pushed together, laden with bowls, platters, and heaped-up plates of food: loaves of rye bread, bowls of apple-sauce, stacks of griddle cakes, racks of crisp bacon, pitchers of milk, flagons of strong, sweet tea, and jars of pale amber breakfast beer. The room was already crowded with sleepy-eyed and hungry warriors.

"Officer?" asked a servant who came to bar his en-trance—not a Northman but one of the castle's staff, Murdan surmised.

"What do you think?" he retorted brusquely and, not waiting for anyone's permission, set about assembling the first hearty meal he'd enjoyed since leaving Overhall five days before.

The servant shrugged and went away.

Carrying his trencher—a flat, hard round of rye bread the size of a large dinner plate—and a mug of bitter but steaming-hot tea, he found a room nearby filled with enemy officers seated at trestle tables, on chests, straight chairs, and wide windowsills. Their conversation rum-bled along like a herd of cattle, punctuated by occasional swearing and sharp exclamations.

Nobody showed signs of being fully awake yet—some were definitely hungover, Murdan observed—so he made himself at home at one end of a crowded table and began to eat. Either the food was surprisingly good . . . or he was hungrier than he'd thought.

"We gotta get out to the field," said a rumpled, red-bearded scarecrow of a man halfway down the table. "GB's ordered an assault on the west gate at nine of the clock. Damn! I was just getting to like this place."

"How's the weather out there?" said another.

His insignia indicated he was a cavalryman. Cavalry didn't take part in frontal assaults on high, strong walls, of course. He was enjoying his breakfast in a leisurely manner.

"Cloudy and mild," growled another breakfaster.

"Heavy going underfoot. Bad for horses, I'd guess. War Chief should wait until it gets colder to mount this attack, I say. Hard to haul mangonels and heavy catapults over muddy roads and wet slush."

Obviously an engineering officer, Murdan guessed. Having tossed down his coffee, the engineer threw his cup to a servant and stomped out, pulling on his sword belt and clutching his white bearskin cap under his arm.

A coterie of younger men hastily gulped their cooled coffee, shoved bits and pieces of food into their pockets, and followed him through the door, chattering like magpies in spring.

"Do you have a spot in the line?" the youthful cavalry officer asked Murdan.

"No, actually I'm a prisoner," Murdan answered honestly. "Captured last night. Good bread, isn't it? Brevory always had a good bakery and a better cellar."

"I wouldn't know about the cellar," snorted the horse soldier. "GB has it under lock and bar, I hear. *We* get nothing better than this here watered-down, wretched, bitter beer! Fine way to repay our assistance in his little adventure."

"You're not Relling, then?" asked the Historian. "Of course not! I recognize your insignia. Bear Totem, isn't it?"

"Yes, exactly!" the other said with some pride. "Our Queen hired us out to this Grand Blizzardmaker—Great Windbag, we calls him—for his war. We get minimum pay and maximum looting, but there's been pitiful little of looting so far."

"Yet you've borne the brunt of the fighting, eh?"

"We Bears led the march all the way from Frontier! He didn't even attack Frontier. Passed it by—although I guess that was a smart move. The garrison was holed up behind their stockade. The Relling rear echelon will starve 'em out eventually, I imagine. Is that real butter I see? Where're you from?"

"The midwest," replied Murdan, pushing a butter

crock nearer to his companion's elbow. "I was on my way to the capital on business when I was taken by a Relling patrol near the southwest gate."

"Note the Rellings are in all the quiet sectors," the other snorted derisively. "If Bear Totem horses could climb walls, we'd be halfway up the ladders right now."

Murdan moved on to chat with several other table mates, most of them Rellings, who seemed more willing to fraternize with their enemy than socialize with their allies.

"Bear Totem cavalry," snickered a loquacious supply officer. "Blue Ice pioneers. Bluewater boatmen from over to Foundlay Bay. I don't trust any of 'em! GB has contracted for their services for a year with an option to renew for another year. Good terms, at least on paper! Not a really good Snowfield campaigner in the lot! What good are horses in snowdrifts, I asks you?"

"Well, you won't find too many deep drifts in these parts, except in the dead middle of winter," Murdan pointed out reasonably.

"Ho! Dead of winter is right! Give me Relling snow-sloggers and their long polar bear spears for this kind of work! Horses may be good for hauling supplies and carrying messages, but not much else."

Fortunately the Bear Totem lieutenant had already gone off to look after his precious mounts or there might have been a fistfight then and there.

"The ones give me the creeps," said a subaltern to the Historian, "is these wicked, slippery, soft-talking ice wizards hanging about old Blizzardmaker, you know. Don't see where they've done anything but take up space and gobble down the best provisions since we left the North Country a month ago!"

"Wizards and mages are better left to their gobbling and swilling," Murdan recommended. "Maybe Grand Blizzardmaker keeps them around for show."

"Show, it certainly is! What kind of *real* man would wear lacy aprons and talk in singsong chantings? Re-

mind me of the traveling-through medicine shows come
to entertain us in summertime. Nasty-tasting medicine
but pretty dancing girls with almost nothing left to
the . . .''

As the hour approached nine o'clock, the dining room
emptied rapidly. Murdan gathered a second trencher of
cooling food and carried it back to the Great Hall, where
Sergeant Spring was just reawakening, rubbing his eyes
and looking about somewhat worriedly, thinking perhaps
his prisoner had flown.

''*I'd* have run for it, given your chance,'' he said
pleasantly as he greeted Murdan. ''Thank you, sir! It's
better commons than we're used to in camp. The good
stuff seems to go to the other guys.''

''Other? Oh, you mean Grand Blizzardmaker's allies?''

Spring dived with both hands into his breakfast
trencher but spared a moment to nod.

''We could've done it all ourselves, you know. I think
His High and Mightiness just wanted to show off for the
neighbors. They've never liked us much.''

Murdan watched him eat for a while.

''I take it you aren't fond of your allies, either?''

''Oh, I suppose they're perfectly good fellows, in their
place. I've got a sister who married a Bluewater fisherman. He only beats her when the fishing's slow and the
liquor's quick. Spoiled rotten, she is, Sir Historian!
Bluewaters are a womanly bunch, for all their brave
boasts of the dangers of seagoing.''

A man in full armor clanked into Great Hall, stopped,
and looked around. Spotting Murdan, he came over,
pushing his heavy helmet up on his forehead and ex-
tending his right hand.

''Lord Murdan! A strange place and time to meet you
again!''

For a moment Murdan was puzzled, but his excellent
Historian's memory came to his rescue.

"Ah, yes! Captain Basilicae, isn't it? Mercenary Knights?"

"The same, Lord Historian! Are you in with this Relling mob?"

"No, I'm just a prisoner of war, I suppose," said the Historian, shaking the hired soldier's hand. "I'm more surprised to see you here than you should be to see me. I understood you had departed Carolna for good and all, after Sir Thomas and Retruance Constable rescued my Overhall people from you at . . . what was its name?"

"Plaingirt," supplied Basilicae. "Well, sir, we had every intention of never setting foot on your fair land again. Two defeats at your hands made for a bad résumé."

"You were offered a contract by this Blizzardmaker person?"

"It's business! His terms seemed generous. My men voted to accept it, and I had to go along. We needed the cash after Gantrell reneged on our fees."

The two chatted beside the fire while Sergeant Spring wolfed down his food and toasted his bread over the coals, broke it into pieces, and stuffed it into a pocket for later consumption.

"I advise you to tread carefully with this lordling from the Far North," Murdan told the mercenary. "There's reason to believe he's allied with or even subservient to your former client, Peter of Gantrell. It may be that Peter's behind this whole thing."

"It wouldn't surprise me, and I'll take your warning seriously. Peter Gantrell was bad news for us! I've attended this Relling War Chief's councils for months—more than a year, in fact—however, I've never once felt Gantrell's presence or even heard his name."

"Hmmm! That's interesting. What would move Peter to hide his light from the world, I wonder?"

"If I hear any word of him, perhaps I could slip it to you, Lord Historian. Professional courtesy, shall we say?

Or a bit of revenge? In case things get too sticky here, I mean.''

''Good enough!'' agreed the Historian. ''It'll be remembered, I assure you.''

''A suit for our full fee was still in court last Sessions, you know. We could use a friend at law. Where will you be, do you know?''

''It depends on what GB intends to do with me. Prison? Maybe even execution? Who knows? At the moment, he seems to have forgotten me.''

''I wouldn't lay bets on that!'' the mercenary snorted bitterly. ''He has a mean streak down him that's fair broad . . . like everything else about him.''

''What does he do with important captives, then?'' asked Murdan.

''I know of several he set out on floes in Blue Ice without food or even clothing. That's considered a merciful death by our dear GB, they say. I've heard some say he chained his most important enemy to an iceberg in the Strait of Athermoral. It'll slowly float south until it melts or breaks up as the waters warm, so the victim will suffer first from the cold, then hunger, and then drowning when the ice melts all away.''

''Pleasant man, this Relling War Chief!'' exclaimed Murdan.

Spring had finished his meal, wiped his hands on his coattail, and stood listening to their conversation.

''Oh, Rellings're all right as such things go,'' Basilicae conceded. ''We get along with them fairly well.''

''Well, Sir Mercenary,'' put in the sergeant, ''it may be because he pays you better than others.''

''What do you mean by that?'' the knight asked, surprised.

''Most of these so-called *friends* came along for minimum pay promised and a free hand at . . . er . . .''

''Loot, rape, and plunder, I suppose,'' furnished Murdan. ''I've heard that already this morning.''

''We Mercenary Knights refuse to fight on a contingency-fee basis," claimed Basilicae stoutly. "Bad business! Cash on the barrelhead; half in advance, or we don't lift a finger. Learned that from old Gantrell!"

"A business policy with much to recommend it," agreed the Historian. "But I still suggest you watch your step. If Gantrell is involved . . ."

"Do you suppose he supplied the capital for this venture?" asked Basilicae. "I wondered where GB got his stake all along."

"Peter may have had hidden resources somewhere over the border," murmured Murdan. "It's possible."

"The state prisoner I spoke of—the one set adrift on the iceberg? They say he was a major participant in the early stages of the planning to invade Carolna, but GB turned sour on him."

"Who is he, then?" asked Murdan.

"Never heard him called anything, save 'state prisoner,' " claimed the Mercenary Knight. "You'll have to excuse me, m'lord. I've a meeting with my officers. We're expected to provide follow-up after the Lexor wall is breached, later today."

"I won't wish you good luck, then, but say to you, be careful!—not of your foes, but of your client."

"We don't trust him further than we could toss his vast carcass," Basilicae assured him, grinning, and he clanked off at a fast pace to gather his men.

"State prisoner, eh? I'd like to talk to him myself, actually," mused Murdan aloud.

"It'd be suicide, sir!" cried Spring. "You'd have to be sent to his ice island and share his cold and wet fate."

"Still . . . ," began the Historian, thoughtfully.

The be-furred Colonel Fraggle appeared, lashing a swagger stick against his boot and scowling darkly.

"Still here, Sergeant? Get you back to your company at once!"

"Yes, m'lord! But the prisoner, m'lord?"

"I'll take him in charge," said Fraggle. "Begone, sirrah!"

"Well, that's the end to being warm and well fed," Spring said, sighing in an aside to Murdan. "Good fortune to you, sir! You've been a gentleman where few are found."

He snatched up his pack and pike and clattered out of Brevory Great Hall.

"Now!" said Fraggle, impatiently. "Come with me, Lord Murdan. His Majesty has asked for you. He will decide your fate this morning."

"At your service, sir," said Murdan.

The officer spun on his heel and stalked away toward the far entrance, sweeping lesser men from his path with his swagger stick and his unhappy frown.

GRAND Blizzardmaker looked rather frazzled around the edges, blinking painfully in the morning light through the high windows and wincing at sudden noises.

Murdan stood at ease before the desk where the War Chief, looking rather green and uneasy, lolled.

"Mordock of Overhill, Royal Historian of Carolna and friend of the cowardly Eduard Ten," growled the War Chief, referring to a sheaf of papers before him.

"Murdan, rather," the prisoner corrected him mildly.

"Eh? What?"

"My name properly is not *Mordock* but Murdan," repeated the Historian.

"Bloody incompetent scribblers! No matter! After this morning your name will really be 'history,' believe me, bucko!" snarled the War Chief.

His heavy humor set his attendants to snickering.

"You're a dangerous enemy, and must be eliminated at once."

Murdan nodded.

"It will be an honor to die for my King and my country," he announced, rather sententiously, for all to hear.

"Bosh, tosh, and mealy rot! Neither your King nor his lousy little kingdom will exist much longer. You might as well die."

"I welcome it, however," said Murdan, affecting a sad look of resignation.

"Oh, don't make me sick!" snapped the War Chief. "You've considerable wealth and influence in Carolna, I'm told."

"I cannot deny that," replied the Historian.

"Then why not foreswear your silly allegiance to this snowflake Eduard? Join me—I mean *us*! Bring your people over to my—our—side, eh?"

"Oh, I think not, really, old Rell," said Murdan evenly. "I have better regard for my King and my fealty oath to him than that!"

"So be it, sirrah! I'll enjoy your . . . what do you people call them? Achievements! I'm about to order your execution by strangling!"

"Better that than set out to freeze in your chill country, like some!" said Murdan, eyes downcast.

"Ha! *Aha*! A quick, easy death's too good for you, Murdam of Coverhall! It occurs to me it may be amusing to keep you alive for a while, although suffering."

"No, please, sire!" cried the Historian in a shrill voice. "A quick, honorable death, I beg of you! I'd go insane in prison—especially a *cold* prison! I cannot abide being cold! I implore you. . . ."

One of the advisers behind the fat War Chief leaned forward to whisper in his crumpled right ear. Blizzard-maker suddenly roared with coarse laughter that shook his entire, obese body like a molded jelly. He caught his breath and began to cough, then choked and spat upon the floor beside his couch.

"Yes! *Yes*! I've got just the place for you, sniveling scrivener! My judge advocate here reminds me that we have a nice, very cold place reserved for important prisoners like you."

"No, good, dear sire! I beg of you . . . !"

"*Silence*! Take him," rasped GB to an officer in black fur standing nearby, "to the nearest seaport and send him by ship to the ice floe and maroon him there. No need to chain him as the other was chained. The berg's too far out in the strait by now for him to swim ashore.''

He pointed a stubby and dirty forefinger at Murdan, chuckling wickedly.

''I hope you *do* try to swim, Burdock! Three minutes in those pleasant waters and you're an icicle, I promise. Drag the yellowed slush out!''

The black-furred soldier, who was not at all looking forward to a sea voyage to the stormy Strait of Athermoral, saluted glumly and gestured to underlings to lead Murdan after him as he stalked out.

ONLY a half-grown polar bear witnessed Murdan's marooning on the iceberg. Three beefy Relling soldiers simply lifted the Historian between them and dropped him onto the edge of the ice alongside the sloop's low midship rail.

The sloop's helmsman turned her away at once, the crew hoisting her mainsail despite the near-gale winds, and the little ship fled the ice-clotted strait as fast as she could safely go.

The polar bear considered investigating the mealtime possibilities of the dramatically cursing Historian but some slight taint in the air pulled him up short.

Sniffing once again, the white bear decided to let well enough alone and dived with a thunderous splash into the icy chop and began to paddle toward the low, white hills of the mainland some distance away to the east.

''Thanks for even small blessings!'' gasped Murdan, watching him go.

He found a handhold to pull himself up the steep slope at the edge of the berg.

''Damnation, it's cold!''

Still, the exertion of climbing up the ice shelf served to warm his body long enough to find shelter from the biting wind in a hollow between two pinnacles of clear green ice.

Even there his clothing quickly froze fast to the ice upon which he sat. As soon as he'd regained his breath he pried himself free and set out to climb to higher ground. It was a clear, cold day and by staying in the sun as much as possible, he kept a little warmth within.

Enough to survive.

For a while, at least.

"A mistake? Well, maybe so, but better than being strangled, I still think," he said aloud to himself.

As much to keep from freezing as anything, Murdan explored the iceberg, slowly circling clockwise, spiraling higher and higher with each turn.

The floe was perhaps a mile across, irregularly round, and it rose a hundred feet in the air at its jagged crest—a large area to cover on treacherous footing.

Where was this state prisoner chained to the ice in punishment for some real or fancied crime against Grand Blizzardmaker and his Rellings?

Entirely possible his particular portion has already sloughed off and floated away, I suppose, thought the Historian to himself. "Hello? I thought I saw something dark moving up there!"

Although he stood in the blustery wind and searched the area above him carefully for some minutes, whatever it had been didn't reappear. He made a fourth and a fifth circuit of the floe, slipping and sliding constantly on the ice, more than once in danger of sliding back down the slope into the sea.

The short autumn day was fast closing down into night. The waxing half-moon was already in the sky and a curtain of ice-bright stars twinkled above him. He used his eyes to watch his step and look for the chained prisoner, but his mind was busy thinking how to survive the coming night as the wind picked up and temperatures plunged.

• • •

AT the start of his sixth lap, now well above the heaving waves of the Strait of Athermoral, Murdan stumbled upon a deep cleft hidden under a cliff. It was as good as he would find for shelter, he realized at once, and he used the very last light of day to explore within.

Fifty steps or so within it came to a dead end, but the air seemed not nearly so cold in here, and no wind entered.

If I could just find something to burn, he thought.

There might be driftwood on the shore, but it was too dark to go back and look for it now.

He tried lying down on an ice shelf at the back of the cave and found it surprisingly cozy, as long as he kept everything covered with his coat, hood, and scarf. Fortunately he'd dressed as warmly and waterproofed as possible for his ride from Morningside to Lexor, and despite the wetting he'd gotten aboard the guard ship from the crashing bow spray, his inner clothing had remained dry.

Murdan fumbled inside his coat until he found an inner pocket in which he had secreted a portion of his breakfast that morning—bread and sweet rolls, some griddle cakes now grown cold and soggy but still powdered with sugar, a fist-sized chunk of some greasy sort of meat or other.

He fell to eating hungrily. It would freeze solid if he didn't consume it soon.

"Oh, where are you wizards and magicians and sorcerers when one needs you?" he asked half-seriously. "Could use a fire-maker, right now!"

By the time he'd finished eating half of his tiny store, feeling rather warmer and better than before, it was fully dark within the cave. He walked to the mouth and looked out.

The waxing moon was near the horizon and the sky was crowded with hard, bright stars, more than he had ever seen, even from the tip of Middletower at Overhall on a midwinter's night.

Returning to the far end of the cavern, he wrapped himself in his fur-lined cloak and settled himself to try to sleep. It was obvious that only a few days of this climate would be the death of him, but for the moment he felt confident and even rather optimistic.

✦ 8 ✦
Hoarling

MURDAN was so exhausted with the events of the past few days that he didn't pause to wonder about the unusual ice cave. If he had, he would have seen that it was smoothly rounded, wide, and high, and its floor perfectly level, looking as though it had been liquefied and then refrozen. There were no sharp points or angles as one might expect of ice calved violently from a massive mother glacier.

He awakened hours later to find himself still in deep darkness, lying on his back on the shelf carved from the ice—yet surprisingly warm!

He blinked, but the darkness was too thick. A tiny bit of light filtered through the thinner walls of ice at the front of the cave. It dimly outlined a fearsome figure, a huge, black hump that sniffed softly and rumbled like a regiment of skaters crossing a patch of rough ice.

"Who's there?" the Historian cried sharply, sitting straight up.

"*I* am here!" said a cold, thin voice from the darkness. "The question is, who are *you*?

Murdan had not expected an answer to his question. He gathered his wits about him as he gathered his cloak. It *was* quite warm in the cave and he could hear meltwater dripping steadily from the overhead.

"Murdan of Overhall," he said through clenched teeth. "Sent here as a prisoner by the Grand Blizzard-maker of the Rellings."

"Ah, that explains a great deal," said the voice, sounding considerably warmer at once. "Another prisoner of the snow-sloggers, eh? Well, well!''

''And to whom do I have the pleasure of speaking?''
asked the Historian boldly.

''*Whom!* An educated, sophisticated gentleman! I'm
surprised and even impressed,'' the dark blob said.
''Well, know then that I am Hoarling . . .''

''. . . the Ice Dragon?'' finished Murdan in great surprise. ''I've heard a lot about you, sir!''

''And I am truly flattered that Murdan of Overhall
has remembered my name, mentioned by his friend
and—what?—adviser? Servant? Retruance Constable, I
mean!''

The Ice Dragon backed slowly out of the cave entrance—he filled it from side to side and blocked almost
all the morning sunlight—so that he could see his visitor
better.

''Well, now, what an *honor*!'' the blue-and-white
Dragon said quite sarcastically, which was his nature.
''That old Great Windbreaker snagged you, eh? I knew
he'd marched his snowmen south into Carolna. How do
you do? Pleased, I'm sure.''

''Vastly pleased, if just for the warmth of your presence,'' said Murdan, now that there was enough light to
see the beast.

Hoarling was somewhat smaller than either Retruance
or Furbetrance, and of an overall deep ice blue color
touched here and there with silver flashes. A handsome
beast, Murdan thought, and somehow more dramatic
looking than the Constables, with their lively red and
gold and green scale patterns.

''I'm forced to give off heat to remain comfortably
cold within,'' explained Hoarling. ''Well, are you finished with my cave? I've been fishing all night and I'd
like to relax a bit out of the heat of the day coming.''

''Yes, I was lucky enough to find your lair when I
needed shelter. I thank you for your hospitality, Hoarling! It saved my life!''

''I doubt that. Although some men have managed to

live a surprisingly long time on this hunk of ice, I find.''

"Ah, yes! The Rellings' state prisoner! Is he still alive and chained to the berg, as I was told so gleefully and at such great length?''

Hoarling laughed a cloud of chilly mist at this and nodded his head. The mist clung to Murdan's cloak and froze at once, coating him with powdery frost, even coating his eyebrows.

"Last time I checked he was still alive and swearing weakly," said the Ice Dragon. "Move a bit more to the left, Lord Murdan, so I can slide by.''

They exchanged places in the cave mouth and the Dragon began backing into the cavern, tail first.

"Where is he, then?" inquired the Historian. "The state prisoner, I mean.''

The Dragon looked surprised but merely gestured up the slope with a silvery foreclaw. He yawned ostentatiously and lay down, cradling his frosted muzzle on his forelegs, and pretended to go to sleep.

"Well and well!" murmured Murdan softly, and he began to climb toward the top of the ice in the direction the Ice Dragon had indicated.

At the very peak he found a man dressed in oily sealskins and heavy, fur-lined boots and gloves, slumped against the pinnacle, either dead or asleep. Two long chains ran from his left wrist and his right ankle through an iron ring set in the vertical face of the peak.

"Hey there! Hello!" Murdan called as he approached.

The man stirred sluggishly and lifted his head.

Murdan slid to a shocked halt.

The face was pinched and blue with cold. His unkempt black beard was rimmed with hoarfrost, and his eyes were red from the wind.

But it was definitely the face of Lord Peter of Gantrell, the exiled enemy.

"Peter, old man!" Murdan cried out in pity, despite himself. He rushed forward after his first pause of surprise. "You're the last person I ever expected to find in such a place!"

Peter's whole body was wracked with convulsive shivers. He stared at the Historian but did not recognize him. His teeth chattered so that he couldn't speak.

"Here, old man," said Murdan, slipping off his fur-lined cloak and throwing it about his old enemy. "I've got some little to eat, too, if you can handle it."

"F-f-f-food!" gargled Peter, bobbing his head with infinite weariness.

Murdan gently fed him bits of cold griddle cake smeared with congealed butter, and a handful of half-frozen grapes.

At first the chained man could hardly swallow, but the juice of the fruit seemed to provide enough moisture for his throat to function. In a few minutes he was holding a piece of fruitcake in both hands, careful not to drop a single raisin, and chewing rapidly.

Some color returned to his sickly blue face. His eyes focused on his rescuer and Murdan saw recognition—and then puzzlement, followed by terror—dawn in them.

"Murdan!" Peter croaked at last, leaning back against the ice wall behind him. "You're here to save me!"

"Of course, Peter! But why were you treated thus? I mean, I assumed from what I learned and heard, you'd gone to the Rellings after you fled from Fall Sessions over four years ago. Our immediate assumption, when the Rellings marched into the kingdom, was it was your doing!"

Peter Gantrell nodded painfully.

"Partly true, I'm afraid. Laid it all out for him, the Relling War Chief. Have you met Blizzardmaker?"

"I wouldn't be here if I hadn't," Murdan told him, handing him the last cold pork sausage patty.

"Well, he lapped it up like . . . like maple candy! He asked all sorts of questions. He would put me back on my lost lands and restore my power in exchange for my assistance and guidance, he said. Ha!"

"And you went along with that? Planning to thwart him after he'd given you back the Gantrell lands . . . and maybe the Trusslo throne?"

"Yes, yes, of course!" said Peter, gesturing with his chained arm, causing the chain to rattle and ring against the ice. "I never intended *him* to take Eduard's place on the Trusslo throne. GB will make a horrible, untrustworthy, wicked, cruel, drunken ruler! I'd never have allowed that, you know. But . . ."

"But you would take the throne yourself, eh? To save us from the Rellings! For I doubt Eduard would have survived the invasion, from what I've seen of the Rellings and their allies. Cold-blooded lot, for the most part!"

"I never let myself think of such an outcome. I was always content to be the power *behind* the throne, you know, Murdan."

"I suppose that's true," conceded the other.

The sun had long since risen and the island had slowly revolved. The side on which Gantrell was chained now faced east. The air had become comparatively warm.

"You always felt you could rule better than anyone else, I think," the Historian went on when the exiled nobleman didn't reply to his last comment.

"But I've twice made such stupid botches of things! I surely have proved my silly, useless incompetence."

Peter began to weep, hot tears scoring the grime and rime on his cheeks.

"And now I'll die," he moaned. "In a day or two, even if you can get me free of these chains, the berg will surely break up and we'll all drown!"

Murdan patted him encouragingly on the shoulder.

"Now, now, don't give up just yet, old boy. I'm here to help and there may be things we can do together to save ourselves, I think, given a little luck."

"How much food did you bring?" asked Peter, sniffing back his tears. "How long can we survive, if the ice stays together that long?"

"Not much. Not long! In fact, food's all but gone, now. So we'll have to act at once!"

He examined the thin but obviously very strong steel links closely.

"The ring in the wall is the weak point," he decided. "Yank it out and we can slip the chain free, I think."

"I've tried for days, until I lost all will and strength," gasped Peter, beginning to take an interest in freedom. "It's frozen solid and deep, very deep, I fear."

"But the wind's switching to the west and blowing warmer. I think the island must be floating southeast into warmer waters. If we both tug hard at it . . ."

They tried, but the ring continued to defy their best combined attempts. Gantrell was too weak to sustain the effort. Murdan brought him a handful of fresh snow—he had eaten all the snow within reach long since—and they rested and nibbled it for its water for a few minutes while they considered what to try next.

"Plume is nearby," exclaimed Peter, remembering suddenly.

"He followed you here?"

"Yes, he found me when I was first at the Rellings' winter camp and I vouched for him as my servant. When GB condemned me to this place just before marching on Carolna, Plume somehow managed to follow me. I sent him off yesterday to try to catch some fish or find some driftwood for a fire, but he hasn't returned."

"He was ever a sneak and a traitor," muttered the Historian angrily. "He betrayed my trust over and over again, and allowed my people to be carried off into captivity!"

Peter at least had the grace to look ashamed and downcast at these bitter words.

"But a third pair of arms might just do the trick. You'd have to carry the chains with you, of course, until we can find a smith to strike them off."

"He must be nearby—I mean, how far can a man walk on this forsaken chunk of ice?"

"Hmmm!" said Murdan. "He may have fallen off, or maybe he holed up as I did during the night. Perhaps I should go look for him."

"Take your cloak!" Peter called as Murdan started to leave. "I'll survive. It's fairly warm, now."

"I'll keep warm just walking about," Murdan assured him. "You must keep moving, too, now—as far as the chain will allow. Either way, I'll be back in an hour or so."

HE began circling the peak again, this time in a downward spiral. The sun shone too brightly. He squinted his eyes almost shut in order to see anything at all.

After a circle and a half he spotted a dark bit of something against the ice farther down the slope. Reaching it, he found it was a ragged bit of coat, and when he pulled it free from the surrounding crust, it revealed a hollowed-out place in the ice lined with pieces of driftwood and half-frozen codfish. The hole was filled with a startled and frightened renegade Accountant.

"Oh, good!" said Murdan, pulling Plume from his nest by the scruff of his neck. "You've got our breakfast and firewood, too. Now you can help pull Lord Peter free."

"M-m-m-murdan?" his ex-employee said, stuttering, though whether from fear or cold, Murdan couldn't guess. "You here? You came to save me—us?"

"So it seems, despite all!" snorted the Historian. "Who else would go to that sort of trouble? Up now, man! Get the old blood flowing! Let's take this wood and fish to Peter's perch. Somehow we'll manage to get a good meal out of it and some much-needed warmth."

He lead the shriveled and shivering little scribbler up the wet and crumbling slope, helping him carry a double armful of salt-bleached branches of trees and splintered timbers from long-lost ships. And somehow Plume had managed to catch three small cod.

"Fire first!" Murdan decided, forestalling Peter's

cries of relief at their reappearance. ''Then some fish steaks, and then get you free.''

He produced sulfur matches in an oiled-silk pouch that usually contained his tobacco—all gone now—and in short order built a small, smoky fire. He laid the three cod right on the blaze to thaw enough to clean for cooking.

''Not that I couldn't eat 'em raw, frozen stiff and whole,'' he grumbled good-naturedly. ''Here, while that's doing, let's see if we can get you free, Peter.''

He and Plume—the latter willingly enough, it seemed—took grips on the chains near the iron ring in the wall and, with and what little help Peter could give, began to pull and jerk and wrestle it back and forth.

At last the ring popped out of the ice and they all fell backward at the sudden release of tension.

The ring had an opening that had been buried in the ice. Once free, it was an easy matter to slip the chain out, freeing the exiled Gantrell.

Peter barely managed not to weep in gratitude. Plume stood by, looking rather pleased with himself but saying little. Murdan brushed his breeches free of snow and bits of wet ice and went to clean and dress the thawed codfish by the fire.

Plume and his master huddled close but—as only the Historian had a pocket knife, which he wouldn't trust his former Accountant to use—they could but watch the preparations with great longing.

By the time he'd finished cleaning the catch the fire had died down somewhat, and he laid the thick, white filets right on the coals to broil.

''They'll be more than a bit scorched, I fear,'' he apologized. ''But good to eat, anyway.''

THE next problem,'' said Plume, speaking for the first time as they finished the delicious—it seemed to them—broiled cod, ''is how to get to a safe shore. This berg, or whatever they called it, is melting fast, sirs. Big chunks broke free yesterday when the sun was hottest, and disappeared out to sea.''

"Perhaps we could ride one of the pieces when it breaks off," suggested Gantrell, licking the last of the fish from his fingers. His spirits had revived considerably with the warmth of the fire outside and hot broiled fish inside.

"Pretty dangerous, but perhaps a good idea," agreed the Historian. "I have something else to try first, before we take that risk. . . . ''

Before he could say what it was there was an earshattering *crackkk!* and fully a quarter of the south face of the floe slid into the sea with a vast splash and crash of waves. The remaining portion wallowed and pitched for several minutes before it became still on the water once more.

"Hurry, whatever it is!" cried Plume in terror. "We may go with the next one, willy-nilly!"

"If we go down," Peter said shrilly, "I'll never swim a yard with this cursed chain attached!"

"Stay here by the fire," ordered Murdan. "I'll be right back . . . maybe with salvation."

The two nodded numbly and watched him toboggan down the north slope on his backside, dragging his arms to steer clear of drops and spires.

It took Murdan half an hour to find the Ice Dragon's cave again, and he would have missed it even then if he'd not seen the frosty vapor of the beast's breath from where he lay dozing in the entrance.

"Here, I say!" the Historian called, approaching cautiously so as not to slip into the sea, which was much closer than it had been that morning. "Better wake, Ice Dragon!"

"For goodness' sake, why?" groaned Hoarling peevishly, rolling his ice blue eyes.

"The floe is breaking up and you'll be in the sea shortly," explained Murdan.

"Who cares? I could use a nice cold bath after my nap," said Hoarling, but he slid himself from the cave and stretched his silver wings lazily.

"Cold water bath is just what the doctor ordered," he said with a wicked grin. "Part of the joy of being an Ice Dragon, Sir Historian."

"I need to ask you a favor," Murdan said, ignoring Hoarling's heavy humor.

"I'm already owed favors," the beast grumped.

But he followed the man back up the hill as another piece of ice calved and dropped into the sea nearby.

"Why is that? Owed what?" asked Murdan when the noise had subsided and the island had stopped rocking.

"Your friend Constable came to me four years ago and I agreed to keep an eye on the Rellings for him. It was I who sent warning to Lexor last month when the Northmen started their silly march, you know."

"No, I hadn't heard that. If so, my thanks, Hoarling! You have more than fulfilled your part of the bargain with Retruance. But now I need you to help us ashore before we have to swim for it in freezing seawater—and we can't take it as well as you, Sir Dragon."

"I could do it easily," agreed Hoarling as they approached the fire where Peter and Plume were squatting in a spreading pool of steaming water about the fire. "But why should I?"

Murdan introduced his companions and the Dragon settled down, just out of the reach of the warmth of the little fire, to haggle.

"My needs are simple, of course. But any Dragon worth his scales likes treasure. Gold! Pelf! Jewels! Dragon moolah! I have a few things hidden away somewhere—don't even bother to ask where or how much!—but I can always use more. I did a favor for Constable out of professional courtesy, but you . . . you can afford to pay in good, old-fashioned treasure."

"Eduard Ten will reward you in the matter of the warning of the Relling attack," said Murdan earnestly.

"You can be sure your reward will be generous."

"I like diamonds particularly, the blue variety that look just like ice. And sapphires, too. I prefer silver to gold myself, as far as metals go. . . . "

Another ice facet cracked away and rumbled menacingly into the water. Half of the floe Murdan had first seen from the Relling sloop was already gone. It was early afternoon and the sun felt quite warm, making the Ice Dragon pant for breath and seek the shade of a precariously overhanging pinnacle.

"Well?" asked Murdan. "Diamonds and sapphires and silver aplenty, if you require them. I give my word as Royal Historian!"

"You are my witnesses, then," said Hoarling to the exiled lord and his spy. "You'll vouch for me, if it comes to a disagreement on this price?"

"Agreed," said Peter, quickly. The ice rumbled under them again. "May we depart now?"

"Let's go," shouted Hoarling over the sound of the ice slide. "Where away, Lord Historian?"

"Toward Lexor," yelled Murdan, staggering as the ice rocked and tipped far over. "Our militia is mustered and marching on the capital even now."

"A problem there," said the Dragon, lowering his neck so all three could climb onto his broad shoulders, slippery with hoarfrost, although it was well after midday. "There's a high winter storm between us and the capital. I must keep away from such stormings—lightning means great heat. Best to avoid it—and avoid the Relling armies, too, I should think, for your sakes. They may have captured Lexor by now, don't you fear?"

"Where can you take us, then?" asked Peter. "We could go for Overtide or my brother's Achievement at Morningside. Granger must be raising his levy of soldiers."

"He is," said Murdan.

"But that far south is highly uncomfortable for me," objected the Dragon, shaking his head. "I can't stand the heat. I suggest we go around the storm to the north and fly north of the Snows. You can make your way south through Summer Pass to Overhall if you're lucky, Historian.''

"Head to Old Place, then,'' decided Murdan with a nod of his head. "It's my mother's Achievement north of the Snows and within a few days' journey of Overhall.''

"We're off, then!'' cried the Ice Dragon cheerfully.

Just as he leapt into the air, the floe split in two right under them, from pinnacle to base deep under the water, and the two sides of the berg fell apart into Athermoral Strait, pushing up tremendous waves and making a racketing roar.

By then the Ice Dragon was airborne and heading west by a bit south, toward dark storm clouds across the horizon.

✦ 9 ✦
Katydid

A DRAGON'S flashing speed was of little use, Tom found, when it came to tracking something, especially another Dragon. No wonder it had taken them so long to find a trace of Arbitrance over the years! Tracking was something you had to do in small steps, very carefully.

Retruance, on leaving Knollwater, began a tortuous flight path, swinging miles to the north and south of the line the soldiers at Knollwater had agreed was the kidnapper's escape route.

"It'll take us forever and a day at this rate," the Librarian complained impatiently.

"No easy way," replied Retruance. "I could go faster only if we had Furbetrance here to help us."

"Can't you call him?" Tom asked. He confined himself to scanning the ground and waterways beneath them. There *might* be some sort of sign there, he thought.

"He's on his way," replied the Dragon tersely. "Now, please, let me concentrate. Papa's trace is recent and strong, but he laid down a difficult trail—purposely, I must think."

Tom apologized for his impatience and fell silent to let his Mount find the way.

He'd been dozing in the soft early-afternoon light for some time when his rest was disturbed by an abrupt change in course. Retruance was swooping to the ground beside a pleasant little lake rimmed with sandy beaches and set among wide, neatly furrowed fields separated by dense hedgerows and scattered groves of fruit trees. Beside the lake was a tiny white cottage and a high-peaked, brown-painted barn.

"What's up?" the Librarian asked.

"Not up. Down!" said Retruance. "Papa must have passed directly over this cottage, and in daylight, earlier today. The country people here might have seen him fly over."

The only person they saw when they landed before the cottage was a little girl with flowing auburn hair, arcing back and forth on a swing hung under an elegant ash at least fifty feet tall.

"Little lady," called Retruance softly so as not to startle the child. "We'd like to ask you and your folks some questions."

But the lovely child continued to swing back and forth, pushing herself with the toes of one bare foot on each pass.

"She's deaf," said a new voice. "Her name is Katy."

A young woman in an eyelet lace apron over a plain gray frock stepped from the cottage door, wiping her hands on a towel. She seemed untroubled by the sight of the huge beast and his armed rider in her door yard.

"Oh, my dear young lady!" cried Retruance sadly, turning to her. "I'm terribly sorry!"

"It *is* sad," agreed the woman, bobbing a polite curtsy to them. "She's been so for several years. We don't know why, sirs."

"If we may, we'd like to ask if you've seen a green-and-gold Dragon pass over—something like this one, but slightly smaller, more golden—this morning or late yestereve," said Tom. He introduced himself and the Dragon and the farmer's wife curtsied yet again.

"I've heard tales of the Constable Dragons," she said soberly. "They seemed like fairy's tales then—but now I see they're quite true."

"Most likely highly exaggerated," said Retruance

modestly. "Have you or your little girl seen a Dragon, ma'am?"

"Not I!" said the woman, whose name was Phoebe. "I would have remembered! But perhaps Katy did. She's always watching the sky as she plays. She makes fullest use of her eyes, since her ears do not serve her now."

She walked around to the front of the swing and smiled lovingly at the child, signaling for her to stop her swing and come to her arms. Once she'd picked the child up, she turned her about and showed her the huge Dragon.

"This is Katy," said Phoebe proudly. "My only child."

Katy's bright brown eyes grew almost as big as pie plates, and her mouth fell open at the sight of the vast beast so near, yet she showed no fear.

"Mama! Mama! A truly, truly Dragon!" she cried in delight, reaching out to touch Retruance's nose, which he'd brought close to her.

"Can you tell her that I am vastly pleased to meet her?" he asked Mistress Phoebe. "I've rarely seen a more beautiful child, ma'am. Tell her that, too."

The mother made a series of quick but graceful movements with her right hand, which Katy studied intently. When the message was understood, she turned in her mother's arms and smiled brilliantly at the Dragon.

"You are the most . . . most . . . pretty and shiny thing I have *ever* seen," she said in an awed whisper.

Retruance blushed bright crimson—Tom had never seen a Dragon blush before—and bowed his head shyly. The little girl smiled serenely at the Librarian while the mother signed to her their names.

"I read," Katy said to Tom when she understood that he was a Librarian. "But I have only three books. Do you have a lot of books at home, Sir Librarian?"

"Hundreds and hundreds!" Tom said with a laugh, his heart warming to the child. "When I get home, I'll send you some. What kinds of stories do you like best, Katydid, my love?''

It was obvious that the child had learned to read lips a bit, for she immediately began to tell Tom what books she would like best.

''Picture books with lots of pictures, of course,'' she cried enthusiastically. ''And stories about knights and castles and, yes, Dragons, and beautiful Princesses, and wicked stepmothers, too.''

''I have a very beautiful Princess as my wife,'' Tom told her. ''She would love to meet you, I know. She even has a stepmother, but this stepmother is very beautiful, too, and kind and generous. Someday maybe my own Princess and I will have a little girl just like you, Katydid. Then you could come and play with her and teach her to speak with her fingers.''

''I'd like that,'' replied the child earnestly. ''But won't your little girl be able to hear? Or would she be all deaf, like me?''

''I don't know,'' said Tom, rubbing his nose to keep his voice from breaking. ''But it wouldn't make any difference. We'd love her just the same, and maybe even more.''

''My Mama and Daddy love me just as much,'' exclaimed Katy. ''Can I ride on the Dragon's back? On Re . . . Retruance, I mean?''

''Of course!'' cried the Dragon, and he lifted the child very carefully to his head, explaining through Mistress Phoebe that Companions usually rode thus, rather than on a Dragon's back.

''If she sat back there,'' said Retruance, ''she couldn't see over my head, you understand.''

''So high!'' crowed the deaf child in absolute delight. ''But you'd best set me down now. Mama might worry about me.''

Once the child was safely on the ground, Phoebe invited the travelers to enter her home and share lunch with them. Her husband Martin, she explained, was working in a far field.

"We came here after the child's illness. We were happy in Rainbow, near the great falls," she explained. "But crowds confuse her. Besides, we all love it here, even if it's lonely at times."

They elected to sit on the neatly sheep-cropped lawn under the dozen or so majestic ashes—Retruance had pointed out that he couldn't even fit his head through the cottage door—and ate bright yellow melon slices and scrambled-egg sandwiches on toast and drank thick, red tomato juice made from the fruit in Phoebe's own kitchen garden.

Katy ate heartily and watched her visitors' and her mother's lips to make sure she didn't miss a thing—and to avoid interrupting the words she could not hear, Tom noticed. She still had much trouble reading the Dragon's lips, however.

Retruance asked her mother to ask Katy about seeing a Dragon, and to their surprise the child nodded her head emphatically.

"Oh, yes!" she cried. "This very morning. I thought just now it was you, Retruance Constable, but it was another Dragon, I think."

"Are you sure it was a Dragon, dear?" her mother asked. "Could it have been a great, big hawk?"

"No, Mother," said Katy, positive as only a seven-year-old could be. "It *was* a Dragon—just like Retruance! Only not quite so big, perhaps. And shining gold, instead of mostly green. Retruance is mostly green, and hawks are brown and white."

"She's very observant, you see," laughed Phoebe, giving the little girl a warm hug and sending her inside to fetch the carrot cake for dessert. "I believe she saw what she says. She has a marvelous imagination and often pretends to see things—like Dragons. I've scolded her for it at times, I'm afraid."

"Which may explain why she didn't tell you about

the Dragon she actually saw this morning,'' Tom guessed.

He remembered his own childhood fancies very well. When Katy returned from the house she was quite as certain that the Dragon she had seen that morning had been heading due west.

"He came toward me with the sun shining through his big bat wings. I could almost see right through 'em,'' she insisted. 'And the gold tip of his tail flashed like . . . like gold, I guess . . . when he flew away across our lake.''

"I've no doubt of it, then,'' said Retruance with a sigh. He explained to the mother why they were seeking this Dragon.

"Don't tell Katy, please,'' he begged her. "She seems to have a good opinion of Dragons and it might disappoint her to learn that one has been so wicked.''

"Oh, I'm most sorry that it's your own papa you're searching for!'' cried the farmer's wife. "Surely, he's enchanted by some wicked wizard!''

"We believe so,'' said Tom.

"We must be on our way,'' said Retruance, "thanking you for the wonderful lunch. I tend to forget that Elves and Humans like Tom require frequent feeding. I'm afraid I forgot to allow him breakfast—or dinner last night, either.''

"I can stand it,'' said the Librarian.

While Katy led Retruance off to see her lambs, Tom asked Phoebe, "Have you sought treatment for the child? I'm sure there are doctors who could restore her hearing.''

"We found it would cost a great, great deal to see a proper doctor, and we're not that rich. We asked the help of Lord Peter of Gantrell, our liege lord in Rainbow. He didn't answer our letter—and shortly after he was exiled.''

"You're richer than anyone I know!'' said Tom sincerely. "To have such a wonderful child! Mistress, tell

your good husband that he is to bring Katydid to Overhall as soon as he can. There's a wizard-doctor named
Arcolas there who's as kind and able as any in the kingdom. If he can't restore the girl's hearing, he'll certainly
know who can. Do you think you could make the journey?''

"Yes, oh! I am sure we can!" cried Phoebe, glowing
with happiness and looking quite young herself. "My
Martin carries his fall produce to Lakehead in a week's
time. He borrows a wagon from a neighbor, you see.
Usually the child and I stay behind, but we could easily
go on from there to Overhall, I would think."

"If we've not yet returned from our quest for Arbitrance, for Retruance's father," Tom added, "tell them at
the castle gate that I sent you. Tell Katy's story to my
wife, Princess Alix Amanda. Something will be done,
be assured, mistress!"

Katy noticed tears on her mother's cheeks as they said
good-bye, and asked what troubled her.

"Nothing at all, little Katydid. Your mother is happy
that you have at last seen a truly, truly Dragon," Tom
told her. "And it's possible we will see you again soon,
if all goes well."

Katy kissed the Librarian on the cheek and the Dragon
on the end of his nose. The searchers flew off westward,
waving until the child, the mother, and the cottage itself
fell too far behind to see.

Neither traveler said anything for a long time
afterward.

THE ground beneath them that evening had changed
from well-watered, black-dirt farmland to wetlands alive
with thousands of southward-migrating birds settling
down for the night. When Retruance tried to engage
them in conversation for news of the rogue Dragon, they
scattered away and filled the air with hysterical squawking and screaming.

"Brainless birds!" snapped Retruance irritably.

"They've been frightened," guessed Tom. "They're flighty at the best of times, of course. But it may be they've been stirred up lately by your papa."

The thought cheered Retruance considerably.

"The scent of Dragon is as strong here as it has ever been in years of searching," he exalted. "Papa *is* nearby, I'm sure of it!"

"But there's all kinds of places he could hide. It's so vast! I've looked at the maps! It goes on for miles and miles."

"More important, it goes on for days and days, at the rate we must fly now!" Retruance now sounded discouraged.

"Well, we'll plug away at it, old friend. For the sake of the Princeling and Arbitrance, too."

"Of course!" choked the Dragon, and he banked sharply, still quartering over the wetlands, checking the direction his renegade papa had carried the Crown Prince of Carolna over what appeared to be endless, empty swampland.

To continue after dark seemed fruitless, for they were close enough now, Retruance said, for his father to become aware of their presence.

"And if we stumble on him in the dark," Tom agreed, "there's no telling what the . . . your papa . . . might do to the boy. At best, he'd fly off somewhere else and leave us to do all our slow searching over again."

Retruance agreed reluctantly and set about finding a bit of higher and drier ground on which to spend the night.

"Hammocks or hummocks," said Tom with a yawn. "That's what they're called where I come from."

"Swamp islands, rather," said Retruance. "Look! That one's big enough for a Dragon and must rise ten feet out of the water in the center. Perfect!"

When Tom looked over the Dragon's brow, he saw a tiny point of light on its westernmost edge.

"Careful!" he warned. "It might be Arbitrance!"

"No," the Dragon disagreed. "It's a campfire like no Dragon would ever need."

He alighted softly a hundred yards downwind of the fire and Tom called out, so as not to frighten the campers by appearing suddenly out of the deep dark under the tangled trees.

"Hoy!" came a reply. "Come up to the fire, neighbors! Supper's just about ready and I don't think I can eat it all myself."

A tall, gangly young man dressed in plain leather leggings and fringed shirt that covered him from neck to knee, despite the humid warmth of the night, jumped to his feet when he saw one of his callers was a Dragon.

"Holy mackerel!" he exclaimed. "The Dragon!"

"Not *the* Dragon, probably," chuckled Retruance, stopping just across the fire from the camper, "but a Dragon very interested in any other Dragon you might have seen recently."

"We're searching for a certain Dragon said to be hiding in these parts," explained Tom.

"Come and sit by my fire! Spend the night, if you will. I haven't had company or any news at all for weeks!" cried the young man. "My name is Findles of Aquanelle."

Tom shook his hand and told him their names and origins.

"I teach agriculture and hydroponics at Queen's College in Aquanelle—that's in Waterfields," the scholar told them.

"We're good friends of Queen Beatrix, your patroness," Retruance said. "In fact, we're here on her behalf, in a way."

He let Tom explain their mission while the scholar busied himself about the campfire, dishing up a savory crawfish stew on tin plates, and slicing bread baked on a metal sheet slanted before the hot coals.

"Yes, I've seen both the Dragon and signs of him hereabouts," he said as they sat down to eat. "I saw

him fly over low, just this noontime. He didn't see me,
I think. Mostly I work under the trees at the water's
edge. I'm tracing the sources of the waters that flow
through Waterfields to learn if they are safe and perpet-
ual."

"Ah!" said Tom, his ears perking up with interest.
"What have you learned?"

"It would immeasurably harm the whole kingdom if
Waterfields should become too dry or the waters were
dirtied. Swamp drainage is not always a good idea, but
most of our good country people wish to do it to make
new fields, as you might imagine."

"Ah, about the Dragon?" asked Retruance to steer
the conversation back to his papa. "Where is he now,
do you know?"

"Oh, in his redoubt, I imagine, unless he's flown out
some other way. In the morning we can look and see if
he is venting smoke. He smokes a lot, usually."

"Redoubt?" asked Tom. "He's built a fort here in
the swamp?"

"Of a sort, yes," replied Findles. "More bread? It
won't keep long in this damp."

"Explain the redoubt, please," asked Retruance patiently.

"Well, this area is called Sinking Marsh, as you may
already know."

"I didn't know. Stinking?" Tom asked.

"No, *Sinking*—it's a vast quagmire. The quicksands
won't bear the weight of a child, let alone a grown
man—or a Dragon. Goes on for miles and miles to the
south and west. Actually, it's a welling-up place where
underground springs come to the surface to form a very
shallow, very broad river."

"We have something much like that at home," said
the Librarian, thinking of Hidden Canyon Lake.

"I'm measuring the flow as part of my study," the
scholar went on. "A fabulous lot of water is filtered
through the sand here. Also this marsh serves as a nat-

ural reservoir upstream from Waterfields.''

"Interesting," said Retruance politely. "How could Papa . . . this Dragon you've observed . . . have landed there, then, without sinking into the quicksands?''

"I'm not sure, for I've never seen him on the ground," admitted Findles. "However, I've a theory he's found or constructed a hummock in the center of it all. Would *have* to be something like that. Pile up logs and brush and anchor it with rocks brought from elsewhere, eh? Take him some time, even for a Dragon . . .''

"A matter of five to ten years?" guessed Tom, beginning to understand what Arbitrance had been doing all those years since he'd disappeared.

"Yes, I'd agree with that. I'd have to examine it more closely, to be sure. Impossible to cross Sinking Marsh on foot, of course. And most boats just bog down because it's too shallow. The sand is entirely saturated, you see. If you can fly like a bird—or a Dragon—you could easily reach the Dragon's hummock, I'd say.''

"Poses us some serious problems," Retruance said, considering. "We'll explore the area tomorrow, Tom. As you said, we can't afford to startle Papa or he might—just *might*—flee again with the boy. He's been enchanted to do such wicked things. No telling what his instructions might be.''

Tom ate another slice of Findles's excellent campfire bread and swallowed a cup of tepid, marshy-tasting tea. The scholar insisted the water from which it had been made was perfectly clean and healthful.

"We may need more than just the two of us to pull this off," Tom decided as they settled down for the night.

Large, voracious swampland mosquitoes swarmed from the still water but such bugs were repelled by the scent of Dragon, Tom discovered. Their shrill whining and humming lulled Tom at last into a deep, exhausted slumber.

He fell asleep thinking not of the kidnapped Princeling or the rogue Dragon who held him captive, but of the flow of water down from the peaks of the distant Snow Mountains, down through deep canyons like his Hidden Canyon Achievement, and then deep into hidden aquifers beneath the Hiding Lands' desert.

✦ 10 ✦
Findles's Hummock

"If *I* can smell *Papa*, Papa can smell *me* . . . if the wind changes to blow east to west . . . and it will! Winter's coming on. Right now it's quite still, but that won't last," Retruance muttered, more to himself than to Tom.

"Before we move farther, we must have Furbetrance here, too," Tom decided. "And I'd like to have Murdan handy, too. Someone must watch the far side of the marsh, in case your poor Papa decides to flee when we move in on him."

"Furbie should be here any hour," his Dragon Mount promised.

They'd broken their fast and were watching as Findles demonstrated the dangers of the quicksands by probing near the tangled edge of his hummock with a ten-foot bamboo pole. There was no firm bottom at that length, even close inshore, although it seemed, when one looked, rather shallow.

"Nor at three times this length, either, I assure you," the young scientist said, paddling his flat-bottom canoe back to the firm soil of his hummock. "That's as deep as I can probe with my present equipment."

Tom nodded absently. "I want to walk over to the other side of your island this morning. I may be able to get the birds to tell me something if nobody else is around to scare them off, Retruance. White Shoulders taught me enough bird-tongue to make myself understood. A lot of them already speak our Elvish, of course."

"Fine with me. I'll just stay here close to guide Furbetrance to us."

Tom said to the scholar, "Tell me, how did you manage to get here yourself?"

"Ten to twelve miles to the east the quagmire is no more. I poled my flat-bottomed boat from drier, higher ground there. I keep my boat moored under overhanging bushes down the shore a way—well hidden. As I said, I don't believe yonder Dragon is aware of my being nearby."

Tom made his way through the heavy, thorn-spiked underbrush across the raised center of the island. Although the going was slow and the air was humid, it was not unpleasant as long as he watched his step. Hundreds of birds sang in the moss-draped live oaks, and lizards of bright yellow, red, and blue scurried hastily away at his noisy approach.

Many of the trees and bushes were fall-flowering and the scent of their blossoms was near to overpowering in the close air. In other trees—some sort of walnut, he thought—he saw what he took at first to be tiny monkeys. They turned out to be frisky, daring black-tailed squirrels—nibbling and gnawing at the brown or gold nuts that grew in huge clusters.

From a grove of smaller trees in the center of the island he plucked oranges of brilliant color and deliciously sweet and juicy pulp.

Exploring and quite enjoying this strange island setting, Tom reached the far edge of the hummock after a half hour's stroll and found a sandy spot of beach among the cypress trunks and knees at the edge of the hummock where he could actually reach open water.

It looked so invitingly cool that Tom shed his clothing without hesitation and took a bracing swim. No birds, animals, or snakes approached him until he climbed out on a mossy-soft, fallen cypress log to let his skin dry in the light breeze and bright midmorning sun.

"I've never seen a grown bird with such an *appalling*

lack of feathers,'' he heard a large, long-legged, snow white bird with a long, curved beak say. Tom smiled and nodded to the bird but made no rejoinder, realizing how strange he must appear sitting naked and soaking wet on the log.

"An exotic of some sort?" another voice asked with a laugh.

The second speaker was a three-foot lizard of dark green with white and bright yellow spots down his back and around his throat. The reptile flicked out a vividly orange tongue, captured a bluebottle fly, and swallowed it with a quick gulp.

"Where are you from and what flock?" asked the white heron, fixing the young man with one beady eye.

"Not from around here, at any rate," Tom replied. "From the north. A place called Overhall."

"Never heard of it," said the white heron with a haughty sniff.

"But that doesn't mean anything," put in the lizard with a lazy grin. "You've lived all your life right here on this hummock!"

"Well, so I have and my mother and grandmothers before me," said the heron defensively. "It's the best place in the world to be, when it comes down to that."

"Care for a dragonfly, fledgling?" the lizard asked Tom politely.

"No, thank you just the same," Tom replied, shaking his head. "I've already eaten. Why do you call me 'fledgling'?"

"It's obvious you aren't yet feathered and ready to fly," replied the lizard.

"Oh, come now!" cried the heron. "How else could he get here? Unless he was brought by the strange water-poke."

"Actually, I came by Dragon," admitted Tom.

"By *what*!" squawked the bird.

She just did manage to keep from toppling off the log by a wild flapping of her long wings. "Dragons eat whole flocks of birds at a gulp! Mama told me so, so I know it's true.''

"Some Dragons do, perhaps," said the lizard, chuckling. "But not the one whose been over in the middle of Sinking Marsh these past few years. That one eats nothing but big rocks and cypress pilings, I've heard.''

"I wouldn't trust a Dragon farther than I could spit," said the heron with a shudder. "But you say one carried you here, youngster? How? Why? Did you manage to escape?''

"Easily told," Tom said, and he launched into the story of the Dragon gone bad and the kidnapping of young Prince Ednoll.

"The thing is, what can you tell me about this Dragon? Is he living on a hummock in the middle of Sinking Marsh, as we surmise?''

"Well, I can tell you that, for I've flown that way several times this week," said the white heron, twisting her head right about to groom her tail feathers with her long, yellow beak. "Yes, there *is* a hummock there— quite large, in fact—and he's added rocks and logs to it, making it even higher and larger and drier. Planted grasses, vines, and full-grown trees, also. For shade, I suppose, especially now he's got the man-child for a visitor or guest.''

"They're all afraid to go closer than that," said the lizard with a slow wink at the Librarian. "Chickens, all of 'em!''

"Sir, if you weren't my best friend, I'd . . . I'd . . . ," sputtered the heron angrily.

"But you've never really *overflown* the hummock, have you?'' the lizard teased her.

"Well, not in so many . . . well, no! But I've seen the Dragon up closer than anyone else, haven't I?''

"That much is true," said the lizard to Tom, who was dressing himself as he listened. "The beast surprised her while she was fishing one evening.''

"No way to get closer to the Dragon but by wing, I

suppose?'' the Librarian asked the bird.

''Unless you've an insane desire to be a Dragon's dinner, you're safe enough. There isn't any other way except flying . . . oh, maybe by swimming.''

Tom considered her words for a moment.

''I wonder if I could get you to do me a favor. Nothing dangerous and it won't take long, I assure you. To help us save the little boy. He's captive to the Dragon, you see . . .''

''I suspected it already! At your service,'' twittered the bird, waving a wing. ''I love an adventure! Children need our protection, 'specially here.''

The lizard snorted in derision and slid off to find some tasty snails to top off the bluebottle flies he'd eaten for lunch.

''Fly as close to the Dragon's hummock as you dare,'' Tom explained. ''Come back and tell us what they're doing, the Dragon and the lad. Look especially carefully at the little boy. Has he been harmed? We must send word to his mother, the Queen of Carolna. And rescue him, if we can, my Dragon and I.''

The white heron wanted to hear the whole story in detail. When Tom had finished the telling, she agreed without further questioning to take a look from aloft at the Dragon's lair in the midst of Sinking Marsh.

''I'll be back at the water-poker's camp by sundown,'' she promised, and, flapping her wonderfully long wings, ran across the shallows off the beach and launched herself into the midday sky.

Tom pulled on his boots, gathered a dozen of the ripest oranges and a bunch of yellow-green bananas, then retraced his steps to the other side of the hummock.

Furbetrance had arrived in his absence, and his brother was filling him in on the latest developments.

''The heron can tell us exactly what we're up against, if she dares to go close enough,'' Tom told them. ''What's for lunch?''

''Small-mouth bass,'' announced Findles, proudly

displaying his morning's catch.

He set Tom to cleaning the fish while he built up the fire and chattered about current flow and water levels and taste and the fact that he'd figured it took a given volume of water several hundred years, at least, to seep from the northern mountains down to the marsh by way of the deep-buried aquifer layers under the Hiding Lands' sand and the Cristol River's stony bed itself.

There was little else the two Dragons and the Librarian could do at the moment, so they responded to Findles's request for assistance, probing several places within the quicksand morass that he couldn't otherwise reach in his boat.

"Out of sight of the other Dragon, of course," said the scholar. "Only sensible!"

Attaching his three ten-foot poles together end to end, Findles attempted to plumb the depths and determine the contours of the open marsh bottom under the watery sand and silt. From that he hoped to estimate the volume of water flowing into the reservoir from the north. Every fact he gained was carefully checked and jotted in a mildewed leather-bound notebook that never left his hands or pocket.

Despite their impatience to finish their mission, the Dragons and Tom found that the time flew by. Tom was especially interested in the estimates Findles had made as to where and how deep the aquifers lay under Hiding Lands.

"Pretty deep for man-made wells, however," warned the young scientist. "A thousand feet? At least eight hundred!"

"I'm not sure how deep man-made wells can be dug with present technology here, but I know they go deeper than that at home," said Tom thoughtfully. "I'll have to check that out. You don't know, do you, Retruance?"

"Not a bit of it!" cried the older Dragon. "We Dragons deal in fire, not water, my boy."

Findles was excited by Tom's proposed practical use

of his information on the deep water's flow.

"You'd dig deep wells to tap the aquifers and use it to water crops in the middle of the desert? No reason why it can't be done, I say!" he enthused. "When you're ready to start, call me. I'll come help all I can. You know," he added, just struck with a new thought, "if the overbearing layer is impervious desert rock, as I suspect, the water must be under considerable pressure. In that case it might gush up through a strong well casing without pumping. What a sight!"

"We'll have to be careful, won't we, not to take too much of the water?" inquired the Librarian.

"I'll have an answer for you on that in a few weeks," promised Findles. "Some care is indicated, of course. Waterfields might go dry! Of course, I've been saying for years and years, Waterfields could stand to have a little less water flowing through!"

As they rested in the late afternoon the white heron glided down to land on a low-hanging oak bough nearby. Tom greeted her eagerly and introduced her to his friends.

The bird overcame her first fears of the huge Dragons and politely exchanged bows with them.

"Now, as to the Dragon's lair," she said. "The hummock is most certainly man made, or rather, Dragon enhanced. It's so large it takes three full minutes to fly across. . . . "

"That would make it six miles wide," interrupted Findles, consulting an ivory slide rule he pulled from his breast pocket.

"That's right!" said the heron. "And as long, too."

"I see why Papa was so long gone," said Furbetrance, nodding gravely. "It would have taken even a Dragon quite a long time to make such a safe, dry haven."

"I flew as low as I thought prudent," continued the heron. "As it turned out, the Dragon was not paying any attention to me. He was playing catch with the man-child.''

"Catch?" cried Furbetrance. "You mean the boy was running away and the Dragon was trying to *catch* him?"

"No, no! They were tossing a ball back and forth. Quite cunningly, I thought, too," replied the bird. "I've played in such manner with my own children, at times, before they learned to fly and left the nesting area."

"So the child seems safe and well?" asked Retruance with considerable relief in his voice.

"Very much so, I should guess," the heron answered. "He, the other Dragon, has built a covered nest—a hutch or a cote, I believe you'd call it—so they have a roof over their heads when it rains or the sun's too hot. The center of the island is smoothly rolling and planted with lawns and flower beds, orchards and gardens of vegetables and fragrant ferns."

"Papa was always a dirt gardener at heart," murmured Retruance with a sentimental sniff.

"That's about all I can tell you, friends," said the heron, accepting a plateful of broiled bass fillets from the scholar. "I can tell you that anything as big as a Dragon or even a grown man couldn't approach the Dragon's island by either air or on foot without being seen when they were yet miles off. At night, perhaps, but I for one wouldn't want to try it."

They thanked the bird sincerely for her help. After they'd finished off the broiled fish and cleaned up the campsite, the researcher sat with his back against a tree trunk, smoothing his rough notes of the day and transferring them to his notebook.

The adventurers huddled on the other side of the campsite to discuss their next moves.

"I say we go over tonight, fly in quick and quiet, and snatch the child straight away while he sleeps," Furbetrance insisted.

"But Papa won't be asleep, especially if he knows we're close by," his older brother objected. "No, what we need is a diversion. Somehow draw Papa away from the boy long enough to slip in behind him.''

"Wouldn't he be expecting just that sort of thing?'' asked Tom.

"You're right, of course. That's just what he would expect and plan for,'' the Dragons said in agreement, sighing.

They fell silent for a long while.

Tom at last said, "What he *won't* expect is anyone to come on foot to his hummock.''

"But that's impossible!'' cried Retruance. "Anyone trying to walk through the quicksands would be swallowed up in a trice! A horrible death and for naught.''

"Still, I recall ways men have managed to cross such quagmires before. I've read of their exploits, at least. A keeled boat would become trapped, but if we used Findles's wide, flat boat that wouldn't sink. I could lie in it and paddle it ashore under the cover of night.''

"I see what you're saying,'' cried Furbetrance. "Or you might use two wide wooden boards and move one ahead while you lie on the other, and alternate like that. Hard work, however!''

"And very slow,'' added his older and wiser brother "It'd take a full night to reach the hummock's edge. Tom'd be exposed to full view once daylight came. Hmmm!''

"Something must be done, though,'' Tom insisted. "What else *is* there?''

"That's good enough for a beginning,'' agreed Furbetrance, rising and stretching his wings. "I'll find a tree to cut up to make the flats, shall I?''

Retruance stayed him with a lifted claw.

"Wait! I suggest what Tom said earlier is still a good idea. It's unlikely, as long as we don't threaten him, that Papa'll move or harm the Princeling.''

"Agreed,'' said Tom.

"We need help. Murdan is, after all, Papa's Companion.''

"I'd forgotten that," admitted Furbetrance. "Yes, he would be most helpful."

"And you've been *meaning* to ask Princess Manda to be your Companion for some time, I believe." Retruance continued.

"True. I'm rather too shy to ask, if the truth were to be known!"

"Go to Overhall . . . fetch Murdan and the Princess . . . propose Companionship to Manda. I have no doubt she'll accept you."

"Nor have I," said Tom. "She hasn't ever really said so, but I know she truly wants to be a Companion."

"If I'd known *that*," grumbled Furbetrance, "I'd have asked her ages ago."

It was quickly agreed that while Furbetrance and Tom returned to Overhall, Retruance would stay on the edge of Sinking Marsh, keeping an eye on his papa. He'd circle the hummock, at a distance, each day, and enlist the herons to fly closer to check on the welfare of Prince Ednoll, just in case.

"We can be back in three days if we fly straight to Overhall without stopping for food, drink, or sleep," decided the Librarian.

"Be on your way, then!" said Retruance gloomily. "Waiting is the hardest part."

✦ 11 ✦
Old Place

As Tom and Furbetrance were departing from the edge of Sinking Marsh, Manda and her parents arrived at Overhall, after an uneventful overland ride north and west.

They were greeted warmly, and with great relief, by Rosemary of Ffallmar. She'd moved to her father's castle after Ffallmar and his troops had marched off to lift the siege of Lexor.

"They've surrounded poor Lexor!" Rosemary told the King. "The Rellings, I mean. According to the last pigeon-post message we've had from your Lord High Chamberlain, the city is yet holding fast . . . at least as of yesterday morning. They've plenty of food and water, according to Walden. The townspeople are manning the wall along with the Royal Guard and maintaining good discipline."

"Good old Walden!" exclaimed the King with a relieved laugh. "How he's improved! He used to be such a stuffed shirt, wasn't he, sweetheart?"

The Queen nodded agreement while handing the sleeping Amelia to Rosemary, who snuggled her down with her own brood in the pleasant nursery atop Middle Tower.

"But, Father, what of Murdan?" asked Manda with concern. "He went ahead alone to Lexor and has since disappeared!"

"So it seems," said the King, shaking his head. "Certainly Walden would have mentioned the Historian if he were safe in the city."

"What must we do now?" Beatrix asked after they'd dined and were only waiting for someone to suggest an early bedtime.

"I'll follow Ffallmar to Lexor," decided the King. "The levees will expect me there, although Ffallmar of Ffallmar Farm will do perfectly well without my interference, I suspect. Sometimes a King must act the figurehead and let the people who know best work. You and Amelia should stay here, my dear. Overhall is the stoutest and safest castle anywhere in the kingdom."

"I've visited here before," the Queen reminded her husband, politely covering a deep yawn. "It'll be as great a pleasure as possible under the circumstances, my dear! Isn't anyone going to say, 'Let's to bed'? I can hardly keep my eyelids from falling shut!"

EDUARD saw her abed and already sleeping soundly before he went to look into the nursery for a moment, and to walk the battlements, inspecting Murdan's orange-liveried Overhall Guard where they stood their posts.

Captain Graham came to him and saluted gravely.

"Bad news, sire!" he announced. "They say Lord Murdan was captured by Rellings and imprisoned on an island in midst of the northern Blue!"

"Who sends this evil news?" cried the King.

"A Relling sergeant was captured by General Ffallmar's scouts during a sortie from the southwest Lexor gate, sire. He said he was the one who captured my master, and that this leader of theirs, Great Blizzardmaker or whatever, condemned him to death by starving or freezing on an island of ice."

The two, captain and King, stood in silent commiseration for a long while. A cold wind whipped the castle's banners and pennants out straight to the east. The chill wind smelled of approaching snow.

"The others can wait until morning to learn of it," decided the King at last, sadly. "Anything else?"

"There's a report that a force of Northmen marches

this way, sire, having outflanked Ffallmar . . . or missed him entire. No confirmation of that yet. We're ready to defend Overhall. We've plenty of food and fodder. Water's no problem, thanks to Gugglerun. My entire force is on alert, as you've seen. I vouch for their courage and skill!''

"Of course you do!" cried the King, clapping him on the back. "Well, we'll just have to wait and see what comes. I was hoping to ride to join Ffallmar this morning, but this will hold me here for a while, I suppose. Somehow I'm not worried about Murdan, though. He's surely a match for a petty Relling tyrant."

"I believe so, too," Graham agreed. "Lord Ffallmar and his main troops cannot reach the capital before tomorrow afternoon, however. They'll have their work cut out for them, especially if it snows yet again."

"Ffallmar can relieve the city if anyone can," the King said stoutly.

"No news from Sir Thomas and Retruance Constable, either, which means, I'm afraid, that they haven't recovered your son, Lord King. If word comes, shall I awaken you?"

"Only if it's good news," decided Eduard, for he was a sensible man. "I need a good night of sleep more than evil tidings about which nothing can be done, save worrying."

Graham saluted and watched him go stumping wearily down the stone stairs to the courtyard below.

"Keep your eyes peeled, you dairy-maid swains!" he barked in his best parade-ground bellow to the lookouts atop the three towers and along the encircling walls.

To his second-in-command he said, "Wake me if they see or hear anything. Anything at all!"

He clumped down the stairs to the outer bailey, making a mental note to have them swept clear if new snow fell during the night, and headed for his own bed. No good was served by staying awake and worrying, as the

King said. Graham had long experience at soldiering to back him on that.

Despite his determination, he lay awake worrying for a long time before sleep captured him at last.

HOARLING, who functioned best in subfreezing weather and winds, stopped twice on his way across the north slopes of the Snow Mountains to allow his passengers to eat, relieve themselves, warm hands and feet over a fire, and stretch their weary legs.

"Only a little bit better than that iceberg," Murdan complained, pounding his hands on his forearms, trying to work up some warming circulation. "*Brrr!*"

"If you'd been chained on that iceberg for fourteen days as I was," said Peter Gantrell, still chained and huddling close to the fire of dry twigs and pitchy pine-wood—lots of light and fragrant smoke but too little heat, unfortunately—"I'm just beginning to feel my toes again, as it is."

Plume nodded glumly but made no comment. He'd avoided speaking to or even looking at Murdan, his former employer, shrinking from contact even when they rode the Ice Dragon's slippery back scales.

"You people just don't appreciate a pleasant season when you see it," said the Ice Dragon, chuckling. "We'd better get up and going again, friends. It'll be blizzarding here in half an hour. The farther west we go, the heavier snow we'll meet. Not that I mind, but poor visibility could cause us to miss our way."

The first night they flew until the Dragon complained his wings were growing weary. They sheltered until dawn in a deserted, half-ruined village surrounded by a sturdy palisade of upright logs.

Murdan recognized it as Plaingirt, once the stronghold of Gantrell's hired soldiers, the Mercenary Knights. Inside its abandoned log huts and halls it was almost as cold as the outside air, but at least there was no wind and plenty of wood to burn.

The last of the Historian's meager supply of bread had long since been consumed, but, poking about in the kitchen storehouse and pantry, Peter found a half sack of wheaten flour and a moldy green smoked ham.

"These must be three, four years old!" protested Murdan.

"It never gets warm enough up this high on the mountainside, even in summer, to cause food to spoil very fast," the Dragon explained with exaggerated patience. "It should be perfectly edible for you lesser types of life."

"I remember how to make bread of a sort, from my campaigning days with the old Gantrell, your father, Peter," the Historian said. "Scrape the mold off and the ham will be quite good, I expect."

He set the Accountant to work on the latter task while he tried his hand at campfire bread—without leavening, of course. Once pared, sliced, and warmed on sticks over the coals, the ham, along with the hot, flat bread and melted snow to drink, made a fair supper.

The fire in the log hall's stone fireplace allowed them to spend the night in some comfort while the storm howled outside and dumped another foot of white on everything in sight.

PETER Gantrell did his share of menial chores despite the dragging chain: cutting wood, tending a boiling pot, or clearing away the clutter left by the Mercenary Knights when they left. Plume, on the other hand, stayed far from doing anything at all, unless ordered to it by Murdan or Peter. Then he performed his assigned tasks with disgust written all over his pinched face.

"I really can't figure that man out," muttered Murdan after he'd sent the Accountant out to fetch a bucket of clean snow to melt for drinking water. The village well had a half foot of ice plugging it. "His life was saved from the ice as surely as yours—and mine, for that matter—but he doesn't seem very grateful for it, does he?"

"You know him better than I," Gantrell said with a shrug. "He was ever very slick, subservient, and callow, I thought, when I had dealings with him . . . er, before."

He meant "before" his defeat and exile, but refrained from saying what they both knew very well.

Plume returned and sullenly hung the bucket of snow over the fire to melt. When it was steaming, all three took turns washing their grimy hands, face, and feet. It was much too cold for further bathing. Razors and soap had been taken from them by their Relling captors.

The Ice Dragon needed little rest, as he slept in glacial ice caves all summer, as suited his subspecies. He was nowhere to be seen when they arose in the morning.

Murdan shook his head in disgust. At least here they were warm, had shelter and some food, and wouldn't have to swim to safety across a stormy sea. If the Dragon had deserted them, they could still hope to make their way back to Overhall in time.

But as they finished eating the last gristly chunks of ham, hard bread, and plain, hot water, Hoarling came swirling down from the overcast sky and poked his head through the front door of the hall where they'd spent the stormy night.

"Just off checking up on our Rellings," he explained, accepting a smoking ham hock to crunch between his powerful teeth.

"Are they near, then?" asked Peter, startled by the thought.

"No, m'lord! The nearest Northmen are in a rough circle about the stockaded fort at—Frontier, isn't it? I'm a stranger here myself. South and east of here, it is."

"Frontier that would be," agreed Murdan. "We'll continue on to my mother's Old Place, if you please, Master Ice Dragon."

"I keep my bargains," said the Dragon huffily, and when they had packed their few belongings, he took them aboard and shot off northwest by west, trailing swirling streamers of ice crystals behind him in the weak winter sunlight.

THE second night was spent under a thick clump of majestic blue spruce. Their haven wasn't as uncomfortable as Murdan had feared it would be. The close-set boughs were layered heavily with snow and, once the travelers crawled under the wide-spread branches that swept the bare ground and lighted a small fire on a stone hearth, the air became quite warm.

Peter had built the fire close to a great bole where the smoke might, with luck, escape to the open air and the heat would not bring as much meltwater down on their heads from the overhead boughs. They wrapped themselves in their cloaks, ate the last of Murdan's unleavened bread crusts, which were toasted over the fire, and went at once to sleep.

Hoarling lay in soft snowdrifts outside, allowing a new, light fall to drift about his sides to camouflage his outline. In a half hour anyone passing within twenty paces of the grove would have seen nothing. Even the glow of their fire was completely hidden by the heavy pine boughs and the snow covering them.

BREAKFAST consisted of a hot tea made from old, dry sassafras twigs Murdan found buried in the snow near the edge of the grove.

"Hot, at least," he said.

"And remarkably delicious," exclaimed Peter. "I always liked sassafras tea. My late, loved Lady Mother used to make it for Granger and me on cold evenings when we were lads."

"I have trouble thinking of you as a little boy," admitted the Historian. "I knew your Lady Mother quite well, of course. Fine figure of a woman, and very, very patient, I remember. Your father . . . well, he wasn't the easiest man to have around, I imagine."

"I've thought about them both often these past few

weeks," said Peter, sighing and pouring himself a spot more of the tea. "Being in mortal jeopardy seems to bring one's memories flooding back, I think. I don't really *know*, but I suspect that much of what I tried to do as an adult was because . . . well, I was trying to best my father. He was a remarkable fighting man, an unquestioned leader. He wanted everything to be done just his way."

"I remember him well," said the Historian, nodding.

"I admired him greatly. He was a perfectionist, so I wanted to be one, too. Goodness knows, he was not easy to *like*."

"Children tend to credit their fathers and mothers for what they become," said Murdan.

They climbed back aboard the Dragon, ready to fly.

"And I suppose that's natural and logical," continued the Historian, "when you consider we also give ourselves credit for having good parents, as well as bad ones. You'll meet my mother soon."

"I've not had the honor before, Lord Historian," Peter said with a smile. "But the court people always spoke very well of Lady Murtal."

"Well, when you meet her you'll know why I'm proud to say I followed in her precepts, ofttimes. But in the end, Peter, we are what we make of ourselves, not what our folks made us into."

Hoarling snorted derisively and leapt into the air, flapping his wings up and then down with a clap like thunder, sending loose snow flying in a great cloud that obscured the wintry sun.

After that, the roar of the wind was too great for conversation, which suited all three of them marvelously well.

Murtal, the lady of Old Place, woke early, as she almost always did, with a strong intuition that important visitors were coming that day.

Her premonitions were so seldom mistaken that she bounced out of bed, despite her seventy-odd years of age, and called at once for her butler, a man even older than she, a great deal more dignified, and almost as spry.

"Garley! Visitors coming! Air out the guest rooms, lay good fires there, and have the upstairs maids change the bed linens and put out fresh towels. In this weather, they'll appreciate warm baths ready when they arrive! Send the cook to me, at once!"

She rushed headlong through her breakfast, volleying orders this way and that, scattering her servants and soldiers to their tasks and trotting about inspecting everything, strewing praise and comments as she went.

"Who would be coming in this weather, I wonder?" one of the grooms asked Garley.

"Haven't the faintest idea," replied the ancient majordomo. "But our lady's never wrong."

"It's almost certainly Murdan," declared Murtal, with growing enthusiasm. "I can feel his nearness stronger than anyone else since his father, my late husband, passed on. A family talent."

She ordered the outer and inner baileys swept clear of new snow and pine-knot cressets set at intervals on the walls. All the lanterns and candles were lighted as the afternoon grew dark toward evening.

Only when all was in readiness to receive Murdan . . . or whoever was coming . . . did the lady sit down before the fire to sip hot tea, eat a jam sandwich, and wait.

When Hoarling at last slanted down to Murtal's snug little keep amid its snow-draped gardens and frozen fountains in the very late afternoon, the whole place was ablaze with lights. Its mistress stood at the main door, swathed in luxurious furs and warm woolens, waving to them cheerily.

"Mother!" shouted Murdan as he dismounted. "Sorry to drop in on you unannounced like this!"

"Give us a bear hug, my sweet son," Murtal cried, laughing with pleasure. "No trouble at all! I had the feeling you were coming since early this morning. My, you look a bit underfed and chilled. Who's with you?''

"You know of Peter Gantrell, don't you?" her son
answered, waving at the frost-whitened lord who had
just slipped stiffly from the Dragon's broad back.

"Ah, of course, Peter!" said Murtal, taken aback at
the sight of her son's archenemy. "Peter of Gantrell!
And in chains! I thought you were . . . ah . . . out of the
country, so to speak.''

"A story best told," interrupted Murdan, taking her
arm, "in front of your best, warmest, most roaring fire
and over hot spiced rum . . . if you please, Mother.''

"Of course! Of course!" she said quickly, and led the
way into her main hall and over to the nearest hearth.
Garley handed them each a mulled and spiced toddy,
and footmen and maids helped them off with their ice-
stiff outer garments and carried them away to beat off
the ice and warm and dry them and make them clean
again.

"This is . . . ?" prompted the lady.

"Oh, you may remember my former Accountant.
Master Plume.''

"Ah," said Murtal, bemused again.

"Mother, there is much to tell, to explain," said the
Historian. "But first, have you a blacksmith? We'll
strike off Peter's chain, please.''

"You certainly travel in strange company, my son! A
dangerous old enemy in chains and a spying renegade,
too, if what I've heard is true!''

The lady of Old Place sent a boy to fetch her blacksmith and his hammers and chisels, and in few minutes
Peter Gantrell was, at last, free.

"Dinner will be served within the hour, gentlemen!"
announced Garley.

"Hot baths and dry clothing await!" added his mistress. "*Then* you can tell me everything over supper!''

BY the time she'd heard the news of the Relling invasion, the capture of her son, and his discovery of Peter

and Plume, captives on the iceberg, supper was finished
and the three winter travelers had largely recovered from
their days' flight.

Hoarling, protesting that he preferred to stay cool and
comfortable in the deep snow beyond the castle walls,
begged the lady's pardon and went off to find whatever
it was that Ice Dragons preferred to eat.

Murdan gave his mother the news from Overhall and
Ffallmar Farm, which she had not heard, due to the in-
clement weather on the mountains.

"I must ask you," said Lady Murtal severely to Peter,
"two important things. First, did *you* plan the kidnapping of the little Prince Royal?"

"No, m'lady, I swear by my own mother's revered
memory, I did not."

"I believe you," said Murtal, nodding her white head
sharply.

"As I do, too," said the Historian.

"Peter, has this experience and ordeal at the hands of
the savage Rellings changed you at all? You've behaved
perfectly awfully over the past eight or ten years. What's
ahead for you? Tell an old woman truthfully."

Gantrell had the grace to look ashamed and paused so
long formulating his reply that Murdan was opening his
mouth to prompt him.

"Lady Murtal, you are very like my own mother. You
ask the hard but appropriate questions at the right time."

"I've been a mother a great deal longer than you've
been a grown man," said Murtal somewhat testily. "Answer me, sirrah!"

"I was dead," said Peter in a flat tone. "I'd given
myself up for lost on that iceberg. Even if Plume kept
me barely alive, in a few hours or a day the ice would
have broken up and I—we—would have been dropped
into the deepest, coldest part of Athermoral Strait!"

Murtal looked sharply at the Accountant but Plume
was staring at the fire, ignoring the conversation altogether.

"I actually saw my whole life again," Peter continued, "but from a different point of view, it seemed. I thought of my lovely mother and my dreaded— yes, dreaded—soldier father, my quiet and competent younger brother, and all the longtime Gantrell servants who raised us and took care of our needs.

"Most of all, I saw the certain consequences of my every action. And suddenly I was terribly, *terribly* ashamed."

He paused to wipe his eyes, which had begun to tear embarrassingly.

"I saw what I was like, truly. What it must have felt like to be Manda, Eduard's brave little girl, sent off all alone when her mother died. Kept from her father in a strange household. *I* did that to her!

"I realized what I demanded of poor Granger, who was as loyal as he possibly could have been, far beyond what a man should expect from a younger brother. Yet, I cursed him for refusing to do evil for me!

"I remembered what it was like to deal with the twisted, lowest levels of Elves, the ones I used and discarded like dulled tools—men like Basilicae, the Mercenary Knight, and foolish, foppish, drunken, bellicose Freddie of Brevory, and—it's true, I can't deny it nor can you, Accountant—with the kind of dog who willingly turned on a kind master! A sneak and a spy."

Plume tried to disappear into the shadows beside the hearth, but Peter speared him with his piercing eyes.

"And here I was depending on such as you to bring me food and keep me from freezing to death! I was reduced to such a slender, fast-raveling string of hope for life."

"So what did you decide about yourself?" Murtal prompted when he fell silent for a long while.

"Ma'am, I'm not sure *what* I concluded. I know I have no desire left now for power over people, nor hunger for greater and greater wealth. I do have a great, overwhelming desire to live in peace and do the things

I always sneered at others for doing before, like build fine houses and plant sweet-smelling gardens; to marry at last and sire children. To have good men admire me . . . for myself, not for my strength and wealth.''

''Admit that sounds pretty unlikely coming from your lips, Gantrell,'' said Murdan, but very gently. ''Given your past record.''

''I know, Historian! And I can't expect you to believe me. I'll have to convince you and the King and Manda and Tom, my brother and his family—everybody—that I truly regret what foolish pride and childish anger made me do. I would make amends.''

''You're still under the King's solemn sentence of exile,'' Murdan pointed out. ''The penalty for returning unbidden to the kingdom is . . . death.''

''Not unjustly,'' Peter sighed. ''I've caused many, many innocent deaths in order to excel, dominate, rule. Perhaps I only deserve to die.''

''I doubt that,'' said Lady Murtal, suddenly reaching out to pat Peter's trembling hand.''

''As for returning unbidden, I believe no Royal Court would convict you on *that* charge,'' said Murdan. ''You came back at my bidding, and the King will agree that I did what was best for him and his people. Don't worry about that. He may even commute your exile, given sufficient proof of your reform.''

''It seems to me,'' said his mother firmly, ''that Carolna and its King and all of us must give you the benefit of a doubt, Peterkins. If you can now exercise power over yourself, it's possible you're worth our forgiveness. Of course, I don't speak for our good Lord King . . .''

''Nor can I, but I'm willing that you shall have a second hearing,'' added Murdan. ''But first we have to find our way to the King's side, to defeat these Rellings and their plunder-seeking allies and send them running for our borders, back where they started!''

''For tonight,'' said his tiny mother, rising, ''I say you need a good night's sleep in a comfortable bed with a

hot brick wrapped in flannel at your feet—all of you—
even *you*, Master Accountant. In the morning we can
discuss what's to do next. Come all! Garley and I will
show you to your rooms.''

MURDAN woke in midmorning, aching in most of his
muscles but able to eat an enormous breakfast of oatmeal
with brown sugar and sweet cream, buttered white toast
and orange marmalade, four fried eggs with two slices
of ham, and six cups of sweetened, tongue-scalding coffee.

That was even before he climbed out of bed and began
to dress in clothes, which his mother's people had dried,
cleaned, pressed, and mended while he slept.

''What's the weather like?'' he asked Garley, who
supervised the service of his breakfast and his dressing.

''Bright as a well-scrubbed copper pot, Lord Historian,'' replied the ancient butler. ''And not quite as cold
as it's been for a week past. The snow on the roof is
melting fast.''

''Not the best news for travelers, however,'' said Peter, who entered just then to hear the weather report.
''I've looked at the road west and it's well on its way
to being one long mud hole already.''

''We must persuade our dour Ice Dragon to carry us
still farther, then,'' decided Murdan. ''I think he's rather
enjoyed his journey so far. Is my Lady Mother up and
about yet, Garley?''

''Up, about, and halfway through her day's work, Historian,'' said the older man with a chuckle. ''No one
here rises earlier than Lady Murtal.''

Below stairs they found the Historian's mother in high
boots and a thick-knit sweater, inspecting her kitchen
garden. Three groundskeeper's boys were sloshing about
in the heavy, wet snow, pulling late cabbages and winter
sprouts from their stalks.

''Soup and sauerkraut and pickled beets,'' cried Murtal, almost singing the words. "Who says winter is without its fruits?"

"I wish I could stay for a roast of pork and your delicious sauerkraut," said Murdan, laughing. "But we're leaving at once, afoot or a-wing. I don't like being out of touch, and Eduard Ten needs me, and . . ."

". . . and you're worried about the bairn, of course," Murtal finished for him, bobbing her silvery head. "I agree! Will the Dragon fly you over the mountains to Overhall?"

As if summoned by the speaking of his name, Hoarling the Ice Dragon emerged from a snowbank just beyond the garden gate, snorting cold mist and shaking ice from his tail.

"Ah, what a pleasant place you have here, Lady Murtal," he said to them in greeting—really quite pleasantly, for him. "Best nap I've had in months!"

"I'm glad to hear you say it," said Murtal, laughing, not at all disturbed by the sudden appearance of a fierce-looking Ice Dragon at her gate. "You're welcome to stay as long as you like of course, Master Hoarling."

"But," said the Dragon with a sigh, "did I hear aright? Your son wants me to carry him back into the fray, just like a silly Companion of yore? Where is your own Dragon-friend, Lord Historian?"

"I wish I knew," replied Murdan honestly. "I intend to go find out as soon as I settle a few other matters, down south."

"Well," said Hoarling with pretended reluctance, "I *should* assist in finding one of my warmer Constable cousins if he's lost, I suppose. I can take you on the next step of your journey, at very least. Haven't seen Carolna in centuries! Too warm, taken all in all. But it's winter there, almost, isn't it? And I suppose I can endure the heat long enough to collect my wages. Are you ready to leave?"

"You can get over the mountains, then?" Peter asked him.

"We must fly through the mountain pass called Summer," answered the Ice Dragon. "The air atop the eastern Snows is too thin to bear me so loaded with passengers. So thin, in fact, you'd fairly choke to death before I could get you to the lower lands."

"Summer Pass," volunteered Garley, "was impassable for horses or men afoot from the time of the first snow last autumn. Won't open until springtime thaws, as usual, sirs."

"We'll fly medium high, then," explained the Dragon. "Deep snows shall not hinder us!"

"BUT there *is* a limit," he said, puffing wearily six hours later, "to what even an Ice Dragon can do in such unsettled weather."

They'd left Old Place in midmorning, loaded with a picnic lunch and dinner rations provided by the lively lady of Old Place. For a while Murdan thought she was going to insist on going along—she was so concerned for the missing royal twin—but in the end her common sense prevailed and she sent them aloft with double-knit pullovers, extra warm socks, scarves, a bright smile, a blown kiss, and one last wave.

By midafternoon, as they approached the north-facing slope rising to Summer Pass, the sky had turned a dark, dismal gray again. When they turned to begin ascending the pass itself, heavy, wet snow suddenly began to fall.

The air remained relatively warm. There was no wind to speak of, so the snow struck and clung—to the passengers' clothes; to the Dragon's back, head, and tail; and, most important, to his long silvery wings.

Try as he might to shake the freezing slush from all his surfaces, especially his wings, the snow fell faster than the Dragon could brush or shake it away, and within an hour it was weighing his body down so heavily that he began to sink toward the rugged ground some miles short of the summit of the pass.

"We're certainly not going to make the top of the

pass today,'' he announced with a worried strain in his voice. ''We'd better find a place to land and take some shelter. If this keeps up, I could crash. Even I!''

''Turn back,'' agreed Murdan. ''Head down for that line of trees there. The firs will again provide us some protection. We can wait it out for days, if need be. Damnation!''

The passengers, even sour Plume, did what they could to brush the fast-accumulating snow from the Dragon's body and as far out on his wings as they could safely reach, but it continued to fall and to cling, fast and thick.

Hoarling took advantage of the terrain to slip down between the walls of the lower pass, barely skimming over a knife-sharp ridge, and plunged into the forest beside a frozen tarn beyond and below that.

He touched down lightly on what appeared to be a clear place . . . and skidded wildly out of control, spinning end for end across the ice of the snow-hidden lake.

With a frustrated screech Hoarling plowed into a stand of cedar and bare poplar saplings on the lakeshore, upsetting and tumbling his passengers head over heels into a deep, soft drift—which broke their falls and prevented serious injury on the jagged rocks beneath.

✴ 12 ✴
Change in the Weather

"Ho!" shouted Furbetrance Constable. "Ha! Hoy!"

Tom was dozing between the younger Dragon's foremost pair of ears.

"What?" he sputtered, coming wide awake instantly. "What d'you see?"

Furbetrance pointed a slender emerald foreclaw down and away to the front as he flew into upper Overhall Vale.

"Something's going on down home," the huge beast rumbled.

Tom peered ahead, leaning out over the beast's scaly brow to see better. There was tall and beautiful Overhall Castle on its narrow, steep-sided ridge, its three slender towers almost scraping storm clouds scudding low against the winter-grim background of the Snow Mountains.

He made out tiny figures dashing about on the crenellated battlements. As he watched, archers on the foregate barbican loosed a cloud of orange-feathered arrows at unseen targets on the ground.

Their targets, he then realized, were wallowing white-clad warriors in the deep snowdrifts below the castle's barbican foregate. Orange arrows peppered their ranks, and in a moment the attackers fell back beyond bow range. Tom could hear their shouts, screams, and their officers' bellowed orders.

"Northmen?" he asked. "Attacking Overhall, it seems."

"Rellings, for sure," agreed Furbetrance, remembering at the last moment not to nod—it would have thrown his passenger about were he to do so. "Shake 'em up a bit, shall we? Ho!"

Without waiting for Tom to agree, he veered and slipped into a roaring dive, spurting a stream of acrid black smoke and white-hot fire from both nostrils. The sight, Tom said to Manda later, must have been like a steam locomotive plummeting out of the gray overcast, hissing at the top of its whistle, belching fire and steam. Manda said she understood—although she had absolutely no idea what a "locomotive" might be.

The Dragon swept low across the Rellings' ragged battle line on the hill below Foregate, blinding the startled Northmen with his smoke and fury and scorching their fur hoods and frosted eyebrows if they tried to stand against his sudden assault.

A few white-clad warriors crouched in the deep snow, covering their heads with round iron bucklers. Some managed to raise their short, heavy swords briefly. Bucklers and swords suddenly glowed red from the heat of the Dragon's breath. The Rellings dropped the incandescent metal and turned as one to retreat headlong down the hillside, across the half-frozen stream and into the trees on the far side.

Most of the attackers took one look at the awesome apparition plunging by low overhead, dropped shields, swords, and all discipline—and fled as fast as the snow would allow.

"That'll keep 'em off our necks for a few hours at least," snorted the Dragon, puffing triumphantly as he pulled out of his flat dive scant feet from the ground. He shot aloft once again and banked toward the high walls of Overhall, where the archers on the battlements were waving their arms and cheering.

"HERE'S my very own Dragon champion!" cried the delighted Manda, running to meet them across the lower courtyard.

Furbetrance landed as lightly as a bit of fluff on the courtyard cobbles, ending his descent with a deep bow that allowed Tom to slip from his saddle and sweep his radiant wife into his arms.

King Eduard arrived somewhat out of breath. He was followed closely by the Queen, the Princess Royal in Rosemary's arms, the three Ffallmar children, and most of the royal and Overhall servants, all clapping and shouting with pleased relief.

"They attacked first at dawn," explained the King, embracing his son-in-law in turn. "Just a probe, I think, to see if we were defended strongly."

"And we were! We were!" shouted young Eddie of Ffallmar, giving Furbetrance a vigorous hug about the right ankle. "We saw them coming across the snowy fields from Sprend! You beat them off, for sure, Furbie!"

"Try to keep *him* in bed at such a time!" sighed his mother. "He's just like his father! Ready either to talk or fight."

"Who are these wicked people, pray?" Beatrix asked.

"Rellings, I surmise, ma'am," said Furbetrance. "Northmen, at any rate. Any word from Lexor? Where's Murdan?"

The King shepherded them all into Great Hall, promising news as soon as they were out of the dampness and chill. Graham rushed up to report the attackers had fallen back beyond the edge of the forest on the slopes opposite the gate. They were milling about in confusion, he added gleefully.

"A good time to hit 'em back," he said. "Permission to sally, sire?"

"Of course!" said Eduard Ten. "Don't wait for me to say. We'll dispatch the Dragon to help you send them packing for good."

The old soldier dashed off, bawling for his Guardsmen to assemble at the sally port.

"Murdan is captured," Manda told Tom. "No word has been heard from Lexor except that they're holding fast under Walden."

"Good for Walden!" said Tom.

"Have you yet found my baby?" asked the Queen, clutching Tom's arm. "We have heard nothing since you left Knollwater."

"Lady Queen," said the Librarian, "we know where he is and he appears to be safe and sound."

"Thank goodness!" cried the royal mother, running to her husband's side. "Will he be soon saved?"

"We've a problem getting close enough to the rogue Dragon—who is certainly an enchanted Arbitrance Constable. . . . "

"Oh, no! It *was* Furbetrance and Retruance's father as they said!" cried the King. "How terrible!"

Tom quickly described the search, ending with stalemate on the edge of Sinking Marsh. The Queen was somewhat reassured by the White Heron's report she'd seen Ednoll happily playing ball with his captor.

"We need some assistance—Retruance, Furbetrance, and I—getting him out of the Dragon's hands . . . er . . . claws," Tom finished. "We'd hoped to find Murdan here. As Arbitrance's own Companion we think he can be of the most help."

"But we don't know where the Lord Historian is!" groaned the King, chewing on a royal knuckle. "He's imprisoned by the Relling War Leader, somewhere. If he were free, I think he would send word, or come to us here."

"Give him a while yet, sire," Tom urged. "He'll find a way to get word to us. But he doesn't have a Dragon to fly him about as I do."

FIVE hours later Graham's troop and Furbetrance returned to Overhall, covered with wet snow and mud and filled with grim satisfaction.

"We ran them hard as far as Fallow Fields, beyond

Sprend," the good Captain reported. "They left most of their supplies and war gear behind, the better to run from us . . . and from Furbetrance."

"They've probably never gone up against a fire-breathing Dragon before," Furbetrance admitted, rather pleased with himself. "We took a few of their officers prisoner, Lord King. They may be able to give us useful information once they're thawed out a bit in Murdan's gaol cells."

"Put them up in Aftertower," directed Eduard Ten. "Give them hot food and warm blankets and let them dry out a bit. I'll question them later in the evening."

After dinner—quite a gala affair, for the residents of Overhall had experienced siege and conquest before and were delighted to be so easily out of immediate danger—and a brief, grim session with the captive Relling officers, the King called his close advisers together in Murdan's study atop Foretower.

A roaring fire drove most of the evening's chill from the cosy, book-lined room. Servants passed around mugs of hot, mulled cider, and a kitchen boy crouched at the fender, popping drifts of corn in a wire basket.

Bushels of the hot popcorn were passed to Furbetrance, standing outside in the bailey with his head through the Historian's balcony door so he could hear and talk—and eat—most easily.

"The prisoners didn't know all that much," Eduard began the discussion. "They were sent against Overhall by someone known as Grand Blizzardmaker . . ."

"That's not what they called him, actually," said Tom, laughing. "But present company is too delicate to hear what they really did name their War Leader!"

"Yes, well, that's better left unreported, as you say," the King said with a guffaw. "They were ordered to invest Overhall and tie up as much of our midland militia as possible. They knew Murdan was prisoner, but not where he's held, I'm afraid. They claim they expect Lexor to fall within a few days. Fortunately, that plan is about to be forestalled. Ffallmar and his troops should be on the scene at Lexor by now—or will be very shortly. I'm ready to entertain ideas and plans for what our next steps should be.''

Everyone looked to Tom to speak first. After trying politely to defer to Manda, who shook her head firmly, and to Furbetrance, who merely grunted and helped himself to more hot, buttered popcorn, the Librarian turned to his royal father-in-law.

''These are our needs, sir. Drive the Rellings from around Lexor and out of the kingdom entirely, as quickly as possible. The history of Carolna I've read tells me that Carolnans seldom fight in wintertime. Northmen, unfortunately, seem to consider Carolna winters as almost summerish.''

''They came prepared and trained to fight here in the south all season, the prisoners claimed,'' Eduard agreed. ''This estimate is confirmed by Captain Graham, who's fought them before, it seems.''

''That's correct, sire,'' said the Overhall Captain. ''As has His Majesty, for that matter.''

''We beat them very badly twenty years back,'' said Eduard Ten, grinning at the memory. ''But they were merely raiding over our border then. Not a full-scale invasion with intent to conquer and hold.''

''Which underlines my point,'' Tom resumed. ''We must strike instantly, for not only do they outnumber us, but they're experienced wintertime fighters, while we're not.''

''Point well taken,'' agreed the monarch of Carolna. ''Go on, my son.''

Tom blushed with pleasure. Eduard's approval meant much.

''Murdan, then. We must somehow find and rescue him. That's priority number two.''

All nodded agreement.

''I can't see how to do it, since we have no information where he is being held—if he is being held at all," Furbetrance pointed out.

"That's the problem, isn't it?" asked Manda. "We need intelligence as to my uncle's whereabouts."

Tom nodded at his wife's words.

"Last, there is the Prince Royal and the enchanted Arbitrance. In that we are better prepared to act decisively. We know where the child and his captor are. Furbetrance believes, and Retruance also, that the help of another Companion should be enough to distract their papa while someone dashes into his lair to bring the child out safely."

"Which explains why I am here," said the younger Constable, trying not to sound too self-conscious. "I have ... It is my pleasure and honor ... er ... I never thought this would be so difficult!"

"Say it," Tom urged, and the King nodded encouragingly.

"Manda ... Princess Alix Amanda Trusslo, will you do me the supreme honor ... ?" Furbetrance began again, blushing brightly crimson about the cheeks.

"Yes, Furbetrance!" Manda said.

"Eh? Well! You mean ... you will?"

"I'd be perfectly proud to be your very own Companion" said the Princess.

Running to the balcony door, she flung her arms about the Dragon's muzzle—or as much of it as her arms could encompass. "It's been ever my dream, believe me, since I was a tiny girl all alone at Morningside!"

"Well, *well*!" mumbled Furbetrance, turning even brighter red. "So, we are pledged, then?"

"Of course!" cried Manda. "We are Companion and Mount, henceforth. I do so declare it!"

Everyone laughed and applauded, especially Tom.

"Like proposing marriage," he commented to his father-in-law. "Should I be jealous, do you think?"

"None of it!" the King laughed out loud. "After all, you *are* a Companion yourself, my boy! This is both meet and just, as the old philosophers used to say. Congratulations, beloved daughter!''

WHEN the meeting eventually resumed, after everyone had given their joyous congratulations to Manda and to Furbetrance, Tom faced the King once more.

''I suggest the following, sir. Manda, Furbetrance, and I should return at once to rescue Prince Royal Ednoll from Sinking Marsh and forestall poor old Arbitrance from doing any more harm to anyone. Arcolas confirms that Murdan is best suited to disenchant his own Mount, but if Murdan isn't available, we'll have to ensnare Arbitrance somehow and hold him until Murdan is found. Can we do that?'' he asked Furbetrance.

''My brother and I will have the great advantage of Companions, and Papa will not. We can control him . . . at least for a while,'' answered Furbetrance with a nod.

''The next move must be to rescue Murdan, then,'' Tom continued. ''To do that, we must move quickly against the Rellings and hope to force them to reveal where they're holding our Historian.''

''Difficult, dangerous, and time consuming,'' Eduard commented. ''So it must begin at once, yes.''

''Begun without help of either Dragon, however,'' Tom reminded him. ''At least until we can rescue Ednoll.''

''Understood,'' the King said, nodding gravely. ''We'll take our chances in pitched battle. Carolnans will be fighting for their King and their own homes, remember. We'll prevail, and quickly.''

''If it comes to that,'' said Furbetrance thoughtfully, ''we'll snatch Ednoll but let Papa go and come to your aid on the battleground. It may be best that way.''

''Oh, but if you do,'' objected Manda, ''you'll have to go through all the anguish of finding your papa all over again!''

''So be it, however,'' decided Furbetrance firmly.

"We owe that much to the King and Carolna."

Eduard clapped the Dragon on the nearside cheek, smiling proudly.

"No Trusslo has ever had even one Dragon by his side in past wars. We *will* succeed, even against these wild Northmen!"

The Queen and Princess Amelia would remain at Overhall, along with Rosemary and her children. Graham would command the castle and hold it if the Rellings renewed their attack.

"They've no experience at castle taking," said Graham. "I foresee no problem, even if they were to send their entire force against Overhall."

Furbetrance would take the King to Ffallmar's camp outside Lexor that very night. Eduard's desire and duty were to be at the head of his army. He would endeavor to wrest the whereabouts of his Royal Historian from Grand Blizzardmaker and rescue him, wherever he was being held.

"It might be better to offer this Blizzardmaker a large ransom for Murdan," Manda suggested. "If you can bring him to negotiate in time. Money might free Uncle Murdan faster than threats, Father."

"I'll keep your wise words close to mind," Eduard answered, giving his oldest child a loving grin. "But this wicked Relling must know at once that we intend to fight and to win."

When Furbetrance returned from Lexor, he, Tom, and Manda would fly to rejoin Retruance on the edge of Sinking Marsh, to rescue the little Princeling.

EDUARD Ten adjourned the war council well after midnight. He girded on the heavy war sword of the Trusslos, kissed his wife and daughters good-bye, shook Tom strongly by the hand, and asked Furbetrance to go as fast as he could to find Ffallmar outside Lexor.

Tom and Manda walked on Overhall's wide outer battlements for a breath of fresh air, chatting with Graham's guardsmen on duty and enjoying the cold, fresh air.

" 'Tis blowing again now from the west," Manda noted when they paused at their favorite spot—between a fierce stone gargoyle that bore a great resemblance to a Constable Dragon and a thick mullion, which hid them from all eyes except their own.

"It's warmer than this morning by a good deal," her husband noted, hitching himself to a seat on a convenient ledge. "That'll bring rain, I fear. Sinking Marsh will be a real mess, if what the scholar Findles says is true."

"But it'll hamper the enemy around Lexor at the same time," said Manda, snuggling against his shoulder. He drew his woolen cloak about them both.

"Furbetrance, my brand-new Mount, insists that Rellings can't fight in warm weather, any more than our people would fight well in Relling cold and snow. That bodes well for father's counterattack at Lexor."

Tom nodded, feeling suddenly very comfortable and private.

"We've most of tomorrow to wait," he said after a long comfortable silence between them. "Let's to bed, sweet Princess! We will need our sleep against tomorrow night and beyond."

"Wait a bit," she protested. "Look! The clouds are parting. And the half moon should be coming up any minute."

"We'll wait for the moon, then," her husband agreed.

A PAIR of Overhall Guardsmen walked their post not far away, keeping their eyes and ears on the deep snow on fields and forests beyond the walls.

"When this is over," said the younger soldier suddenly after a long, companionable silence, "I shall resign and marry and settle down."

"For heaven's sake, why?" cried his watch mate, a confirmed bachelor. "What can marriage offer that barracks life and frequent leaves cannot?"

"That," said the other, pointing his thumb over his

shoulder at the young couple seated on the parapet.

His partner sighed and nodded.

They swung away to patrol the rest of their section of wall top before Captain Graham came to check on them.

LADY Mornie of Morningside, wife of the fur trapper Clematis of Broken Land, vigorously plied a willow-twig broom to clear newly fallen snow off the slated front porch of their sturdy log cabin.

"We may be here all winter!" she called to her husband.

Clem appeared at the door, gazed at the white world without, then glanced up at the overcast sky.

"Entirely possible," he said. "And not the worst fate we could suffer, I say. I've spent many a long winter cozy in this cabin, snug as a bear in his cave."

"Well, I won't complain—except that we promised Manda and Tom to go to Hidden Lake with them this wintertime," replied his wife, handing him the broom. "Here, I must wake the boys. They'll want to make snow-people on the lawn and tell the animal and bird tracks in the first snow."

"Best sort of life for them! Better than being held prisoner by winter in a stony, chilly old castle," exclaimed their father.

He quickly finished the sweeping, clearing a path also to the stable and the high-lofted barn, and down to the wellhead near the edge of the steep cliff.

"Better'n crammed in a stuffy castle, I adds," he repeated, resuming the conversation when he came back indoors after stomping the wet snow from his boots.

He placed on the kitchen counter two brimming-full pails of milk he'd just coaxed from the family dairy cows.

"There are things to be said for both, castle and cabin," his wife insisted.

"But," Clem went on, "if we're to help Tom and

Manda with their house building, we should leave here before the really deep snows begin.''

Gregor, aged four, and Thomas, two and a half, tumbled out of the cabin door and raged across the soft snow, ignoring the swept path their father had made, shouting joyously at the tops of their voices, causing great dollops of wet snow to plop from the pine boughs at the edge of the forest clearing.

"Will it be safe, love?" Mornie said worriedly. "I mean, to travel in this snow over Summer Pass?"

"As safe as anything we might do, I suppose," said Clem. "If we waited for a safe day, we'd never do anything."

"You have me to consider, however," said Mornie. "And the boys, too."

He thought a moment of her objection while she laid a hearty woodsman's breakfast on the smooth-scrubbed plank table—toasted sourdough muffins and wild berry jams; strong, steaming coffee in white mugs; and sausages with fried eggs.

"There *is* some danger, but we can withstand it, Mornie," he said at last. "And I've a hunch . . . a feeling, that . . . well, that things are happening that call for us to go east now, rather than wait for spring."

"I do respect your intuitions," Mornie said with a sigh, "and I for one would dearly love to sleep behind stone walls again, and laugh at the cold and snow."

"You agree to leaving at once, then?" asked her husband.

"Never any doubt!" she said laughing aloud, and she kissed him on the top of his head as he bent to sip gingerly at the steaming coffee.

"It'll snow no more this week," her husband said. "The wind's turned to due west, and it's already warmer. We'll leave as soon as the boys are fed and I can saddle and pack the horses."

•   •   •

IT always surprised the woodsman how much faster time and work flew, now that there were others sharing his once-lonely life. He was used to great, empty, silent spaces, and having the world to himself. To have Mornie and the bright, noisy little lads to love and help and to do for made the hours whirl by like leaves in an autumn gale.

Before noon all was ready. Each was mounted on a sturdy, shaggy forest pony. For each saddle pony, there were two pack horses, and during their journey, especially where the going was rough, they would switch horses frequently.

"We'll soon look like four of your snowmen on horseback," said Mornie to her older son, Gregor Clemsson.

The boy grinned up at her from a deep nest of woolen scarves, down mufflers, and a fur-lined parka hood.

"We'd better go, or we'll become too hot for comfort," said the father, swinging into his saddle. "All right, Hedy! We'll break the trail for these city-and-castle folk, shall we?"

"I'm a *woodsman*!" protested little Thomas Clemsson, stoutly. "I live in Broken Land!"

"But it'll be nice to stand once more between the fireplaces in Overhall Great Hall," his mother reminded him, tucking an errant cloak tail under his saddle blanket.

"No more talk!" cried Clem, waving his arm and touching Hedy with his heels. "Keep your eyes open, lads! You, too, Mother! Snow changes things in the woods and sharp eyes are needed to avoid missteps or hidden deadfalls."

The four saddled ponies and the eight pack ponies filed from the clearing in front of Clem's winter quarters, down a long, wind-cleared slope, across the creek, not yet frozen over but rimmed with clear, starred ice.

Once across, they rode into the dense pine forest

where everything was still and soundless. The normally raucous blue jays and the energetic brown squirrels slept in trees coated with a fresh blanket of snow.

Even the little boys fell quiet, impressed with the wintertime hush.

GREGOR insisted on taking his turn at breaking trail when they started out the next morning. The family had spent the night in a cozy camp under the lee of a bank of broad-leaved rhododendrons.

Under the trees the snow sifted through the boughs was only a few inches deep, so Clem allowed him to lead the way while he checked the pack ponies once again.

Every hour or so they paused while the father and his sons scraped the horses' hooves free of caked ice and pine needles. The going here was relatively easy and they made good time, ever climbing toward the open meadow at the foot of Summer Pass.

In the open, however, drifts were deeper where the wind had been trapped about clumps of bare-limbed birch and outcrops of stone. Under the icy crust, the snow was clinging and wet. The west wind was almost warm, and the travelers shed and stowed away their heavier outer clothing before noontime.

"Lunch soon!" Mornie called to her menfolk.

She knew her husband would go without lunch if he had his way, pressing on in order to reach the bottom of the pass before dark.

"If you say so," Clem sighed. "We'll stop over there, where the alders edge the tarn, you see?"

With their destination in view, Gregor and Thomas urged their mounts into a quick trot and quickly disappeared into the grove of leafless trees beside the mountain lake.

A moment later Gregor reappeared, waving silently for his father to come to them, fast.

Clem spurred Hedy forward along their track and

quickly closed the gap between them. Little Thomas had joined his brother, waiting just inside the edge of the alder grove.

"Men on the lakeshore," whispered Greg. "I heard them talking."

"Well, we'll move with some caution, then, sons," directed Clem. "No telling out here if they're friends or foes. Most likely they're friends. Maybe lost in the snow. We can help them, then."

He dismounted, leading Hedy by her reins, and followed Greg and Thomas's beaten track through the close-set trees.

"We can go ahead on foot, I suggest," said Hoarling to Murdan. "Not nearly as pleasant as flying, but . . ."

"We'd better camp here for the night," decided the Historian, shaking his head. "It's sure to get colder after the sun sets, even though it's gotten somewhat warmer, if you'll notice. The slopes will be slippery at night. By the morrow we can fly up to the top of the pass, if the day is clearer."

"It'll still be mighty deep underfoot," predicted Peter of Gantrell. "But I agree we shouldn't press on tonight under the circumstances."

Neither man thought to consult Plume, who sat in a clear spot under a pine, nursing a bruised knee and an elbow scraped in their crash landing.

"Hello!" came a sudden cry from the fringe of bare alders behind them.

Murdan and Peter spun about in surprise. Plume slunk deeper under his tree.

"Hoy!" cried the Historian. "Here we are!"

Clem's mount came plowing through belly-deep drifts, churning her powerful legs to keep balance over rounded stones hidden under the cover.

"Lord Historian!" Clem cried in surprise as he dismounted in front of them.

He and Murdan clasped each other, as much to keep from falling as in greeting.

"This is Clematis," said Murdan to Peter. "I don't think you've met before. This is Peter Gantrell, Clem."

"Ha!" snorted Clem, drawing back a step in surprise. "The exile?"

"Yes, the exile, but much humbled now by great adversity," said Peter, shaking the woodsman's reluctant hand. "I've heard naught but good report of you, Clematis of Broken Land."

"Anyone living in these parts learns to forgive and forget," Clem observed slowly. "If you say he's to be trusted, Lord Historian, I'll accept your word on it."

"And yet keeping your eyes peeled, I suppose," said Murdan with a chuckle. "We hoped to cross Summer Pass. We must get to Overhall quickly."

As Mornie rode up and the boys stared curiously at the strangers from behind her, Murdan recounted recent events—the Relling invasion, his arrest, and the escape with Peter and the Accountant by way of the Ice Dragon.

Clem glared at the former Lord of Gantrell, saying, "We'll see how you work out, shall we?"

He turned back to the Lord of Overhall.

"We were headed for the pass ourselves, and down to your Ramhold, then to Hidden Lake to meet Tom and Manda, Historian. Not today will we make it over the pass. With luck, perhaps tomorrow. Hello! What's that?"

Hoarling, who had been exploring the surrounding countryside, had just now plowed into view.

"Our noble rescuer," said Murdan dryly. "Hoarling the Ice Dragon, meet Clem the Woodsman."

"Pleased, I suppose," muttered the ice-hued Dragon, nodding his head as cordially as he ever did to anyone. "Lovely weather you've got here, Clem! Could be colder, however, for my liking."

"Wait a few days, at most," said Clem with a dry laugh. "It'll get almost as cold here as it does where you come from, Ice Dragon. My old friend Retruance Constable spoke of you, of course."

"We were attempting to fly over the pass to Overhall," explained Peter. "But the beast's wings got too heavy with ice and forced him—and us—down here."

"Unlike the Constables," said Hoarling in his own defense, "I cannot generate internal heat to melt ice from my wings."

"What can you do, then?" asked Clem, who was really quite interested.

"Freeze just about anything I breathe on, if I choose to," snorted the Ice Dragon. "Turn anything . . . or anyone . . . to solid ice."

He blew on a patch of tarn that had melted in the afternoon sun. It at once shivered, blurred, and solidified.

"Impressive," admitted Clem, "although I fail to see its usefulness when you live in a place where it's below freezing most of the year anyway."

Hoarling chose to ignore his comment and sat down in a convenient snowbank instead. Actually, the thought had occurred to him in the past. Why should an Ice Dragon live in a land of ice?

"Wait until morning, what with this change in the weather," Clem advised Murdan. "By noontime, when we reach the summit, you should be able to fly without danger. If not, he looks capable of plowing our way with ease."

"Hadn't thought of that," said Murdan, shaking his head.

"I had," muttered the Ice Dragon. "Hoping nobody else would think of it."

Clem and Murdan ignored the beast's boorishness. "We'll make camp here among the alders and get an early start in the morning," decided the latter.

"Children? Out here in this terrible winter wilderness!'' cried Peter, catching sight of Gregor and Thomas for the first time when he turned to greet Lady Mornie politely. Mornie was cool but proper, as they had met before at Morningside.

''Our sons—Gregor and Thomas Clemsson,'' she said proudly. ''My lads do fine as fish hair in this lovely country. They'll fairly keep your ears from frostbite with their chatter alone.''

MURDAN, who had spent the previous night huddled miserably under a giant fir before a tiny and rather smoky fire, was amazed when, within an hour after their meeting, the woodsman had assembled a clean, dry, and cozy camp in a sheltered nook between tumbled boulders the size of houses.

Supper was soon bubbling merrily on the fire. The smell of fresh-baked biscuits filled the air and even the sullen Plume moved closer, licking his lips while still trying not to be noticed by the newcomers who knew him of old at Overhall.

After the generous and hot supper, spare fur robes furnished by the Broken Land trapper, and a sleeping place of soft pine needles out of the worst of the night's cold, the joined parties set out at dawn greatly refreshed, to climb drift-clogged Summer Pass.

Despite his dire grumblings, Hoarling broke their way through the deepest of these heavy drifts, and swept lesser accumulations away with his batlike, silvery wings. Where, in sunny places, the snow turned to deep mush, he blew his frosty breath on the path, refreezing the slush for firmer, if slippery, walking.

By high noon the party had topped Summer Pass and were looking down on the tops of clouds concealing the hills and plains to the south.

''Now will you tote us?'' asked Murdan of Hoarling. ''No snow falling and it's all downhill to Overhall.''

''It's pretty hot! Suppose we call our deal quits and I

go my way north again,'' the Ice Dragon suggested. ''Or you could increase my fee.''

''I'll do no such thing!'' shouted Murdan indignantly. ''I've had plenty and enough of your lousy, un-Dragonly carping and complaining, icy beast! If you're not prepared to carry us to Overhall—well, just say so and we'll proceed afoot, and save the fee you've already extorted from me!''

''Now, now, now, *now*!'' sputtered Hoarling, taken quite aback in surprise. Few ever spoke thus to any Dragon, of course. ''Calm down, fiery old Historian! I'll do my best to carry you onward. No need to get angry! But even if I wanted to, I can't carry all these new people, the woodsman and his lady wife and the tireless little boys who've been playing jump rope with my tail all morning, not to mention the horses.''

''I suspect he's telling truth,'' sighed Peter.

''We're headed to Ramhold anyway,'' said Mornie. ''You must fly quickly to aid the King, Lord Historian. Clem and I and the boys will ride on, just as we originally intended. We'll be perfectly safe, I assure you. My husband knows how to make travel easy, even in the worst conditions.''

''As we've already seen, Lady Mornie,'' said Peter, bowing deeply to her.

''Let's go on, then,'' said Hoarling impatiently. ''The sooner we reach this Overhall place, the sooner I can get back to the comforts of my ice cavern.''

Before they parted, Clem laid a fire in a sheltered cleft and warmed the last of Mornie's good soup. The boys toasted bread from the day before on cleft sticks, offering some to the Dragon in apology for playing games with his tail.

When they'd all eaten, Murdan followed Peter and his sour sycophant up onto the Dragon's broad back, turning to wave good-bye to Clem's family.

''I'll send word to Ramhold as soon as I can, so you'll know whether to come to Overhall or go on to the canyon,'' Murdan called. ''Stay cozy with Talber for a few days. I'll send a Dragon to fetch you, if we need you.''

Clem and Mornie waved farewell and the boys jumped up and down with excitement to see the Dragon fall off the steep mountainside in a long, shallow glide, heading south and east beyond Summer Pass before turning due east toward Overhall Castle.

✵ 13 ✵
Back to Sinking Marsh

A SOLDIER carefully stamped his cold feet on a narrow and slippery walkway atop tall Middletower, sixty-five feet above the inner bailey, and shouted the news to the sergeant of the guard, below the wall. The sergeant in turn leaned over the inner parapet and relayed the warning to Graham, seated on Gugglerun's curbing and picking his teeth after an early dinner.

"Dragon a-coming!"

Graham shouted, "Man the battlements!" and sent a runner to tell the Queen and her party, just finishing their evening meal in Great Hall.

"Which Dragon, I wonder?" asked Manda, putting down her dessert fork.

"Furbetrance, I suppose," said her stepmother. "Returning from Lexor. We'll get news, at last!"

Tom was out of his seat and through the door when a second call came from above.

"*Another* Dragon! A second Dragon! From the west!" they heard the tower-top sentry scream.

"Not Retruance," said Manda to the Queen. "Certainly not Arbitrance, would you think?"

She caught up with her husband when he paused on the steps outside.

"Here's Furbetrance, at least," cried the Librarian.

The younger Constable brother bumped to a stop in the center of the courtyard.

"I don't know who he is," Furbetrance shouted, even before he was asked. "Stay under cover, all! I'll check him out."

He crouched, then leapt back into the air, roaring his wings and climbing steeply to meet the unknown beast coming from the west.

"Whoever it is," said Tom, shading his eyes against the westering sun, "he's carrying passengers. He doesn't have the coloration of the Constables, do you see? Silver and black, it looks like. Hard to tell in this light."

"How exciting!" cried Beatrix, who had followed them out into the bailey, trailed by the Ffallmar children and Rosemary with little Princess Amelia. "A stranger Dragon from goodness knows where! Can Furbetrance stop him? Is he planning to attack?"

"Trust old Furbetrance, Stepmother," Manda told her. "But just in case, maybe we'd better take the children back indoors."

Between them, the ladies herded the wildly excited young ones back into Great Hall. Young Eddie of Ffallmar insisted on peering up through the narrow clerestory windows, hoping to catch glimpses of the airborne Dragons.

"Maybe they'll fight!" he shouted, pressing his nose against the glass. "Oh, no! Look, Aunt Manda! Mama! They're circling each other almost overhead!"

"THIS is Hoarling," called Murdan to Furbetrance. "You may have heard of him."

"Both good and not so good," replied Furbetrance Constable with some distaste. "My brother bespoke him some time back about keeping an eye on the Rellings, didn't he?"

"Not the Rellings, actually," said the silver-and-blue Dragon, eyeing the Constable Dragon warily as the two circled each other slowly, high over Overhall Castle. "He asked me to watch this exiled lordling Gantrell in case he tried to sneak back into your precious country. He never did, and I fulfilled my commission."

"Huh!" snorted Furbetrance with disgust. "It never

occurred to you we'd like to know about the Rellings'
attack?''

"Well, actually," admitted Hoarling, looking rather
sheepish, "I was still in summer sleep when they made
their move. I *did* send word to Lexor, you know. The
King was on vacation but the message went to someone
named . . . Chamberlain, I think it was. When I went to
see where Gantrell was, I found him—and the sour little
Accountant and the Historian, too—on an iceberg."

"That much is true," agreed Murdan. "He warned
Lexor and rescued us, all three, from certain death by
freezing or drowning."

"Come along, then," said Furbetrance, relenting.
"Better let me go first, however. There may be some
itchy bowstring fingers on Overhall's walls."

WHEN pleased greetings and shouts of surprise had subsided, explanations and exchanges of experiences were
demanded by all sides. Tom, Manda, and the Queen con-
gratulated the Historian on his narrow escape. Furbetrance was given the floor—so to speak, as his body
remained outside Great Hall—to report on the siege of
Lexor.

"But first," insisted Graham, who had immediately
taken Peter Gantrell and Plume into custody with a platoon of archers, "what's to be done with these fine so-
called gentlemen? By royal law, Peter Gantrell must be
held for reentering the kingdom without the King's permission. And I imagine Lord Murdan has some questions to ask the Accountant."

Murdan waved a hand and said, "No time for that
now. Put 'em up . . . in Aftertower . . . but not with the
Relling officers. I promised Lord Peter I'd speak for
him, when his case came before the King."

"I accept imprisonment willingly," Peter said
quickly. "It'll be so nice to be warm and dry once again,
I'd agree to almost anything."

"Put them to Aftertower, yes," said Beatrix. "Keep

them close, Captain Graham! I deem it's a matter for the King to decide when he returns from battle.''

"Grand Blizzardmaker double-crossed Peter," Murdan explained to Tom and the rest as the exiles were being led away. "It seems to have changed his attitude, somewhat."

"I don't trust him, nevertheless," snapped the Queen. "We'll be wise to hold him and his nasty little flunky close until we can sort this out properly."

"Now, about Lexor?" reminded Furbetrance, mildly.

"Yes, yes! Speak of the King and Ffallmar," commanded Beatrix, dismissing Peter from her thoughts at once.

"His Majesty and I found your husband, Lady Rosemary, at the head of seven thousand troops of levees, marching on Lexor. The Relling host was drawn up about the walls of the capital, evidently preparing to storm the city. All is well! I was able to give Ffallmar some badly needed intelligence after flying over the Relling lines to spot their weak and strong points.

"Early yesterday, Eduard and Ffallmar attacked them from the southwest and west. Walden saw us coming and sent a sortie in force from within the city. I helped as best I could—much fierce roaring and fire-belching smoke and flame—and the Relling allies to the south of the city withdrew after only a brief fight."

He waited for a rumble of approval and applause to die down.

"The main Relling force was in the northeastern quadrant, however, and they resisted for a few hours longer, but surprise and the unseasonably warm weather proved too much for them.

"When I left Lexor early this morning the Carolnan army, which had been billeted inside Lexor, and our levees, too, were preparing to chase the Northmen, molting their furs all the way, toward Frontier. If they aren't rallied, they'll be forced to flee into the cold wastelands over the border. They won't be able to mount a counterattack before spring, if then!''

He paused while his listeners cheered and applauded even more.

''And Grand Blizzardmaker?'' asked Tom when the hubbub had subsided.

''Nowhere to be seen,'' Furbetrance admitted dolefully, reaching for a hogshead of ale to wet his throat. ''He must be in at the after guard, somewhere.''

Said Murdan, ''This Blizzard-faker, or whatever they call him, was War Chief of the invaders, promising his men and allies all sorts of looting and pillage and . . . well, you know what that sort wants.''

''I wouldn't be too quick to trust Uncle Peter,'' warned Manda. ''He had a hand deep in this from the very beginning, I'm positive.''

''The King and Ffallmar will see to it the Rellings and their friends are kept headed north,'' promised Furbetrance. ''As instructed, I hastened back because of the other matter.''

''Indeed! My poor child!'' cried Beatrix.

TOM took Manda by the hand and beckoned to Murdan, who was talking to Mistress Grumble, the Overhall housekeeper, about supper.

''Nothing frozen or even chilled, dear lady,'' he was saying. ''I want hot! Hot! Pepper soup! Spicy wine! Steamship round of beef, eh?''

''Yes, sir,'' said Grumble. ''Puffy-crisp cinnamon pudding and dilly carrots?''

Murdan sent her off to begin supper and followed the Librarian and his Princess to where Furbetrance's great head was resting on a rug just inside the door.

Manda said, ''We must leave for the south at once.''

''After supper!'' begged Furbetrance and Murdan in unison.

''We've had several very long days of short commons, you know,'' the Historian added.

"If you insist," said Tom, grinning broadly. "We missed you, Master!"

"Ah, the rescue of the little Princeling," cried Murdan to hide his pleasure at the Librarian's sincere words. "You say it's certain old Arbitrance is at the bottom of it all? I scarce can believe it!"

"Not at the bottom, certainly, but used as a tool, likely unwillingly enchanted," said Tom. "Arcolas maintains if anyone can break such a spell, it'll be Arbitrance's own Companion—you, Murdan. Do you feel up to flying on to Sinking Marsh tonight? You've had a rough journey."

"I'd come at once," agreed the Historian, "but a night of sleep might make all the difference in the world, too. What to do?"

"Tom and I can go ahead, as Retruance will be anxious for news and also need our help at watching Arbitrance's redoubt," Manda suggested. "You get your rest, Uncle, and come tomorrow morning. You really look worn out."

"How will I come, though? Furbetrance will carry you . . . but I have no Dragon of my own handy."

"How about yon Ice Dragon?" asked Tom.

Hoarling had not joined the party within Great Hall, preferring to take a reviving bath in ice-cold Gugglerun, much to the delight of the castle children.

"Will he do it?" Manda asked.

"Leave him to me," cried Furbetrance, who had been listening all the while. "Dragons have certain obligations, no matter if they are Ice Dragons or not."

"I'll just have a bite to eat and a short nap and join you in the morning, then," suggested Murdan. "Be off with you, youngsters!"

He yawned vastly, and when Furbetrance and the Librarian left Great Hall to speak to Hoarling he was already nodding over his roast beef. In a few moments Rosemary and two servants were struggling to strip off his dirty, wet clothing and wrap him in warm blankets.

• • •

"Ho!" called Furbetrance as he and Tom trod out to the drawbridge over Gugglerun. "A word with you, Ice Dragon, if you please!"

Hoarling, who had surprised himself by enjoying the applause and calls of the castle children who were watching him swim, turned on his broad back, spread his wings from bank to bank to hold himself in place, and blew a jet of frozen crystalline mist high in the air.

"You're looking for me, brother Dragon?" he gurgled. "Ah! You must be the young Tom Librarian Murdan spoke about, eh? Nice, ice-cold moat Murdan has here! Ice cold and fresh running, direct from the high mountains!"

"Hoarling," Furbetrance began. "Hoarling . . ."

He crouched on the edge of the drawbridge looking down at the chilled water and the chilly Dragon.

"You were about to say?" Hoarling chuckled, grinning up at them from the water.

"Hoarling . . . I don't think you're as nasty as you'd like people to think."

"I can be pretty nasty," said the other Dragon, snorting, shaking frozen drops from his wings.

"But you saved Murdan and the others. And carried them to Murtal's Old Place. A long way to go on a begrudging favor, I'd say."

"Ah, but perhaps Murdan forgot to mention that I extracted my price!" crowed the Ice Dragon. "My pick of jewels and gold coins and spare diadems for my secret hoard. That's why I agreed to make the trip, old Furbetrance! No other reason!"

He swam off around the edge of the castle, puffing steam with each stroke of his powerful legs until the whole castle was surrounded by a slowly settling ring of dense, cold mist catching the rays of the setting sun.

"Wait!" Furbetrance said quietly to the Librarian.

The two settled down on the drawbridge and watched

the sun strike gold and crimson and purple from the low clouds overhead.

Hoarling returned around the castle wall, no longer steaming or puffing but slowly stroking, breasting toward the drawbridge in a more thoughtful mood, it seemed to Tom.

"I really should be getting home," he announced when he reached the drawbridge and stopped, treading water with all four feet. "I really can't abide this tropical climate at all! Give me ice and snow any day."

"Understandable," said the Constable Dragon, nodding graciously. "Well, if that's what you need and want, old icicle. We'll understand."

Hoarling heaved his enormous bulk out of Gugglerun onto a narrow stone jetty used by the moat cleaners to moor their scrub boats. He streamed icy water and sloughed thin sheets of clear ice, which had formed on his back and tail.

"I know you Constable people!" he barked. "A smooth answer and a trick up your sleeve! Say what you're thinking, old Furbie! But know that I'm going home as quickly as pinions can carry me!"

"It's your right," began the other Dragon.

"Of course, my *right!*" snarled the Ice Dragon, shaking his head fiercely. "We've said it all there. I'm about to leave!"

"And we're not all that sorry to see you depart," admitted Furbetrance solemnly. "It sadly confirms a growing opinion my brother and I have been forming of your sort for some years, old snowball!"

Hoarling stopped in the middle of turning away and stared over his shoulder at Furbetrance, scowling.

"I don't need your damned approval, Constable! You live your way—I intend to live mine!"

"Of course, ice creature!" said Furbetrance calmly. "No real civilized Dragon expects splinters like you Ice Dragons to be otherwise."

"Otherwise! *Otherwise?* I just wish you'd explain

that base canard, Constable!''

He whipped around to face Furbetrance and Tom on the narrow draw span.

''I'm my own creature. I owe nothing to you or any other simpleminded hot-gutted Dragon, let alone any Elf or Human! I come and go where I wish! I am Hoarling the Frigid, the Awesome Ice Fog, the—''

''The fool!'' snorted the other Dragon. ''You confirm our opinion of such northern trash! Go! No matter that the honor of all Dragons is concerned with the reputation, maybe the very life, of one poor Dragon, sorely enchanted and helplessly bound in magic toils. Who needs you! Certainly not Dragonhood at large. Certainly not me or my brother or my poor, gentle papa! Or my own five kits!''

Hoarling opened his mouth to roar a retort, but Furbetrance's final shot had told, at last.

''I . . . I . . . didn't know you were a father yourself, old cinderhead! *Five?* Five kits! I'd not heard of a Dragonkind birthing in centuries. This is great news! Congratulations, Furbetrance!''

Furbetrance solemnly bowed his head.

''Thank you for your courtesy, Ice Dragon. I had hoped to take you to our Obsidia Isle nest after this is all over and decided. My kits would be all agog to meet a real live Ice Dragon. Why, my son just recently asked me if Ice Dragons were truly real. 'As real as rocks!' I told him, but I couldn't prove it. Young ones believe what their fathers have to say, at least until they grow old enough to doubt his words.''

''The little boy-kit should see proof for himself, I say!'' cried Hoarling. ''I . . .''

''But maybe you'll allow us to visit your snow lair and frozen hills one day?'' asked Furbetrance. ''Say, in a century or so? The climate is much too harsh for young kits up there, their mother'd insist.''

''Nonsense! Any Dragon worth his scales can withstand the very worst the arctic sends his way.''

Hoarling suddenly lay down in the middle of the draw span and turned to gaze north, to where the peaks of the Snows were blazing with the last of the sunset.

"I ask myself," he said softly, after a long silence, "which is worse? To suffer the terrible heat of your southlands? Or be alone and miss the joys of dandling a kit or two or three on your tail and hear them cackle and chortle."

Tom and the Constable Dragon stood unanswering.

"And you're right in one thing, at least," continued Hoarling. "If I run away from Arbitrance, I'll always be remembered for that deed, among all Dragons, including the very young."

"Probably true, although my family will never repeat the tale, I assure you," said Furbetrance.

The Ice Dragon nodded slowly.

"No, I do believe you people would never blame me for stopping short of the common goal. I'd feel better about it if you would rant and rage and curse my bones!"

He laughed then, a deep, rough rumble that reminded Tom of distance ice in a river fracturing and beginning to slide of its own weight out to sea.

"Well, you're right, of course! I was being mightily selfish—part of my lonely nature, I guess. I suppose I should see this adventure to its end. I *will* see it to its ending! Count on me, Dragon and Librarian! I may be sour and sound bitter and cold, but I'm not at all insensitive. And I'm not a fool, either!"

"Nobody ever said a word to that effect, at least in my hearing," said Tom. "We're more than just pleased to have you come with us to rescue the child. His mother and father will be overjoyed! And we welcome you as a friend, not just a passing acquaintance, Ice Dragon!"

"Thank you, Tom Librarian! And I don't even ask for more fee than already agreed to, to show my *bona fides,* or whatever it is the scribes and lawyers call it. Well . . . now that's settled, I think I'll cool off with another swim around this delightful moat. Be some time before I am that cool again, I'm afraid.''

He rolled over and crashed flat into Gugglerun, soaking the watchers on the draw to the skin.

''Ah, well, he'll always be the same sassy old Hoarling, I suppose,'' said Tom, laughing. ''I'm going to go rub down with a hot towel before I catch a bad cold!''

And he left Furbetrance watching the Ice Dragon making designs in thin, crystal-clear ice on the surface of Gugglerun below the drawbridge.

MIST shrouded Sinking Marsh as Furbetrance glided silently over Findles's hummock the next morning just after dawn. Lightning lit the black-and-gray western horizon, but above, the sky was clear and intensely blue. So far the autumn storm had held off.

Retruance's deep booming voice rose from the dark trees below. ''All quiet!''

He showed a bit of clear red flame to guide his brother to a safe landing between two huge oaks heavily festooned with moss, hung to hide the scholar's camp from the eyes on the redoubt island across the way.

''The herons say Papa and the boy went to bed at sunset after a long game of hide-and-seek,'' the older Constable told them once they were safely aground.

''Oh, my! How does one play hide-and-seek when one is a fifty-foot fire-lizard,'' asked Manda with a giggle despite the seriousness of the situation.

Findles of Aquanelle bobbed bashfully to Manda and welcomed Tom back to the marsh with a firm handshake.

''Anything's possible to a four-year-old boy, I guess,'' said the Librarian. ''Murdan will be here in the morning aboard your old friend Hoarling the Ice Dragon, Retruance. Perhaps then we can do some serious rescuing.''

''Hoarling! Not one of my favorite Dragons,'' said

the older Constable brother, growling. "Still, I suppose . . ."

"He's been very helpful, if rather snide and sarcastic about it," Manda admitted. "I think he may be the kind who groans and growls so nobody will know he has a good heart within. A bit like Uncle Murdan, you know?"

"That," grumbled Furbetrance, "remains to be seen. Is that breakfast I smell?"

Findles had made a huge meat loaf baked within a thick, brown crust of bread, enough to satisfy even two Dragons' appetites. After three days and nights of fish and freshwater clams, Retruance had flown east to purchase meat and produce from Phoebe and her farmer husband.

They all ate, talked, and admired the neatly designed shelter Retruance and Findles had built while Tom and Furbetrance had flown off to Overhall.

"What keeps the mosquitoes away?" asked Manda as she and Tom settled for a short catch-up nap, for they'd flown all night to reach the scene of action. "I can hear them snarling and whining. I expect to be eaten alive in my sleep!"

"Something to do with the smell of Dragon, I understand. One of the many advantages of being a Dragon Companion, tenderfoot," Tom teased.

Manda kissed him and snuggled into the crook of his left arm. In moments they were both asleep, totally unbothered by the hungry mosquitoes or anything else.

TOM had been prepared to lie awake thinking of the problem of the kidnapped child less than five miles away on the redoubt hummock built by the rogue Dragon in the midst of deadly quicksand. But good sense and weary limbs prevailed and he slept long and peacefully beside his wife.

When he woke in late morning to the sound of rain drumming on the broad banana leaves Retruance had used for his roof, Tom found a plan for the rescue of Ednoll fully formed in his mind.

They brunched on filets of fresh-caught bass breaded in egg and cornbread crumbs, fried over the scholar's cook fire. Findles found an eager student in Manda and explained his study of the sources of the waters that kept Waterfields fertile and lushly green.

Tom listened also, asking questions at the right moments, and filing all the information away in his librarian's memory.

Furbetrance dozed in a patch of watery sun after the rain stopped. His big brother went off to consult with the white herons, who had thrown themselves eagerly into spying on the Dragon's island.

Murdan, on Hoarling, dropped from the sky just then.

"It must have been a short nap you had," said Tom to greet his master. "No more than three or four hours, at most."

"Hard to sleep in these circumstances," agreed the Historian. "I'm glad to be here. I've heard little but bad-tempered fussing and complaining since we took off from Overhall."

Hoarling lay panting in the deepest shade he could find, waves of frosty vapor rolling off his back and shoulders and even the tips of his nose and tail.

"What a terrible, awful, dreadful climate!" he gasped. "It'll be the death of me, sooner than late, gentle sirs and beautiful Princess! May I please go home, now? I'll even forgo my fees, if you wish."

"He must really mean it!" snorted Murdan. "Well, he's served us well. We should let him go, I think."

"Sorry, but we must extract one more favor from him," Tom said, shaking his head firmly.

"No! No! No, no, *no*!" howled the Ice Dragon, thrashing about in the reeds until they were covered with hoarfrost.

"I've a plan," Tom insisted, "and it *requires* an Ice Dragon."

"Let's hear it, then," Murdan said.

Tom outlined what had occurred to him between that good-night kiss and deep sleep.

"Very good!" cried Retruance. "I've been lying low here for three, four days and never came up with even the glimmer of a plan. That's what Companions are supposed to be for!"

Tom blushed at the praise from his Dragon. Even the Ice Dragon, despite his acidulous comments, was caught up in the urgency and excitement of the rescue.

"I can do it!" he murmured softly. "I *know* I can. Despite the puny heat!"

"I hope you're right, old ice cube," said Manda. "For if you fail, I'll be sunk in the swamp!"

"Quicksand," Findles corrected her with scholarly precision. "A swamp is a body of *stagnant* water. The water here . . ."

"Yes, of course, it *flows,* as you told me," Manda said kindly. "My husband will have further questions about that, as soon as we can snatch back my little brother, capture his captor, and shoo the Rellings out of the kingdom for good and all."

"My great pleasure," responded the scholar, bowing. "When shall we begin?"

"As soon as I've finished lunch," said Murdan rather grimly. "Flying always gives me a grand appetite."

"I ate before we left Overhall," said Hoarling. "That nice lady . . . Grumble? Gave me ten gallons of the most delicious food I've ever tasted. Ice cream! Chocolate was my favorite, but the strawberry was every bit as good!"

"*Woosh!*" said Tom, sighing. "Wish you'd brought some along. It gets hot here."

"See, it's getting to you, too!" the Ice Dragon teased.

Murdan, wiping his lips and complimenting the scholar on his cooking skill, settled himself on an open bit of sand dune under the arching willows, where he had an unobstructed view of the fuzzy line of cypresses that marked Arbitrance's low island sanctuary across the placid lake.

He relaxed and began to hum softly to himself, not words but a slow melody from some distant place and time. He was calling out to his long-lost Dragon Mount.

"He hears me, but . . . ah . . . refuses to answer," he said after a quarter-hour of plaintive singing. "He knows it's me, but he seems unable to say my name. It disturbs him greatly, I think."

"Don't push him too hard!" warned Tom. "Just keep him preoccupied for as long as you can."

Findles brought his flat-bottomed skiff around and tied it to one of the ancient weeping willows, hidden from view if the rogue Dragon should decide to fly.

Manda climbed aboard and settled herself on the midship thwart. She was dressed in the warm sweater, heavy woolen skirt, and thick stockings she'd worn the day before at Overhall. She was perspiring freely but bravely refused to complain, except to say, "Let's go! Before I melt entirely into a puddle."

"Good girl!" cried Furbetrance. "I'll be pushing your boat from behind. Ready, Master Hoarling?"

"Swimming isn't the worst part of all this," griped the Ice Dragon. "At least it's a little cooler than the air in this furnace of a tropical swamp!"

"Where is he now?" Tom asked a white heron who flew down to report at that moment. "The Dragon, I mean."

"Pacing nervously back and forth on the near shore. You could see him if you flew up twenty or thirty feet."

"He'd see me, then," Tom explained patiently. "And the child? Where's Ednoll?"

"Playing in the shade of blooming lemon trees near the Dragon's nest. Building a sand castle, I think."

"Return quietly and tell us if there's any change. If Arbitrance goes back to the nest, or if the child wanders off somewhere. We really must know exactly where the Prince is *at all times*. It's very important! Manda won't have time to go looking for him!''

"Willingly!'' the great white bird chirped softly, and flapped off, taking a roundabout course, flying just above the water.

"Now you're off, Manda my love! Remember, direct your thoughts to Furbetrance when you want to contact us. Your Mount can hear you at a distance, as you already know. Retruance and I will be on the far side of the lake, in case Arbitrance flees with Ednoll. Murdan will keep Arbitrance distracted as long as he can. Furbetrance will be there to take you and the child off the rowboat once you've brought Ednoll away from the Dragon's nest. Any questions?''

"Only one,'' said the Princess. "Have Dragons ever been known to kill?''

"Not to my knowledge, Princess,'' said Furbetrance, gently. "It's not generally in our nature to take life.''

"It's not in a Dragon's nature to kidnap babies, either,'' Manda reminded him.

Without further comment she pushed the skiff away from the shore with its long oar. The boat floated free among thick-matted hyacinth, but the lass made no attempt to row.

There was a sudden ripple behind the boat and a Dragon's muzzle appeared just a few inches out of the tea-dark water. Furbetrance began to swim underwater, pushing the skiff easily along with his nose.

"Tell him to take it easy! Making a bunch of noise!'' whispered Tom, sending a mental message to Furbetrance through Retruance.

The skiff slowed and the slight sound of its fast passage died away altogether.

"I'm off, too,'' announced Hoarling, sounding more cheerful than usual.

He slid down a slippery sandbank and disappeared under the water with hardly a ripple. A trail of misted bubbles showed where he swam. They looked like nothing so much, Tom thought, as floating electric lightbulbs. They quickly popped and melted into Sinking Marsh's almost-still waters.

Tom clambered aboard Retruance, grabbed a pair of ears, and held fast when his Mount hurled himself into the now-clear afternoon sky, streaking in a roundabout course for the black bank of rain-fat clouds to the south and west.

Good! They'd be screened from Arbitrance's sight by islands and later by those black clouds, Tom fervently hoped.

MANDA steered the scholar's light skiff toward the south-facing shore of the Dragon-enhanced islet, circling well away from the point where she now could occasionally glimpse him pacing nervously back and forth on the eastern shore.

Furbetrance lifted his head from the water, high enough to assure himself of their course. The Princess waved him back under the water, signaling to him that she was in control. No spoken words were necessary between Dragon and Companion. It was her first experience with this strange rapport, and she found it both disturbing and comforting.

Astern at some distance, a chevron of ripples and an occasional puff of vapor that clung coldly to the water surface showed her where Hoarling swam.

A white heron glided down to land on the forward thwart, startling the Princess.

"Ah . . . the child?" began the bird shyly.

"Yes, my dear?"

"He's tired of playing alone and has lain down to rest under the lemon trees. You can't miss him. The lemons are loaded with bright green and yellow fruit."

"Thank you, mistress," said Manda. "Go back and keep a close watch, please."

"Yes, Princess!" replied the bird, bobbing her head several times. And she was off, flapping rapidly for altitude.

• • •

I *know* you!'' groaned Arbitrance, suddenly loud in the Historian's thoughts. ''But . . . uh? . . . can't think of your name! Yet you are a Companion! I *had* a Companion myself once . . . didn't I?''

''I *am* your Companion,'' said Murdan calmly, evenly, silently. ''Don't you remember old Murdan of Overhall? Your grandfather Altruance built my castle for me, remember? You lived there much of your youth.''

''Overhall . . . I seem to remember,'' quavered the Dragon's thought uncertainly. ''I was told not to remember you, whatever your name is. I'm not to say your name or even imagine your face.''

''What *is* this terrible barrier that separates us, my dear Arbitrance?'' asked the Historian, almost sobbing. ''Who gave you such wicked, wrong commands?''

''I *cannot* tell you, Voice of the Past!'' cried the great beast in very real anguish. ''Don't ask me, I beg of you, unknown sir! It causes pain to even think of it!''

''I do not wish to cause you pain, old fellow! You're distraught. Why don't you lie down in the warm, soft sand for a while and close your so-tired eyes? You're very tired.''

''The Prince . . . the boy-child. So innocent! So trusting! I must go to him, mustn't I?''

''Not right now,'' replied Murdan, struggling to sound calm and unconcerned. ''He'll be all right, dearest of friends. Stay with me yet awhile. We're old, old friends, you and I. Rest there, where it's warm, so very warm and cozy. You've provided a safe nest for the kit-Princeling, there in the middle of this great marsh. Tell me! How long did it take you to build your island, Arbitrance Constable? Your grandfather would be proud of your work!''

The sound of his name seemed to calm the beast on the other side of the lake. Murdan sensed he had lain himself down wearily, lowered his head to the ground, and closed his eyes.

Good!

Dragons are proud and capable builders, Murdan thought to himself. *Get him to talk about building that wretched island.*

"Well, it took me most of four years, once I decided to hide the Princeling here rather than in the Isthmusi Mountains," Arbitrance began, matter-of-factly. "First I had to build a firm retaining wall and lay a foundation of huge boulders from far to the west, south of Obsidia Isle. I laid them carefully, one at a time, just below water level. That was the hardest part, stranger! I brought them round about, over the Isthmusi highlands, one or two at a time."

He rambled on, dreamily describing the enormous problems he'd solved, and the materials he'd brought from afar. Murdan listened with all his attention. Was it necessary to build so carefully? With such precise materials? Was the Dragon subconsciously delaying the next phase of a distasteful task—the actual kidnapping of the royal children?

"A task, in its way, even more difficult in many ways than building Overhall," he told his Mount. "Go on, please! Tell me all about it."

Tom and Retruance had the hardest task—waiting and watching. The great green-backed Dragon relayed snippets from his brother, who was in the water behind the skiff, and conveyed some idea of what Murdan and his enchanted Mount were saying to each other.

Retruance soared in great, lazy figure-eights along the western and southern edges of Sinking Marsh just in front of the storm front. Rain would move in at any moment. Occasionally the west was alight with fierce flashes of blue lightning, and their rumble reached them over a long distance, slowly coming closer.

"Manda has reached the point near the south shore that we selected, screened by the young mangroves," said the Dragon finally. "The next step is up to Hoarling."

"He'd better do it right!" Tom ground between his teeth.

They passed through a pelting rain shower, which soaked him to the skin. He didn't notice it.

HOARLING was not at all happy, even in the cool of the marsh's upwelling water. He was a creature of arctic wilds, ice and snow and everlasting wind chills. To an Ice Dragon, the marsh water felt like live steam.

The very air burned in his lungs. Vapors rising from the marsh made his eyes water and blurred his vision.

But the task he had been asked to perform would provide some relief, he knew. He was eager to begin.

"Through the mangroves here to the stones that bind the island," said Manda, gesturing to him as he floated, just submerged at the edge of the mangroves. "The ice will float, I presume?"

"Ice floats," Hoarling assured her, forgetting to be sarcastic. "Your husband was correct about that. I'll use the mangroves here to anchor the ice, the bridge, so it won't drift if the wind rises."

"Begin then, please," she urged him.

She wiped sweat from her eyes with a soaking handkerchief.

"It won't take long," said the Ice Dragon.

"I'll be ready!" the Princess assured him.

Hoarling wheezed great sub-zero gusts from his wide, frost-rimed nostrils onto the still lake surface, making it shudder, glaze, and crackle.

He increased the chill severalfold.

The water began to glisten, hair-thin ice widening to squares of clear blue rime around the wide-spreading boles of the nearest mangroves. An incautious movement from Furbetrance, waiting nearby, shattered the delicate film.

"Keep still, for goodness' sake!" Hoarling hissed irritably.

"Sorry!" whispered the other Dragon. "I'll fall back a length or two, shall I?"

"No, no. Curl yourself about me from behind. Make a water-break to keep wavelets away from my nice new ice, at least until I get a good thickness here."

Furbetrance moved very carefully to shelter the Ice Dragon's work area.

It went faster all of a sudden, with the skin of fragile new ice spreading after Hoarling as quickly as he could swim in the mixed sand and water. Manda in her skiff was fascinated by the beauty of the freezing water, the clear, flat crystals forming straight lines and smooth planes, rayed stars and webs of cracks.

"Not thick enough," she heard Hoarling say to himself.

He slowed his forward progress and concentrated on increasing the ice's thickness. The Librarian and the Ice Dragon had estimated Manda required at least two inches of hard ice to hold her weight.

"Better make that four inches," Hoarling muttered, "just to be safe. If you fall in here, and the quicksand catches hold of you . . . you'll just keep going down and down. . . ."

Fifteen minutes later the waiting Manda, shivering now in the cold mist rising in billows from the ice, leaned from the immobile skiff and pounded the ice with her fist.

"Now!" said Hoarling. "I'll keep on ahead, Princess. Watch your step, please!"

Manda stepped cautiously out onto the frozen surface, resigning the little boat to Furbetrance's care. The surface was smooth as glass and very slippery, but she managed quickly to get the hang of moving forward without slipping or falling sideways.

She fervently wished for ice skates, remembering skating with her foster brothers on the lakes and ponds near Morningside in the winters when she was growing up.

As she moved closer to the wallowing Ice Dragon the ice became colder and even firmer underfoot. It cracked and snapped like fireworks as the warm water rapidly cooled and congealed at the touch of the Dragon's breath.

She prayed that the sounds wouldn't attract the attention of the rogue Dragon.

Poor Arbitrance!

A WHITE heron skimmed in low, trying very hard to look nonchalant, keeping the mangroves and the more distant columns of young cypress between her and the still-reclining Dragon across the low hummock.

"You're more than halfway to firm shore," she whistled encouragingly. "The boy is playing again under the lemon tree, Princess."

Manda nodded, not trusting herself to speak softly enough to reply.

"The beast seems to be asleep now," added the heron. "His head's down, his eyes are closed, and he hasn't moved in ten minutes or more!"

"Thank goodness! Good for Murdan! He can talk anyone to sleep when he wants to," Manda whispered to herself.

The stray thought almost made her giggle dangerously aloud.

Several species of water birds were attracted by the sight of the ice bridge surging forward across the quicksand shallows. A brace of mallards tried to land in the surface, only to shoot ahead without stopping, narrowly missing the cypress boles.

The white heron rushed about, squawking and shooing them off and away.

"THESE rocks are the edge of the hummock," puffed Hoarling, rolling aside so she could see her way straight ahead. "I'll await you here and keep the way back to the boat open. You're on your own, Lady Princess!"

"It's a mile and then some," squeaked Manda nervously. "It shouldn't take more than half an hour, at most."

She took her first step onto solid ground. The Dragon had frozen, and she had safely crossed nearly two miles of the deadly quicksand!

"Head for the lemon trees!" the heron called, swooping by and away again. "Follow my lead!"

Manda's feet were like frozen stumps, so cold were they from walking on the ice. Once on the hot gravel strand beyond the retaining boulders, they began to tingle and then to burn painfully, indicating that she'd come close to frostbite.

Have to protect the baby from that on the way back, she thought to herself. She began to run as quietly as she could, despite the sharp pains in her arches and ankles, dodging trees and rocks in her path.

She slowed for a breath, perspiring again in her Overhall clothing. She stripped off her sweaters and the two outer skirts of wool, and felt better at once. She folded the clothes neatly and hid them under a heavily fruited currant bush, to be picked up on the way back.

If there was time!

The heron had flown ahead, so she had to believe she was on the right path. She saw no sign yet of the lemon trees.

"They're just small trees, after all," she said half-aloud. "Fortunately, Arbitrance's hummock is fairly flat."

There were few large trees in the center of the hummock, unlike the center of Findles's natural island, in which the trees grew quite tall and tangled and very close together.

She scrambled to the top of an angled block of reddish granite in her path and peered forward, looking for trees with green and yellow fruit.

There they were!

Did she spy the tiny figure of her half brother playing alone under it? Impossible to know for sure at this distance.

She began to run as fast—yet as quietly—as she could, now that her feet had stopped aching, leaping clinging briars and skirting tall clumps of bulrushes that marked low spots filled with stagnant water the color of strong tea.

She paused for a breath behind a plant climbing a rough trellis of deadfall. It had large, bronzish green leaves and bore plump purplish fruit—ripe wild grapes—which stained her hands when she plucked a bunch and ate them for their tart juice. Her throat was raw and her mouth felt like a desert.

Ednoll, Prince Royal of Carolna, was sitting under a lemon tree, rubbing his eyes and looking about for his huge playmate. At that moment he saw Manda and waved joyously.

"Ednoll, little brother!" she cried softly. "It's Manda! You remember sister Manda, don't you?"

The Princeling smiled brilliantly and trotted toward her, holding out his arms to be picked up. She scooped him up and spun about to plunge back behind the grapevine.

"Come on!" she whispered to the child. "I've got a true marvel to show you!"

"*I* have a *Dragon,*" cried Ednoll. "His name is Arbitrance."

"I remember Arbitrance. We'll see him shortly, I'm sure. He's napping on the shore. But what I have to show you must be seen quickly, before it melts!"

"Oooooh!" sighed the boy, and he clung to her neck as she jogged back down the path along which she had just come.

"I can walk," he said after a bit of jostling and a lot of jiggling.

"Of course you can," puffed his half sister.

He was quite solidly heavy at four years. *Almost* four, Manda remembered. She set him on his feet, took his right hand firmly, and walked more sedately toward the south shore of the Dragon's hummock.

"SHE'S got him!" exclaimed Retruance. "Furbetrance caught a glimpse of them coming back across the redoubt!"

"*Woosh!*" said Tom, gasping in pure relief, "*Woosh,* again! Keep your eyes open now, Retruance. Better move closer in, just in case! Fly low and slow!"

"Murdan's still speaking," Retruance agreed. "That means he still has Papa's full attention and Papa doesn't know what's going on behind him . . . yet."

"Closer," urged his Companion. "There! I see Arbitrance asleep on the beach! I see Manda and the boy trotting! Oh, no! Arbitrance is on his feet!"

"THE Prince!" Arbitrance cried out, breaking off in midsentence his detailed description of the deep-rooting shrubs, trees, and grasses he had brought to anchor his island's sandy soil.

"No, no, no problem!" soothed the Historian, a trifle too quickly. "But go on. Rhododendron, you say? But they are mountain shrubs!"

"No! *No!* Someone's stealing the little boy!" roared Arbitrance, emitting a vast cloud of black smoke.

Murdan heard and saw him even across the still, evening water.

"They're stealing him away! I must go to him at once!"

He lumbered to his feet, stumbled, and fell on his side.

"Damn! My left hind-foot! It's asleep!" he cried in agony.

He heaved himself painfully to his other three wickedly clawed feet and snapped up his wings.

"I'll fly after them!" he said. "Now!"

✦ 14 ✦
A Princeling Saved!

"DIVE! Dive!" Tom screamed into both pairs of Retruance's ears.

The green-and-gold Dragon collapsed his long wings flat against his body and dropped like a stone toward the artificial hummock.

Hot wind shrieked about the Librarian's ears. He wrapped both arms about the Dragon's left, aftermost ear with all his strength and gritted his teeth.

Before him he saw the golden shape of the older Dragon hurtling at right angles to Retruance's collision course.

From the right Tom saw an explosion of water as a second green-and-gold form shot out of the lake, aiming for a point just ahead of the frantic rogue's snout.

Furbetrance!

At the very last split second Retruance boomed out his wings and twisted ahead of his father, flashing directly before him, terrifyingly close. Arbitrance shied away automatically, but loosed a white-hot stream of fire. Only a quick flick of Retruance's port wing saved his Companion from a serious scorching.

Before Arbitrance could draw a breath to shoot fire again, Furbetrance, screaming like a whole flight of eagles, struck his father's left shoulder just in front of the powerful wing, sending them both spinning out of control across the uneven ground, crashing through a ticket of brambles, tossing rocks and pieces of plant high in the air.

Tom held his breath, waiting for both Dragons to

crash into the water at the edge of the hummock and sink in the quicksand.

With bare inches to spare, the wily old flier somersaulted over and up, coming parallel to the ground and turning again to intercept Manda and Ednoll, now nearing the end of the ice bridge and the waiting boat . . . and Hoarling.

Hoarling reared up on his hind legs and shot a blast of sub-zero cold at the attacking Dragon. Arbitrance's wings froze at full extension. Unable to finish his downstroke, he streaked past the runners at less than ten feet, crashing through a dense hedge of tangled, tough vines.

He hit the sandy level beyond with a pained squeal, slid on his back across a clearing, just missed a thicket of green-and-yellow bamboos, and slammed headfirst into a clump of the young mangroves at the edge of the water.

There was a terrible crash, a scream, and a fearful *snap* . . . then silence, except for the excited screaming of the flock of watching herons and other water birds, which quickly died away into stunned silence.

"Pick up Manda and the Prince," ordered Tom, struggling to regain his seat.

"I'm on my way . . . but . . . ," said Retruance.

"I'll see to poor Papa," screamed Furbetrance, flashing overhead. His voice was filled with worry and strain. "He's hurt!"

"Don't be fooled!" croaked his brother, harshly. "I've seen Papa pull the 'dead Dragon' trick before."

He landed with a jerky hop and a skip beside Manda, who threw the child and then herself into Tom's outstretched arms the moment they were within reach.

The little Prince, lifted to a seat, bravely clung to Tom's waist. Retruance launched himself again immediately.

"Is Arbitrance hurt?" the child asked, his voice muffled by Tom's cloak.

"I don't know, Ednoll," Tom said, smothering the

worry from his voice for the child's sake. "We'll know
in a moment. First we have to get you and Princess
Manda to a safe place."

"Which is where?" asked Retruance, circling down
to where Hoarling awaited, maintaining the ice bridge
to the end.

"Back to Findles's hummock," decided Tom.

He shouted to the Ice Dragon as they swooped over
his head, "Head back for the other island, Hoarling!
Leave the skiff. We're taking the Prince over there."

"If you don't need me," called the Dragon, "I'll stay
and try to help Furbetrance and the old Dragon.

"*I* should go to Arbitrance," Manda said to her husband. "Maybe I can help if he's hurt."

"No," said Tom. "Retruance thinks his papa may be
playing 'possum,' and if he is, his vicinity is going to
be dangerous until we can get Murdan closer to him.
Your job's to take care of the laddy."

"You're right!" agreed the Princess, hugging the little boy. "Come on, Ednoll, my heart. You'll like the
beautiful little hunter's hut of grass and leaves we've
built for you over on the other island."

"But what about my *friend*?" the Prince insisted,
looking about to cry—or become royally angry.

"Come with us, then," conceded Retruance. "Plenty
of room for all, and you can see how my papa fared
from his unfortunate crash landing."

"Your *papa*?" asked the little Princeling, forgetting
his anger. "Arbitrance never told me he was your
papa!"

"Well, he probably just forgot to tell you, Ednoll,"
observed Manda. "Here's Uncle Murdan!"

The Historian greeted them anxiously as Retruance
plopped down beside him on the beach.

"What happened? I couldn't stop him. I'm sorry! Is
he all right?"

"Hop up! We'll take you across," said Tom. "Now

is the time to break his spell, I think. He must've been knocked out by the crash.''

FURBETRANCE nodded as they landed beside the mangrove trees, among flung boulders and torn vines, shattered palmetto fronds, and coarse grass. There was neither movement nor sound from the Dragon.

Said Tom, peering into the dark shadows under the trees, ''We'll have to go in and see. He may be playing with us . . .''

''. . . or he may be badly hurt,'' Retruance finished for him. ''No, I'll go in and find him. Come with me, Lord Murdan? As his Companion . . .''

''Yes, of course,'' replied Murdan.

''I'll guard from above,'' decided Furbetrance. ''Hoarling, you watch from the lake side of the grove, please. He may try to burst out or up, you know. Call if you need us, Murdan!''

The Historian and the older Dragon son walked side by side into the deepening shade beneath the mangroves. Retruance flared his nostrils, to light their way.

''Arbitrance, old fellow!'' Murdan called out. ''It's Murdan of Overhall. Are you hurt?''

There was a movement in the deepest blackness, and a low groan.

''Who calls?'' came a weak voice. ''What's your name again? I remember . . . remember . . . who is it? Who calls Arbitrance Constable?''

Retruance started forward but Murdan put out his left arm to stay him.

''Let me talk to him awhile. I don't think he's hurt badly, just shaken.''

''Shaken? Yes, shaken—that I certainly am,'' rumbled Arbitrance. ''Must save the little Princeling! Carry him off. But I don't want to hurt him, oh no!''

''Listen to me, Arbitrance Constable,'' barked Murdan sternly. ''I am your Companion, and you cannot forsake or deny me, now or ever! I am Murdan the Historian, Lord of Overhall, and your Companion, bound to you for life. No spell can stand against our long, tough bonding! Listen to your heart, Arbitrance Constable! Hear it tell you who I am and what is right!''

"Oh, oh, oh, oh . . . ,'' moaned the elder Constable.

He loosed a feeble, yellowish green jet of fire by which Murdan saw the great golden beast crumbled in a scaly ball against the bole of the largest mangrove. His splendid fifty-foot-long left wing was bent at an awkward angle. His eyes were glazed with pain and confusion.

"You are . . . are . . .''

"Say my name, Dragon! Say Murdan! Murdan!''

Arbitrance gasped a great breath, and the Historian—and Retruance, also—braced for a searing blast of fire.

But the older Dragon, instead, let it out in a long, shuddering sigh.

"Mur . . . Murdan! Old Companion! What am I doing here, dear friend? My wing is broken, Companion. Can you help me rise and leave this dark, nasty place? Dear Murdan . . . good old Historian! I'm so glad you've come! I had a terrible, awful, endless dream!''

From the jumbled meadow outside the mangroves Tom, Manda, and Ednoll heard the unforgettable sound of a grown Dragon sobbing as if his enormous heart would break.

THE three Dragons managed to set the injured elder on his feet and, carefully supporting his broken wing, led him, limping painfully, from the grove into the sunset light outside.

Tom, Manda and Ednoll rushed forward to help. The Prince now wept to see his friend in pain.

"There, little Princeling,'' gasped Arbitrance, wincing as Murdan and Retruance carefully straightened his broken wing. "We must be brave, mustn't we? I appreciate your tears, because I know they are of love, but . . . well, I'll be fine in a day or two, I promise you.''

He put his right foreleg claws gently about the child's waist and soothed him even as the Historian and his two Dragon sons examined his injury.

"I'm terribly sorry, Papa," wailed Retruance, wringing his foreclaws in anguished regret. "But it was the only way I could think of to stop you, just then."

"Ah, well . . . I'm a tough old Dragon, after all. Hello, Hoarling. Haven't seen you for a century or more."

"Of course," replied Hoarling softly. "Good to see you again, old friend."

"I seem to remember you, young lady," Arbitrance said to Manda when she brought him a pail of water to drink from a clear pond near his cave.

"I was a child, young as Ednoll, here, when we last met, Arbitrance Constable. I am Princess Alix Amanda Trusslo."

"Ah, *ah*! Little Manda! Yes, of course!" said the Dragon breathily, with as respectful a bow as he could manage, lying on his right side. "I've missed too many years and you've grown to be a beautiful young woman, I see."

"Married, too," Manda said, chuckling as much in relief as humor. "This is my handsome husband, Sir Thomas Librarian of Overhall, to be very formal. We call him Tom, for short. He's Companion to your older son Retruance."

"Honored to meet you, Sir Thomas," said Arbitrance Constable, nodding his head in formal greeting. "You're a very fortunate young man to have this lovely lass as your bride and my son as Dragon friend. Your father, the King? In good health, my dear Princess? Otherwise, I would expect you to be Queen, rather than Princess."

Replied Manda, "My father, the King, is well and has remarried. This is his son, Prince Ednoll."

"Oh, yes, Prince Ednoll and I are old, old friends! Aren't we, laddy?"

"Yes, oh, yes, Arbitrance!" the little boy said, sniffing manfully. "Does it hurt a lot?"

"The wing? Well, I guess so, but seeing so many old and new friends makes it feel much better. We'd better ask the experts how I'm doing."

Arbitrance and the boy turned their attention to his port side, where Retruance and Hoarling were binding heavy cedar trunks to hold the fractured wing immobile while it knitted.

"Lie still for a while, old fire-snort," Murdan was saying soothingly as he rubbed the Dragon's neck and shoulders.

"Comes from having husky, grown sons bigger than I am," sighed the Dragon father. "Oh, well . . . I know you didn't mean to hurt me, young Furbie!"

Furbetrance shook his head to dash tears from his eyes.

Retruance returned from the cave in the center of the island with a large, woolen blanket, which he spread over his injured papa with infinite tenderness. It was beginning to rain in hard, cold drops.

MANDA shook her head at Tom, saying, "He doesn't remember what he's done these past four, five years!"

"Seems to me for the very best, for his sake and for the Prince's sake, too," Tom said, putting his arm around her shoulder. "Eventually they'll both have to know, but there's no hurry that I can see."

"I think I'm married to the wisest, sweetest, kindest, bravest man in all Carolna," said Manda, sighing.

"And I, the bravest and most . . . most . . . light-footed lady," Tom said. "You were wonderful, Manda! I was petrified when the Dragon awoke and chased you."

"I'd no time to be afraid," Manda confessed. "Beside that, I remembered I was a Princess, and Princesses shouldn't show fear, should they?"

But she let her husband seat her on a flat stone in the shade of the fragrant lemon tree, the quicker to recover.

Murdan tried vainly to brush sticky, fragrant cedar

resin from his hands as he came over to them.

"Clean simple fracture," he reported. "Painful for a while, I'm sure, but Dragons can handle a lot of pain and they heal very fast. He'll sleep shortly, and the process of healing will be well under way."

Retruance nodded his agreement with the Historian's prognosis.

"We should get him to Overhall, perhaps," said Tom. "There we can watch and care for him."

"No, I think we'd best leave him here. He needs only quiet and some curing sleep. Sleep for a week or so, now, or I've missed my guess," said Retruance. "It'll keep him out of trouble, too, in case he has a relapse into his enchantment."

"Retruance and I will take turns watching over his convalescence," said Furbetrance. "And perhaps we can prevail on the brave Ice Dragon to lend a hand, if we need it."

"I'm sure you can," said the Ice Dragon, forgetting to be sarcastic for the second time in a quarter hour.

"He'll probably enjoy your company once he's awake," Murdan said. "Having flown alone for so long. You've been more than just a help, Ice Dragon. A true friend, I'll be the first to say."

Hoarling came as close to blushing as ever he had.

MANDA picked an armful of lemons and made lemonade with sugar borrowed from the scholar's stores. They sat in the evening dusk around a comforting fire Retruance had ignited to warm them and the patient, who was still sound asleep, breathing greenish-tinted puffs of smoke as he gently slept.

"He'll be all right?" Ednoll asked with a worried frown.

"Yes, my dear," Manda reassured her half brother. "His wing will take a week or so to knit properly and at least that long again to get its full strength back. After that he'll be the same, wonderful old Arbitrance Constable.''

"I want to show Amelia to him," said Ednoll, with a five-year-old's logic. "After he's well again, I mean. When are we going home, Manda? My mother will be worried about me, I know."

Tom answered for her, "In the morning, Princeling. We'll fly off to Murdan's Overhall, where your lady mother is worrying about you. Amelia is there and the Ffallmar children to play with, too."

"Never been to Overhall," the Princeling said, yawning.

"You have, but you were too young to remember," Manda told him. "Here, Arbitrance made this downy bed for you to rest upon. Go you to sleep, little Prince. Tomorrow will be busy and very exciting."

"I was," murmured the Prince, fighting the good fight against falling asleep, "looking forward to sleeping in the hunter's hut over on that other island."

He slept between one thought and the next.

Murdan wearily wrapped his cloak about his shoulders against the evening dampness, pillowed his head on his Dragon's warm flank and fell into deep slumber also.

Retruance, Hoarling and Furbetrance chatted softly about family matters and how they would divide the nursing care between them these next few weeks. Furbetrance decided to send for his wife, Hetabelle, from their home in the far west to assist them.

"We've still got a whole nation of Rellings to chase home," Hoarling reminded them.

"That's our final concern," agreed Tom.

"Except for one," said his wife.

"And that is?" Tom wanted to know.

They'd found a soft, sandy spot near the fire on which to spread their blankets.

"Why is it nobody has asked any questions about Arbitrance's terrible enchantment?" she asked. "Who enchanted him? Who wanted Carolna to suffer so? Who *is* our enemy? So far we've dealt only with his tools and fools.''

''I agree. Someone or some force seems to be interfering,'' her husband nodded. ''Murdan has been quietly working on it for some time. He also seeks to learn who or what brought me to Carolna in the first place.''

''Is that connected with this, does he think! With this business of invasions and kidnapping babies?'' his beautiful, sleepy wife asked.

''I don't know, but the Historian may have some ideas.''

''There are obviously two forces at work,'' Manda reasoned. ''It was a *friendly* someone who brought you to us five years ago. You helped save the kingdom then.''

''Well, perhaps. Are you suggesting that a second person enchanted the Dragon to kidnap the Prince?''

''And that makes at least two interferers. One good, one evil,'' replied Manda with a slow nod. ''I think it's time we found out who's playing with our lives this way and force them to stop.''

''Perhaps,'' repeated Tom. These things were very far from his realm of experience. ''Well, it can wait until we get back to Overhall. The library there and the Royal Library at Sweetwater Tower may have clues. Maybe even answers.''

''Once a Librarian, always a Librarian,'' giggled Manda, snuggling even closer to her husband's side. ''Is every answer in a book somewhere?''

''Of course not, else why would anyone ever write a new book?'' replied Tom. ''But a whole lot is hidden away in a good library, if you know where and how to look.''

The train of thought this started kept him awake for a while after everyone else in the camp was sleeping. But only a little while.

✴ 15 ✴
Retreat of the Rellings

RETRUANCE handed Manda a red and a green stone, each about the size of a wren's egg.

"Now, Princess," he said. "We need to decide which of us will stay here with Papa and who will fly everybody to Overhall."

Manda hid the stones behind her back and shuffled them from hand to hand several times.

"Brother," said Retruance, "which color do you choose?"

"Red stone I stop, green stone I go."

"Agreed!" said the older Dragon. "Let Hoarling pick! We agree he should return north as soon as possible. This is not his kind of climate."

Hoarling carefully touched Manda's left fist with a long, silver claw. She opened it to show them the red stone.

"I'll hang around, then, at least until Hetabelle arrives," said Furbetrance. "Can you handle the passenger load, older brother?"

"I'm not *that* decrepit!" snorted Retruance. "I once carried a fully armed platoon of soldiers, youngster. Hauled a whole boatload of pirates, too! Besides, Hoarling will be flying with us."

Manda left them to their good-natured squabbling to go find Tom and Ednoll. The Librarian had borrowed Findles's fishing rod and was showing the Princeling how to catch his breakfast. The two were sitting together on a log fallen half in the water, casting for largemouth bass among the offshore lily pads.

"No breakfast fish, today," Tom told her. "I think the fish were frightened by all the commotion yesterday afternoon."

"Besides, fish never bite just before a rain," said his Princess, pointing at the leaden skies again rolling over Sinking Marsh. Her odd bits of knowledge often surprised her young husband.

"In Iowa," he insisted, "fish bit before, during, and after rain. Or so I remember."

"I doubt it," she scoffed. "Come and have some flapjacks with syrup and wild blueberries, instead. Findles has it ready."

Ednoll, knowing a good thing when he heard about it, reeled in his line and set off for the open-air breakfast table, shouting with a five-year-old's enthusiasm. A flock of white herons who had been watching the fishing and making delighted (and humorous) comments, followed them, hoping for some table scraps in lieu of the promised bass.

"You're quite good with children," Tom's wife said rather thoughtfully.

"Thank you! I come from a large family in which I was the youngest," he explained. "Youngest children of large families know very well what it takes to amuse other little ones."

"I was all alone, a little girl with two faster brothers, which I guess is the same thing."

"*Foster*, rather," Tom corrected her automatically.

"Boo to you, sirrah! They were *faster* as well as *foster*, you see. I used to pretend I was the eldest of a large family, left to care for my younger brothers and sisters in place of our mother. Poor mother always had perished in very tragic, very romantic circumstances."

"Who will ever understand little girls or their dreams?" asked Tom, rolling his eyes in pretended mystification.

They walked arm in arm across the hummock to Findles's campfire under the arching willows. The smell of bacon and pancakes met them halfway.

"I'm glad you like children," resumed the Princess after a long, companionable silence.

"I love children," said Tom, looking at her sideways.

"Good!" she said, and would say no more.

THEY waved good-bye to Findles and Furbetrance, swooped low to check on the still-sleeping Arbitrance once more, and shot away to the northeast as fast as Dragon wings could flap. Murdan rode the Ice Dragon's back, after conning all the warm clothes he could garner from the others in the party.

Manda, Tom, and the little Prince Ednoll sat on Retruance's broad brow.

The day had turned faultless, the autumnal rain having passed on over the waters thereabouts while they ate breakfast and prepared to depart. It was a gem of a midday, cool and diamond clear.

"Bright as a new penny," Tom said.

Manda and her half brother wanted to know what a penny was, and the resulting conversation about money, metals, and coinage lasted for more than an hour.

They crossed wide Cristol River during the middle afternoon.

This great stream almost divides Carolna into northern and southern halves, Findles explained to the boy. Retruance turned to follow its course eastward until they reached the confluence of the Cristol and Overhall Stream some time well after midnight. The Prince had fallen into a deep, child's sleep. Manda had tied him to Retruance's forward right ear for safety.

"What are you thinking about, my love?" Manda asked Tom.

They watched dawn come up off toward Lexor and Rainbow.

"Water," he answered. "A major concern for those of us who live on the edge of a desert."

"Oh, you mean Findles's ideas about water flowing

deep under Hiding Lands? What use is it to us at Hidden Lake Canyon?''

''Not so much at Hidden Lake, but it was never my intention that we should live alone and isolated, always, there. How to get farmers to take up our land and make it green and grow? What if we were to draw up water from below the desert itself?''

''It would all evaporate away in the heat,'' she replied, quite reasonably.

''Maybe . . . and maybe not. In my home world, men cleverly dug wells or diverted rivers and made dry deserts bloom. Given a reliable, year-round supply of water, we could grow crops right in the middle of Hiding Lands and attract good, practical farmers like Ffallmar's to come and establish their own Achievements near us.''

''A very pleasant thought, even if it'll rather spoil the peace and quiet I love so at our lake,'' murmured his wife. ''If it'll work, that is.''

''Worth trying someday. First, we want to build our house. Murdan says Clem and Mornie are already at Ramhold. When we finish with the Rellings I'd like to go back to the canyon with Clem and begin building. Start digging and pouring foundations before springtime . . . if you can be there, Retruance.''

''Papa will be completely well by then, yes,'' answered the Dragon, who had been listening, as Tom knew he would be. ''I'll come with you, of course! Probably Furbetrance and his Hetabelle, too. More hands, quicker done!''

''It'll be nice having Mornie and the boys with us. We have Fall Sessions first, of course,'' Manda reminded him.

''I'd forgotten! It'll be a long and busy Sessions this year, what with the war and all.''

Murdan called over to them to look ahead where Overhall had just come into view as the sun rose out of the distant Blue.

''It's a special pleasure to see home after a long, arduous adventure,'' he said to the Ice Dragon sentimentally.

"So it is,'' agreed Hoarling. "I look forward to deep summertime sleep myself. Winter's *my* kind of time and place.''

Manda began pointing out the local sights to her just-awakened half brother, who fairly jumped with excitement as they gazed down on farms and fields, orchards and woodlots and trout streams, and the magnificent castle towers, gay with pennants and flags and banners.

"There are three towers,'' she told him. "Foretower—that's where Uncle Murdan has his apartments. Middletower—that's where we have our place, me and Tom . . .''

"Tom and I,'' the Librarian corrected her.

"Well . . . and that's where the nursery and library are, and the workroom of the late, great Dragon architect, Altruance.''

"My own grandfather,'' put in Retruance proudly.

"What's in the third tower?'' the boy asked.

"Aftertower,'' said Manda. "Uncle Murdan uses it for storage and as a prison, sometimes. Your great uncle Peter is living there just now.''

"Ugh! I was hoping he'd stay in exile for a century or so,'' said Tom, making a face.

Ednoll thought this very amusing, and wanted to know what else was housed in the wonderful tall towers. Tom told him of the time he and Retruance had sneaked into the castle after it'd been captured by Mercenary Knights to find Altruance Constable's construction plans—and a way to drive the Mercenary Knights from Overhall by diverting Gugglerun into the castle itself.

OVERHALL was fairly brimming with people and excitement.

Word from the front was of sharp skirmishing near the northern city walls between Carolna's forces and the Relling invaders. The Rellings and their remaining allies had concentrated to the north of the city and at first refused to give way. At the moment they had begun to retreat, according to daily messages received from Eduard by pigeon post.

The smaller force that had attacked Overhall was slowly retreating also, raiding and marauding as they fled, burning farms and villages whose men had gone to fight around Lexor. The womenfolk had run from their homes, many of them coming to Ffallmar Farm and Sprend, and even to Overhall Castle, for safe refuge.

"They need a second lesson in Dragon war," decided Retruance, a hard gleam in his eyes. "I think I'll see if I can convince them to go away quickly and permanently."

"They fight on because they'll never make it back to their own country before the northern winter sets in," said Murdan. "I've a plan. It'll serve two purposes."

He sent Tom and Retruance, accompanied by Hoarling, who was going that way anyway, loaded down with his fee for assisting them, to herd and harass the raiders to Plaingirt, the deserted log-walled town that had once been the stronghold of Basilicae's soldiers for hire.

Isolated here, they'd be allowed to settle in for the winter, unable to rejoin the main Relling force in their own withdrawal. In spring they would be allowed to return to their frozen Northlands homes, never to return again.

Murdan guessed that a number of them would elect to stay in Plaingirt. A deserted town was always a temptation to soldiers weary of fighting. True, he admitted, they might be a problem in the future, if the wrong sort took the leadership there.

"We'll have to see to it that the 'wrong sort' doesn't get control." said the Historian. "The Rellings as a whole are not a wicked people—just adventurous and restless at times. A few of them in a nice, solid little town like Plaingirt might be a welcome addition to that part of Eduard's kingdom. They might even appreciate good government, for a change.''

"You're far too lenient with them," complained Retruance. "They started this war. They deserve to be punished more than just a little for it. We can drive them right into the North Blue, if you and the King but say the word.''

"Only Eduard Ten is empowered to make such decisions. The important thing is, the King and Ffallmar can use you at Lexor. Men are being hurt and killed there, yet. Secure this raiding party at Plaingirt, leave some of Manda's foresters to watch them over winter, then report to the King at the capital.''

AFTER seeing the Relling raiders, short on weapons and nearly out of food, safely holed up and snowed in at Plaingirt, Tom and Retruance flew to Lexor to find the King and Ffallmar.

"We're preparing a major counterattack against the remaining enemy in the hills just to the north of the city," Ffallmar told Tom.

"Do we call you general, now?" Tom teased the Historian's solid, bucolic son-in-law.

"No, no! I'm but a patriotic countryman," answered Ffallmar, blushing. "I just did what I could to relieve the capital and assist the kingdom. Somebody had to take charge.''

"No matter what he says, I've made him a Baron-Knight and commander in chief of all my forces, outranking everyone except me," said King Eduard. "He's superb in the field, understands his enemy almost as well as he does his own men. Never has the Carolnan militia fought better or served so willingly, even against great odds.''

"They fight for their families, homes, and lands, just as I do," said the modest farmer-soldier. "I admit it's nice to hear people call me 'Lord Ffallmar' once in a while. It'll sound nice when they introduce My Lord and Lady of Ffallmar at the Sessions Ball next month.''

• • •

THE Battle of Near Hills proved sharp but mercifully short.

With the Dragons appearing early in the day, striking justifiable terror in many Relling hearts, the forward works were stormed and the makeshift defenses scaled and breached in double-quick time.

"I suspect," said Tom to Eduard during an afternoon lull in the attack, "that they have already made their plans to escape."

"I have that feeling, also. What can our Dragons tell us?"

Retruance and the Ice Dragon went aloft to have a look behind the Rellings' ragged lines and returned to say that it was packed to overflowing with armed men, moving off to the north.

"And they've packed wagons with all sorts of loot," Hoarling added. "Their stolen horses are in the traces, even now!"

"Then you're right," said the King to Tom. "They're preparing to break off, taking at least some of their spoils home with them."

"That'll be their downfall, then," exclaimed the Librarian. "Order the final assault, Lord King. Leave the wagons to us Dragons and Companions!"

When the Carolnan soldiers burst into the inner fortifications, hastily thrown up by much hard digging, they found the Rellings were even then escaping in good order, taking the heavily loaded wagons with them.

Soldiers spent more effort pushing the carts through the drifts still blocking the woodland road north of Lexor than they did fighting Ffallmar's cheering troops pouring into their camp in triumph.

Grand Blizzardmaker rode in one of the first carts, chuckling over the thick, soft robes and blazing gold, silver, and rare jewels he'd assigned to his own account, trusting his own loyal bodyguards to avoid pitched battle.

"On! On!" he screamed. "Whip those nags harder!
Clear the way. Head for home!"

Seeing all of their hard-won loot disappearing northward with their fat War Chief, many Rellings threw
down their weapons, found dry places to rest from running and fighting, and waited to be captured.

STILL, Blizzardmaker had a good chance to make his
escape, moving quickly over roads his men had shoveled
clear, working feverishly all the night before . . . until a
dark-winged shadow fell over the sixty-odd horses,
straining, cruelly lashed, pulling the ten remaining wagons filed with heavy plunder.

One sensible lead mare stole a glimpse upward.

Barely ten feet over her head she saw gleaming emerald claws, long and curved and thin and sharp as
scythes. She felt a fiery breath on her neck.

Before her wild eyes, a deep snowbank melted to
steaming, streaming water in a flash.

Screaming in abject terror, she bolted sideways into
her off-side teammate, who slipped on the icy road and
fell on her side, tangled hopelessly in the leather harness.

The following pair pulled up to avoid piling into the
tangled heap of struggling legs and screaming horse-
flesh.

The wagon they had been pulling lurched wildly, and
the enormously fat Relling War Chief pitched headfirst
into the snowbank on the right-hand side of the road.

He never touched frozen ground. When he opened his
eyes and shut his mouth from a long, drawn-out scream,
he was being carried aloft by shiny green talons, high
into the cold air, away from the city he'd hoped to sack
and burn and rule.

NO one ever really discovered what became of Grand
Blizzardmaker.

He was never seen again in Carolna or in the Northlands. Retruance told Tom years later that a certain float-

ing iceberg had been washed ashore on a rocky island
in the central Blue, a lonely, stormy place in the widest
part of the eastern sea.

The island fishermen found a crazed, all-but-frozen
man clinging to a last bit of shattered, wave-washed sea
ice. They kindly nursed him back to health, if not complete sanity, the Dragon said. The crumpled, wizened old
derelict couldn't even remember his name. The self-
reliant fisherfolk gave him a new name, and healthful,
useful work drying and mending their nets and packing
salt herring.

They thought his great rolls of fat had kept him just
barely alive in his months adrift. He slimmed down considerably while a castaway, Retruance had heard.

"Heard rumors also that the Relling Allmoot pro-
claimed the Grand Blizzardmaker an outlaw. Not for his
failing of victory in battle, but for deserting his men and
attempting to steal away with their loot," Retruance
snorted in disgust. "Hoarling listened in and had a great
laugh about it."

THE King's homeward way was a triumphal progress.
Everywhere the women and children and the jubilant
veterans from all the Small Achievements and farm villages lined the road to cheer their King and Queen, the
little Prince and Princess, and their soldiers.

The route, which had taken but five days westbound,
took them nearly twelve on the return trip. Every village
and farmstead wanted to share the moment of glory and
bask in the King's warm smiles of gratitude.

In places, of course, there were solemn memorials to
be observed, and the King's royal presence made many
a wife and child feel comforted for having lost their
soldier in brave and worthy battle for King and Carolna.

Each of twelve nightly bivouacs called for a gala ban-
quet, and every stop along the road to Lexor meant a
speech or two or more. Tom sent messages back to the
few who remained at Overhall, describing the slowness

of their march and the joy of the people, but promising to return to Overhall as soon as Fall Sessions were over.

The last day of their eastward progress was blustery with a soft and lovely fresh snowfall. The soldiers still under royal arms were those from Overhall, Morningside, and Manda's foresters of Greenlevel Forest, and the Royal Army, stationed at Lexor or at Frontier, a mere handful compared to the entire force that had responded to the call to arms.

All the same, they made an impressively long four-abreast line as they wound through Lexor's west gate; tramped along broad Trusslo Avenue, lined with cheering citizens; and passed at nightfall into the bright, torch-lit and banner-decked Palace Square, which was located between Alix Amanda Alone Palace, with the great Sessions Hall opposite.

Little Prince Ednoll at once described his adventures all over again to anyone who would listen.

"Obviously, it didn't harm him at all," Eduard said to Beatrix.

"Oh, he had a *marvelous* time!" she said, laughing. "It was you and I who suffered, my beloved! Now, our Amelia wants to go spend the summer with Arbitrance Constable on his swampy redoubt island! She's a little jealous of her brother's adventuring, I'm convinced."

"Well, and why not?" rumbled Retruance, who had accompanied the returning King, also. "Papa loves children, and he's very good with them . . . as we found out."

"We'll have to wait and see about that," said Eduard, with some doubt. "It's pretty far out of the way, the Dragon's island."

"Oh, now, my dear! When has there ever been a Princess, other than perhaps our Manda here, with a Dragon for a friend and nursemaid?" exclaimed the Queen.

"Besides, it might be a fitting punishment for old Papa," Tom suggested. "After all, he *did* kidnap a Prince Royal!"

✦ 16 ✦
Lexor Fall Sessions

On the far edge of the ecstatic crowd in the square, Tom recognized a pretty young countrywoman holding aloft a beautiful child to allow her to see the pageantry and celebration. They were accompanied by a rather uncomfortable-looking young farmer wearing painfully neat clothes and the wary manner of a countryman amid city splendor.

"There's someone I want you to meet," he said to Manda.

He drew her off to the side and greeted Phoebe and little deaf Katy.

"I'm so glad you decided to come now," he cried. "Introduce us to your husband, Mistress Phoebe."

"This is my wonderful, understanding, hardworking Martin," said she, blushing bright red under her farm-yard tan. "Katy's father. Sir, if we've come at a bad time, with the great victory celebrations and Fall Sessions and all, we can come again in the spring."

"Never think of it, not for a single minute!" insisted the Librarian.

He cordially shook the young farmer by the hand and clapped him on the back, introduced them all to Manda, and told her the deaf child's story.

"Next to Dragons," said Katy, lisping, eyeing Manda carefully, "I think Princesses are the most beautiful people in the world!"

Manda shed tears as she hugged Katy and then Phoebe as well.

"You must come and meet the King, my father, and

my stepmother, who really is the kindest and best lady in the whole kingdom, no matter what the old stories say about stepmothers. And my uncle Murdan, who's heard all about you, Katy. Between all of us we can surely find a way to help the child.''

"I'm not sure I need helping," murmured the little girl, carefully reading Manda's lips. "I know I miss hearing all sorts of good things, but I can still see . . . and *everything* is so beautiful! Maybe I'd better stay as I am.''

"Well," Tom told her very seriously, "there's always the possibility that your lost hearing is incurable, so it's good you feel that way. However, I think, Katydid, we should let some good and wise people see if they can help. Don't you agree?''

"Yes, Sir Tom Librarian," the child said with equal gravity. "Can I ride on Retruance, do you think?''

"He'd take you anywhere you asked him to, sweetheart Katy!" Manda assured her.

They waited until the cheering crowd had somewhat dispersed—some to Sessions Hall, and others to try the savory sausages toasting over the bonfire coals in the middle of the wide square despite the snow that continued to fall.

"Come along and meet my own papa," Manda invited them all, taking the little girl by the hand. "Sooner we see what can be done, the better. There'll be a lot of good music and singing and street plays and carnivals and such for days here during Fall Sessions, and you wouldn't want to miss any of it if you can help it, sight *or* sound!''

IF they know anything well at Alix Amanda Alone Palace, they know how to put on a grand party.

Lord High Chamberlain Walden, despite his reputation as a fully stuffed shirt, had the happy ability to make everyone feel completely at home, whether a reigning monarch or a farmer's little deaf daughter.

He expertly orchestrated all sorts of strange and wonderful sights, sounds, tastes, smells, textures, and pleasures.

The celebration started, when Fall Sessions adjourned after the first long day, with a wonderful wintertime picnic. Despite the snowstorm without, Alix Amanda Alone Palace's servants spread rich carpets and soft cushions on the floor of the vast King's Hall. Everyone sat on the floor and dined on crisply fried chicken and spicy hot sausages, hot loaves of various breads fresh from the city bakers' ovens . . . some of which had marvelous treasures baked in them . . . and three kinds of potato salad.

The Constable Dragons had brought bushels of bright yellow lemons, and everyone marveled at the full, rich taste they gave the fruit punch dipped from eight vast crystal basins, each with a silver-and-blue enamel ice statue of the awesome Ice Dragon in their center, spouting the drink from its mouth and keeping it cold for hours and hours.

The royal couple's special guests, the next evening, piled into sleighs drawn by the most experienced and surefooted horses in Eduard's stables and pulled along the ice-slicked streets to Rosemary and Ffallmar's new town house for the Sessionstime Dinner, stopping at the famous Lexortown Inn, halfway there, to warm themselves in front of glowing-red sea-coal fires, to sip warming cups of hot, spiced rum, and listen to the delightful singing of the children of Spread, a tiny village near Ffallmar Farm.

The next evening, despite a second heavy snowfall that made the entire capital look like a sugary confection two feet deep in pure, white silence, Eduard Ten, King of Carolna, held court in Sessions Hall, which had been draped with the most expensive and colorful tapestries the Queen could find, and hundreds of lanterns and torches that burned forever with the wonderful odor of cedar and spruce and juniper woods.

"Friends, brave soldiers, dear countrymen all!" began

Eduard, grinning broadly. "It is fit and right to honor those who have saved our homeland from the northern armies, our kingdom from foreign invaders and cruel warriors."

The crowd cheered lustily.

"Once again my sweet bride and I have a single knight to thank for warding off great tragedy and horror from our family—which we like to think is your family, too."

There was more cheering, stomping, and much nodding of heads to show him his listeners agreed.

"You know, of course, that Sir Thomas Librarian of Overhall and my oldest daughter, Princess Alix Amanda—Tom and Manda, with their wonderful Dragons—were instrumental in rescuing our little son, Prince Royal Ednoll, from a most dangerous captivity."

Now the audience went wild, cheering and yelling, clapping and waving, stomping their feet and clashing their cups together. Tom and Manda were ever great favorites at Sessions . . . or wherever in Carolna they might be.

"I know! I know!" cried the King above the clamor. "They will say they couldn't have done it without the help of their great Dragons, Retruance and Furbetrance Constable . . ."

Loud shouts of approval rose for the Dragon brothers.

". . . and they are right! I want officially and publicly to speak of my fatherly gratitude to them, all four, beloved Dragons and beloved Companions. Their deeds and their names will be engraved into the *Official Records of Trusslo,* never to be forgotten as long as men can read words on paper.

"Some might insist I give them material rewards, but these two young people say that they already have everything they could possibly wish or ever will need. They won't hear of additional titles, rewards, and benefices."

He took a sip of rum punch before he continued.

"As a token of our love and gratitude, the Queen and I have decided we will ask to share with these two young people the cost of building their Achievement at Hidden Lake, above Hiding Lands. We hope they will accept our gift, for it is given in light of the truest love and fullest admiration!"

Tom and Manda stood to the uproarious acclaim of the assemblage, blushing with pleasure, pride, and modesty.

"Speak! Speak!" the crowd chanted as one.

Princess Manda pushed her husband forward to do the honors for them both. Tom stood, bowing and nodding for long moments as the great audience roared their approval.

"Well, of course, *any* household just starting out welcomes help when it comes to paying the really big bills," Tom began. "Our house at Hidden Lake Canyon will take not a little money and a lot of time to complete. I wish you all would come and see it, as soon as you can. If you bring a hammer and a saw, we will put you to work, come next summer. . . . "

A hundred men promised at once to come, even those who didn't know a hammer from a frying pan, or so said Retruance to Graham.

"Hidden Lake House will not be a castle like Overhall," Tom continued when they had quieted. "There can be only one Overhall, and we will always love it best of all. Our home at Hidden Lake will be but two or three stories tall, long, low, rambling, fitting itself into the magnificent setting of lake and forest and canyon walls. It will be, I think, uniquely ours, Manda's and mine, where we will live when we are not serving our King here in Lexor or off adventuring with our friends and companions, the Constable Dragons.

"There we will bring our children into the world, and rear them to be as strong and good and true as we possibly can manage."

Manda turned to him with a fierce hug and a kiss before them all.

"Speak! Princess, speak to us!" the crowd clamored.

"Oh! Well," said Princess Alix Amanda Trusslo, Dragon Companion, when the cheers had at last died down a bit. "My husband speaks for a family. He will need the practice. Our family will shortly become larger!"

There was suddenly a complete silence, as if each listener caught his breath and turned to a neighbor to raise his eyebrows, asking silently, Did I hear her a-right?

Then, if the earlier cheering had shaken the sturdy rafters of Sessions Hall, this new shout of pure delight that leapt up from the assembled friends, noblemen, soldiers, servants, Dragons, and family was so loud it shook the deep, wet snow from the steep-set roofs of the enormous hall and was heard by guardsmen on the city walls and far beyond.

Even the deaf child Katy, who had been eating it all up with her big, wide-set blue eyes, sprang up with surprised wonder, for she had heard the glad shout as clearly as she saw sunrise each summertime morning!

"The child's ears are responding to treatment," said Arcolas, Murdan's magician-physician, to Phoebe and Martin. "I venture to say in a day or two at the most . . ."

Laughter and tears mixed freely and the evening was a tremendous success.

KING Eduard had one further award. He apologized to Ffallmar and Rosemary for leaving them until the last.

"If I had known my daughter's wonderful news, I would have known to speak praises of you, Ffallmar, before I spoke of Tom and Manda. I intentionally kept you for last, to give you the greatest share of praise."

"Nothing you can say would make me happier than I am," said the soldier-farmer, beaming proudly. "Tom

is like my dearest brother, which I never was lucky
enough to have! And, Manda . . . well, what more can I
say?''

"However, as your sovereign, I have the pleasant duty
and the intense gratification . . . ,'' Eduard went on, "of
declaring, subject to the certain endorsement of this present Fall Sessions, you now and henceforth my Royal
Champion, Sir Ffallmar of Ffallmar!''

When the new Royal Champion could get his breath
he thanked the King simply and suggested that all that
cheering and declaring and, yes, weeping for joy, called
for a round of strawberry ice cream (thanks to the abun-
dant early snow, ice cream was available in quantity that
Sessionstime), with some of the absolutely tremendous
layered chocolate-and-raspberry cake Mistress Grumble
of Overhall Castle had baked, and now stood ready to
slice at the other end of Great Hall.

EDUARD and Murdan closeted themselves in the King's
comfortable study early the next morning, and shortly
called for Tom and Manda to attend them.

Retruance had gone off to relieve Furbetrance and Hetabelle at Sinking Marsh and tell them all the latest news.
Ffallmar and Captain Graham were in attendance, however, as well as Clem of Broken Land, who had arrived
from Ramhold the morning before with his wife and
sons, despite the heavy snow on the road east.

"We still have a few loose ends to fold over and tuck
in,'' said Eduard Ten, seated beside Murdan, his oldest
adviser and most trusted friend.

"First, the matter of the exiled Peter Gantrell. Murdan?''

"Sire, it's my firm conviction that Peter Gantrell has
finally begun to learn his lesson. He will always be a
man to keep close tabs upon, but I don't believe he will
cause the throne any further trouble.''

"I'm of the same opinion,'' the King agreed at once,
"but you must remember he is under official sentence of

lifelong banishment—punishment for his past, most serious crimes.''

"It was an open-ended sentence, however, as I recall," remarked Tom. "And up to you, Lord King, to continue or relieve, at your will."

"I realize that, my son, but I'm asking for your advice. You know Peter better than any of us, you and Manda. What do you say?"

Tom deferred to Manda. Of all those present, Peter Gantrell had harmed her life the most.

The Princess stood, eyes cast down, thinking for a long minute.

"Father . . . sire, it's a difficult question you ask me."

"I realize it, but I know you are strong and fair enough to answer it honestly, oldest child."

"So I will, then. In all justice, I suggest that Peter . . . my uncle Peter . . . should be kept on a short leash until my half brother Ednoll reaches his majority and assumes the Trusslo Crown. Uncle Peter should not be allowed any say in how young Ednoll or his sister are trained and educated, nor have any say as to who will serve him, as he once tried to do with me."

"Strong and fair, as I said," her father said, nodding approvingly.

"I suggest also that Peter Gantrell, bereft of all but his name, be allowed to return to your kingdom, sire, and be encouraged to make a new life for himself."

The King nodded again, then turned to Tom. "And you, Sir Thomas Librarian? Your counsel is always worthy of close heed."

"I think we should do as Manda suggests, on the condition that Peter's aid be enlisted to solve the other great riddle of the time."

"Which is?" the King prompted.

"Which is the question of my strange and sudden appearance in Carolna six years ago, which is also the question of who was responsible for the kidnapping of the Princeling by the enchanted Constable Dragon.

Someone or *something* is interfering with our history, ladies, gentlemen, and Your Majesty! We must find out who and why and put a stop to the interference, if possible.''

''And guard ourselves against it in future, if the intent is evil—or even if it is good!'' added Manda. ''Tom says, and I agree, that our lives are just that—our *own* lives. No one has a right to *force* us to spend it for his . . . or her or its or their . . . unknown purposes!''

''I agree again,'' Eduard Ten said, nodding to his firstborn child. ''As for Peter Gantrell, he must spend his basic term of exile, seven years less the five already served, in close warding. For the next two years, we decree that he be held a prisoner in Overhall, under the supervision of Murdan Historian. Do you agree, Lord Murdan?''

''Well, yes, sire, I have to agree,'' said Murdan, surprised by the King's decision. ''And at the end of two years?''

''You will turn him loose, with suitable mount, arms, and armor, if he so wishes, to mend his personal fortunes as he can. We will not damage his brother Granger of Morningside by giving Peter back his old titles, lands, and property, given in judgment of him to Granger and his heirs. Peter must prove to us he can be as loyal in our support as he was cruel in opposition.''

The King turned to Captain Graham.

''Fetch your prisoner Peter Gantrell from Overhall Castle, to appear before us within the fortnight, so we may explain his imposed sentence and circumstances to him, face-to-face.''

''Sire!'' said the captain of Overhall's guard, saluting sharply. ''I leave at once!''

✦ 17 ✦
The Missing Plume

A BEDRAGGLED hunched little figure on an unkempt calico pony drew rein with a nervous jerk that made the shaggy pony shy and snort unhappily.

This rider is a great trial and a sore temptation to nip on the knee, the pony thought to himself. *Now he'll expect me to swim this river I see before us, I suppose.*

Rider and tiny horse stood, heads bowed into the steady wind and rain, gazing down from the low riverside bluff at the wide, gleaming, brownish gray Cristol River.

They had ridden from the calico pony's comfortable stable at a freehold farm not far from Overhall Castle, without pause except to catch a few hours of sleep under some stand of pine or later, as the weather warmed somewhat, hidden in the lee of a lone haystack in a field distant from its farmhouse.

What's he looking at? wondered the pony crossly.

His rider had given little thought to his mount's needs, not even a decent meal with time to digest it, since they had set out. Riding half the night, each night, and hiding half the day for five cold, windy days!

It isn't a horse's business what his rider does or thinks, the pony thought, noting a rumbling deep in his belly. *I've heard awful tales of riders who killed their brave mounts when urgent business spurred them ever on. No matter the waste.*

But this one? He has a goal somewhere to the south. He doesn't quite dare to slay his only horse. Not yet! He must feed me and give me a bit of slumber sometime during the hours of day or night—or I might just give up, lay down, and let him beat me!

He was shocked at the appeal of the idea of collapsing in a weary heap, just giving up, but shuddered it off.

What is *it he's looking for, I wonder?*

Never been this far from good old Overhall. I don't like it, this windswept riverbank. Sure, I don't like this mean and nasty rider! Perhaps I could give him a toss and run away! Or stumble on a gopher hole and pretend to break my leg?

Would he have the humanity to slice my throat, if I did break *a leg? Or let me lay there and die in agony of pain, thirst, and hunger?*

This one'd probably enjoy someone else's agony!

AFTER a long wait, the pony and the former Overhall Accountant named Plume caught sight of a low-sided, clumsy craft moving across the broad river from the unseen other bank.

It had a lantern burning at its blunt prow, a second one—colored red—along one side, and a third at the top of its stubby mast.

"Here it comes, at last!" grunted Plume wearily.

A ferry? the pony asked himself. *Well, enough! At least for a few hours I will ride and let the boat carry me onward.*

"Up!" snarled the Accountant, jerking the reins cruelly in the animal's tender mouth. "Down the hill there. Careful now!"

Anything, thought the pony wearily, *to get you to get off my back and leave me alone for a night or a day!*

When they reached the bottom of the low bluff the Accountant guided his mount onto a rough plank dock reaching out over the slowly sliding waters of the Cristol. The strange odors of the river and the feel of solid planks underfoot bemused the pony until the thought of tossing his rider into the river came too late to act upon,

even if he had found the strength and the will after all
those weary miles.

Plume pulled him to a halt and dismounted—an act
which brought a deep sigh of relief from the little horse.
The cruel Accountant was a particularly bad horseman,
all sharp ankles and sharper boot toes, always kicking
or kneeing when there was nothing to kick or knee about
by any horse-sense standard the pony ever learned.

Plume watched the ferryboat—for that was what it
proved to be, long and low of the sides, bluff of bows
and wide of beam. Its single square sail pushed it slowly
up to the dock, where it came to a sudden stop with a
plumpety!

The sail dropped, as if it too were dead weary, and
fell in untidy folds amidships.

A boy scarcely older than the pony's farmer's oldest
son ran forward and hopped to the dock, looping a heavy
hawser around a worn bollard of tough tree trunk, and,
turning, gave a call to the helmsman in the stern.

The ferry swung slowly so its prow pointed upstream.
A moment later the stern bumped, less sharply, against
the dock. A tall, spindly steersman tossed another loop
of thick, oily hemp rope over a second bollard and, putting his foot against the ferry's low side, drew it up
close.

The ferryboat gave an almost-Human groan of relief,
the pony thought.

Six men and a woman climbed warily ashore, stretching their muscles and twisting their legs painfully from
side to side. The thwarts had been very hard; unyielding
and uncushioned. The river crossing had taken some
hours.

"I'll light us a nice, warm fire in the hut," called the
helmsman to his passengers. "Warm yoursel's before
you go on. See to it, Duggan!"

The lad waved and trotted ahead to open the lop-
hanging door of the dockside cabin on the marshy shore.
A moment later, as the passengers shuffled that way, the

pony saw the bright spark of struck flint and a moment later still the boy had a blaze started in the fireplace inside the building.

The acrid smell of damp cottonwood twigs burning came to the pony and he wished, very hard, that the shed had a back lean-to for sheltering passengers' mounts. The wind from downriver was not as cold as the wind across the farmlands they'd been secretly crossing for several days, but it struck through his damp coat, which was wet with the sweat of a full day's hard riding and made him shiver miserably.

"Captain!" called Plume, approaching the ferryman. "I want to cross to the southern shore tonight!"

"Not *this* night!" the ferryman answered roughly. "Next trip's at dawn!"

"Tonight!" insisted the Accountant firmly, and rather shrilly. "I'll trade you this valuable horse for a special trip across, *right now*. By morning the price will fall to half!"

The ferryman, who was also the boat's helmsman and the boy's father, considered the offer, neither smiling nor frowning.

He could surely use the money. Traffic was slow this time of the year. His wife was about to give birth to his fourth child, and she couldn't work the ferry as she had once done. And the boy was asking for some sort of wage—or he would run away to work on the new Achievement in the dry mountains, he said, north of the desert.

"If you'd but wait an hour . . . ," the ferryman began. "To tend my passengers and get them off to night's shelter. It may snow again tonight. Don't want their lives on my conscience, you sees, sir."

"Just an hour or two at most, but I must cross this night!" insisted Plume.

"All-fired eager to get over the river," grumbled the ferryman, whose name was Parank. "Well, in exchange for this . . . er . . . horse, you call him? *Pony* is what they calls these little fellows where I come from!''

''Pony or horse, of more value than a special crossing, I swear,'' said Plume, sneering. ''He's my offer. Passage to the south bank, safely, less than two hours from now! Take it or I'll ride up to Fiddlehead and get some squatter to take me across in a skiff for the price of a quaff of stale ale.''

''Right!'' said Parank, deciding at last. ''Give us an hour or a bit more to settle these here incoming passengers. We'll unhook before ten o'clock,'' he promised, consulting an enormous pocket watch he drew from the fob pocket in his greasy, tattered trews.

''I'll go inside, then,'' said the Accountant, turning to walk down the dock. ''Little horse or big pony, he's yours to keep now! His day's been long and hard! A few days on good feed and he'll be strong enough to pull your boat, ferryman!''

''Lot you know about horses,'' sneered the riverman, after his nighttime passenger had gone inside to join the weary people in front of the fire.

''Take care of the horse, Sonny,'' the ferryman said, not unkindly, to the waiting lad. ''We'll take the little squirt across before we quit for the night. He's traded the horse for a night crossing.''

''Yessir, Pap,'' said the boy, sketching a sort of salute.

The ferryman swung a big, scarred fist his way but the boy dodged good-naturedly aside in time and gathered up the tired pony's reins.

Small horse, indeed, thought the pony with an angry snort The ferryman's boy led him gently, speaking kindly to him on the way, toward the rear of the tumbledown cabin at the far end of the dock.

Better'n standing about on the open riverbank, I guess, the pony thought, snorting.

To his surprise and everlasting gratitude the ferryman's lad filled a feed box with sweet riverside clover and a generous double handful of real oats to crunch.

Friends for life! the pony thought gleefully, nosing the feed box eagerly. *I swear it, my boy!*

THE Captain of Overhall's Guard returned to Lexor a week and a day later with Peter, unchained and well dressed, if somewhat subdued and evidently ill at ease in his former enemy's presence.

"Here is Peter Gantrell, the prisoner from Overhall, sire," declared Captain Graham. "However . . ."

"What is it, Graham?" the King asked.

"Sire," said Peter. "He is escaped!"

"Who? Who is escaped? What do you mean?" the King cried, startled from his usual calm.

"The . . . the Accountant Plume, sire," explained Graham, wringing his hands in concern.

"When Captain Graham came to fetch me, he noted the Accountant was not in his cell," explained Peter, gravely. "Yet his door was locked from without and he couldn't have climbed out of the window. Too high above the ground—sixty feet from the top of the bailey wall—and a good three hundred and fifty feet straight down to the floor of the valley below that!"

"But, then . . . ?" started Murdan.

"He knew of a secret passage!" exclaimed Tom, suddenly realizing what had happened.

"Secret passage? Atop Aftertower! Nonsense! There are no secret passages in my castle. None that I know of, that is," sputtered the Historian.

"Sire, Retruance and I've been studying Altruance's plans for Overhall off and on for five years," Tom said earnestly. "For some time we've known that they sometimes keyed to diagrams showing hidden passages, stairways, and secret doors. But all details were missing—stolen, I think now, by Plume!"

"What? What?" cried a distraught Historian.

"The walls of Overhall are honeycombed with hidden passages and stairways, it seems," Tom explained. "Altruance Constable meant them to speed service and allow servants to move about without interfering with castle life. The servants seldom used them, and the secret ways fell into disuse in a few years. They've been forgotten now for a lifetime! You, Murdan, for some reason, never were told they existed.''

"But secret passages in the Historian's own castle! How did Plume . . . ?'' The King gasped.

"Plume long had access to the Dragon-Architect's archives in Middletower,'' Tom replied. "He must have discovered, memorized, and destroyed the plans for the hidden passages and secret rooms and doors.''

"He never told me about them!'' cried Peter. "If he had, things would have gone differently there at Overhall! What I mean is, he'd never have escaped, the little snail-wort!''

"Old Plume was always a great one for carrying a spare card or two up his sleeve,'' said Graham thoughtfully.

"Secret doors! Hidden passages! It's so hard to believe!'' said Eduard, shaking his head angrily. "Not a bad idea, however, when I think of it again.''

"I'm sorry I didn't think of it first,'' Tom said, shaking his head angrily. "But Plume, with his inquisitive, acquisitive ways, must have been into old Altruance's files years ago. He certainly hid his trail carefully, sir.''

"No harm done, except that the knave has escaped us,'' growled Murdan with a shrug and a rueful shake of his own head. "Good riddance, I say!''

"Just a wicked, heartless knave,'' agreed Manda. "Yet, I've wondered . . . why so loyal to Uncle Peter for so many years? Even went into a very dangerous exile with him. Why? Does anyone know?''

"We can't question him about it,'' said her husband. "But I don't really think anyone knows who or what the Accountant really was.''

"It occurs to me,'' the Queen thought aloud, "that Plume was . . . is perhaps more than he appeared to us.''

"Smart as a whip, I'll give him that, the infernal little

sneak!'' said Graham. ''He saw that Retruance had left, Furbetrance gone away, and even the Ice Dragon flown off homeward, so if we are to chase him, we'd have to do it on horseback, not by Dragon!''

''How much of a start has he got, do you estimate?'' the King asked the Captain.

''If he left Lexor after dark the night before I arrived, sire, he can be a half continent or more away already, sire. Farther, if he found a horse to steal.''

Murdan said, ''Good riddance! I am inclined to let him go—''

''Except,'' Tom interrupted, ''I agree with the King. I'd like to ask him a few pointed questions myself.''

''It's entirely possible he knows the answers—don't you agree?'' Eduard asked Murdan.

''Entirely possible, Lord King,'' said the Historian. ''But I for one cannot begin to guess what his role really was. Peter here tells me Plume came to him, offering his services as a spy within Overall. Not the other way around.''

''Plume's part of the problem, no doubt,'' Tom agreed. ''Maybe part of the answer, too? *Someone* brought me here to Carolna, to this Elfin world. And someone unknown tried to shuffle Peter aside and use the Relling invasion to destroy the whole kingdom. Does anyone have the least idea who and why?''

''Not the least, as yet,'' admitted Murdan. ''But I intend to nose him out, if I possibly can. With your permission, sire?''

''Of course, but with extreme care, old friend,'' said the King after a moment of consideration. ''It should not allay our happiness of the moment, however. Call the servants to send in something hot to drink. All this talk of mysterious *interlopers* has given me the chills!''

RETRUANCE and his papa in the quiet middle of Sinking Marsh said they would keep their eyes peeled for the fleeing former Overhall Accountant. If Plume fled south, he should perhaps pass close to the Dragon's Island position.

Furbetrance, about to return with his Dragon wife to Obsidia Isle, said they would begin a search for the fleeing spy farther west.

Arbitrance assured Murdan that he was well enough to take care of himself, so his sons could concentrate on the hunt.

"In another week I'll join them," he insisted. "My wing is almost healed. Dragon bones heal quite fast, as you know."

Two weeks later, as Manda, Tom, Clem, and Mornie and her sons prepared to lead a long train of horse-drawn sleighs heavily laden with tools, furniture, and materials for Hidden Lake Canyon, Retruance came to Overhall to report the four great Constable Dragons—seven, if you included the Obsidia Isle kits—had enjoyed little luck in their search for the runaway Accountant.

"A ferryman on the Cristol says he traded passage for an Overhall pony two weeks past. He recognized the description of Plume when I gave it to him. Said the rider had proper documents *and* a bill of sale for the horse, but would offer no cash to cross the river."

"Old Plume was ever a clever counterfeiter," Tom recalled. "He traveled faster than news of his escape, I see."

"What else did the ferryman say?" Clem asked.

"Just that the man went on afoot, heading south through the marshy country east of Waterfields—as far as he could tell. If he swung to the west after a short way, he avoided the wetlands entirely," Retruance told them. "A bit farther south and then west and he'd be lost in the hardwood forest of northern Isthmusi. Once under the dense trees in the forest proper, as I can attest, he could hide or run forever without ever being seen."

"We'll have to do it the hard way, then," sighed Tom. "Track him afoot."

"We Dragons will continue to search and ask for him," Retruance promised. "Papa's particularly eager to recapture Plume, for obvious reasons. But . . . nobody has even rudimentary maps of that area far to the south. There are said to be terrible beasts and dreadful chasms and . . . well, so they say."

"I think he's escaped us this time," said Manda with a sigh, climbing into the sleigh and pulling the thick, warm fur robes about her, for it was by now full winter at Overhall. The day was bitterly cold, diamond clear, and still. "I think all we can do is watch out and play a waiting game. We can only be ready to spot him, when and if he surfaces, again. He *may* be gone forever. Who can tell?"

"Well, well," said her husband. "I suppose you're right, sweet mother-to-be. Meanwhile our lives must proceed. We've the baby to consider. I can't go off on a wild-goose chase and leave you to bear our child alone."

"If it were necessary," said Manda stoutly, "I'd insist you go. But for now let's move to where it's warmer and drier. It would be nice to have a roof over our heads when the baby comes next summer."

"We'll keep in touch, of course," said Tom's Dragon. "Especially as your time draws near, Princess. If you need anyone fetched to the canyon, or need to be taken anywhere . . . I mean, if the birthing proves difficult . . ."

"I'll call on Furbetrance, of course," said Manda, grinning happily. "He has the right to pamper his own Companion."

"Of course," Retruance apologized. "I was really thinking more of the father of the child. My experience is, first-time fathers need more care than the new mothers. You'll remember Eduard Ten before the twins were born, Tom?"

"Off with you, then!" cried Murdan. "I've got work to do, and so do you. Write often! Keep your feet dry!

Don't get too much sun! I can recall Arbitrance and be there in a couple of days at most if you need me—any or either or all of you!''

The four young people and the two little Clemssons, highly excited about riding in a horse-drawn sleigh, transport seldom used in rugged Broken Land, waved as the four-horse rigs filed down the slope from Overhall's foregate, and turned southwest along the frozen course of Overhall Stream.

The morning sun struck the snow-carpeted landscape with almost painful brightness. Tall pines and wide-spreading, brown-leaved king oaks, all covered with heavy frost, sparkled like trees of diamonds. The horse's hooves were almost silent in the snow, but the harness bells jingled pleasantly and the sleigh runners hummed a high-pitched winter song as they dashed along.

✦ 18 ✦
Hidden Canyon Spring

PRINCESS Alix Amanda Trusslo-Whitehead of Hidden Lake Canyon—a herald's mouthful, she always thought—squirmed and giggled aloud.

"What is it?" demanded her young husband in sudden alarm.

Spring had already come to their canyon. The alders and the birch along the lakeside were all but in full summer leaf. Tom was resting in the shade with his wife for a moment before going back to supervising the work of erecting the thick sandstone outer walls of their house.

The weather was summer hot but perfectly dry and clear as far as the eye could see, even way out over the flat, sandy desert to the south.

Off to one side, Clem was instructing a party of workmen on the uses of broadaxes in squaring great redwood beams and rafters brought by Dragon from the upper west coast.

On the rim of the canyon, high overhead, Arbitrance and his father argued about some esoteric point of architecture. The youngest Dragon and his wife and children, up for a long visit as the equinox approached, were making themselves useful bringing in the great tree trunks or running the treadmill that drove the big buzzsaw in the mill a short way downstream.

They had proved themselves much more efficient than the mill's undershot waterwheel Clem had built back in midwinter. Things were going well and fast.

Manda giggled again.

"Oh, just the baby kicking against my side," the Prin-

cess said, gasping, when she could stop laughing. "He's
strong and determined, I swear. Like his papa."

"Of perhaps *she's* eager and excited, like her mama,"
said Tom, smiling a bit foolishly down at her.

A shadow moved in the aspen wood nearby and Tom
caught sight of the graceful, somewhat menacing form
of Julia, the canyon's resident Jaguar. In a moment the
big cat was beside Manda, who reached out to stroke
the soft fur behind her ears.

Julia purred delightedly, eyes slitted half-closed.

"All goes well, I see," the cat murmured. "I'll sit
with the mother-to-be for a while, Sir Tom, if you've
work to do. The sun is not too warm here, Princess?"

"Absolutely delightful. But I've work to do, also,"
answered Manda, bouncing to her feet. "Come along,
Julia! You can help me decide the colors for the nursery."

"Beige and fawn, of course," said the cat instantly
and firmly, walking beside her, close enough to touch.
"No kitten should have to look at just pink or pale blue
when she wakes!"

" 'She'? Is that a guess or a prediction?" called Tom
as he watched them go, but they were already out of
earshot.

Tom watched the two—three, really—until they disappeared into the half-finished building. Manda bore her
inner burden gracefully. He had never seen her more
glowingly beautiful.

Another shadow, dark against the sky this time,
caught his attention.

Furbetrance raised a cry. Arbitrance and he dropped
down into the canyon on wide-spread wings.

Retruance had arrived, calling out to them all.

"What news?" shouted Tom, running to meet his
own special Dragon.

"Nothing new on Plume if that's what you mean. He
definitely did go south into Isthmusi, however. I've got
all the Lofters watching out for him. I just came by to

tell you Murdan, Rosemary, and Ffallmar and their kits are but a day's ride away. They should be here by afternoon tomorrow.''

"Good!'' cried Tom. "I was seeing myself delivering a baby with the assistance of a Jaguar.''

"And half a dozen Dragons,'' added Arbitrance with a loud guffaw. "The Dragon way is better! Eggs laid in a soft nest and Papa as far away as possible, until hatching time comes!''

Retruance went on as if never interrupted.

"The King's declared the Relling War officially at an end. Except for the Relling colony at Plaingirt—they're still there, petitioning the King to be allowed to stay permanently, as Murdan guessed they would—all our late enemies have been driven well beyond Frontier.''

"All *is* well, then!'' the Librarian exclaimed with some satisfaction.

"As well as things ever are in real life,'' agreed Retruance Constable.

"There's always something coming along, somewhere, you can bet,'' said his father. "Come up to the rim and see if you agree with me—or Furbie—about the roof line of Great Hall. I say it should be square with side hips for lighting. The boy wants it three times longer than it is wide, in the old-fashioned mode.''

Arguing good-naturedly, the three Dragons, father and two grown sons, flapped up to the rimrock, leaving Tom to walk toward his house to tell his wife of approaching guests.